# THE HOUSE
IN WALES

RICHARD RHYS JONES

A Ravenous Roadkill Publication

Published by Ravenous Roadkill in 2016

Copyright Richard Rhys Jones 2016

ISBN-13: 978-1539817604

ISBN-10: 1539817601

*Second Edition*

*All rights reserved under the International and Pan-American Copyright Conventions. No part of this book may be reproduced or transmitted in any form or by any means, electronic or mechanical, including photocopying, recording, or by any information storage and retrieval system, without permission in writing from the publisher.*

*This is a work of fiction. Names, places, businesses, characters, and incidents, are either the product of the author's imagination or are used fictitiously, and any resemblance to any actual persons, living or dead, organisations, events or locales, or any other entity, is entirely coincidental.*

*Warning: the unauthorised reproduction or distribution of this copyrighted work is illegal. Criminal copyright infringement, including infringement without monetary gain, is investigated by the FBI and is punishable by up to 5 years in prison and a fine of $250,000.*

*This book is for Stephanie, Daniel and Chelsea.*

*Mam, Dad, brothers and sis.*

*I love you all.*

# PROLOGUE

The door slammed shut, and instantly Danny was awake, instincts screeching at him in alarm.

His breath wafted steamily in the moon's faint watery light and a slight tremor passed through his bladder. Pulling up the bedclothes and covering his mouth, his eyes slowly grew accustomed to the dark corners of the room. *It* was back and at that moment Danny didn't feel as brave as he did earlier. He'd been ambushed by sleep, and now after being bluntly woken by the slamming door he was vulnerable and scared.

It was freezing again and the small voice at the back of his mind needlessly reminded him the window was closed. Not daring to move, waiting for something to happen, his mind raced in unspoken prayer nothing would.

Slowly the temperature changed and it seemed the cold was retreating towards the closet. He could feel it ebbing away, almost pulsing as it withdrew. *It was leaving*, he willed it to be true.

A puff of cold air hit his face and he jerked back as something whispered hatefully into his ear, "Make no mistake, your mother's with me Danny, and she's burning in hell for all the bad stuff she did for you."

Instinct overcame reason and Danny retreated under the covers, knuckling his mouth in silent and absolute terror, wishing for death so this horror could end.

# 1
## TWO WEEKS EARLIER
## EN ROUTE TO OLD COLWYN STATION
### on the North Wales coast

Though older than the other children on the train, and knowing others suffered as great a loss as he had, Danny Kelly was withdrawn, ignoring them.

Having lost his mother to the German bombs only six weeks earlier, the grief was like a cancer in his psyche, unmoving, pitiless and heavy. That his father left when Danny was five, to find work back in 'the old land', never to return, wasn't a concern. Danny could barely remember his face. Only the indelible impressions of drunken rages and frequent slaps gave any authority to his memory.

But his mother, now that was different.

Softly spoken and always cheerful, her eyes showed the burden of a daily, weary, survival. She had given her all for him, and now she was gone. All his toughness in the school yard, and all the hours in the boxing club, could not have prepared him for this. Disoriented and out of his depth, he was unable to deal with the pain and bewilderment of his sorrow.

Pulling along the coastline toward their destination the mood in the carriage was one of holiday excitement. Ignoring the jubilant cacophony and the lull of clacking train-tracks his gaze went to the window instead; he pondered the morose reflection.

His tears blurred and distorted the postcard view of the sun coaxing colours from the deep blue of the sea before him. Turning away, he pored over the one remaining picture of the only person he ever truly loved, and who truly loved him.

"Hello. You don't look happy."

Danny looked up to see a pretty blonde girl sitting before him, roughly sixteen or seventeen - his age. She smiled as she nodded at the photo in his hand. "Your mum? She looks nice."

She sounded sincere. He dropped the defensive scowl, nodding, "Yeah, thanks, she was."

He stuffed the precious memory back in his jacket. He knew who the girl was and had often seen her at the orphanage, but the burden of his loneliness and the guilt of feeling any pleasure had stopped him from any interaction with the others.

"I'm Sandy, or Sandra if you want to be formal. I noticed you some time ago but I guessed you wanted to be alone, so I didn't say anything. I lost both my parents too, so I know how it is." She smiled.

Danny smiled tiredly, nodding, "I'm sorry. I pretty much grew up without a father, so I only lost my mother, but she was all I had. It was just six weeks ago."

"I'm sorry," the girl frowned. "So recently ... that still has to hurt a lot. It's been awhile for me, so it's not quite as painful. And I had quite a lot of time together with them. There are some kids on the train who lost their parents at such an early age. You haven't told me your name yet, and seeing as we're the oldest on here I suppose we should get to know each other, in case we have to help the younger ones."

Feeling vaguely disappointed she only wanted to know his name so they could work together, he relented, "I'm Daniel."

"Well Daniel, I hope wherever we end up we'll be able to be friends, because if we haven't got families what's left but friends, eh?"

She smiled again and Danny brightened up a bit. Before he could reply she stood and pointed excitedly, "Look, there's the station. I've to get my case. See you later." And she was gone.

The party atmosphere evaporated at the sight of waiting adults on the platform. The children filed silently into line to walk the mile to St. John's church. A few adults accompanied them, but up to now the only one who'd said anything was a very tall, broad-shouldered vicar, who had demanded quiet while reading out the register. His angry demeanour spoilt his film star looks and Danny smirked at the girls admiring his rich black hair, spiv moustache, and racy eyebrows.

"Now I know you're from the city of Liverpool, but I will not have you being disobedient or disorderly while you are here. Do I make myself clear?" he'd bellowed in a strong Southern Wales accent, frightening some of the wee ones.

Coming from a school where teachers depended on the whipping cane to stress their authority, Danny experienced anxiety at the vicar's menacing demeanour. Danny hoped with his whole heart he didn't have to stay at *his* house.

As the other children left with families after having their labels inspected, Danny found himself in the last group of three. A kind-looking middle-aged couple entered the church hall, and after a brief greeting to the vicar and a look at his list, moved on to inspect the orphans.

Sandra, who was still waiting, looked back at him as the couple read her label and pulled her out along with the other two, and then Danny was alone with only the angry vicar for company. He groaned inwardly as the vicar approached, hoping against hope there had been some mistake.

"Now then young man, you seem a bit old to be an evacuee. Shouldn't you be helping the war effort by working somewhere?"

Danny bristled at the jibe. The fact was he did feel guilty about being evacuated like a kid, but the authorities had thought it better for his mental health to have him away from the city, and he didn't have the fight in him at the time to debate their decision.

"The orphanage sent me as I lost my mother

recently. They'll probably find work for me in the next few months and call me back, sir," he answered.

"Well, it seems like you're to stay with me for the time being. Now, I have other business today, so just sit down there and wait for Miss Trimble to come. She's my housekeeper and will take you up to the house."

Danny plopped down and waited.

On the verge of nodding off, he was abruptly brought back to alertness by a sharp cough. Standing automatically, he was greeted by a stern woman of indeterminate age.

Slim and tall, she looked over her glasses at him like a school marm. With her severely pulled-back hair, tight mouth, and large black rimmed spectacles, she looked the very soul of severity.

"Daniel Kelly, I presume," she said, her crisp English accent reinforcing the school mistress impression. "Sleeping during the day? Well, we won't be doing that very much from now on Mister Kelly, let me assure you of that. Now, come on, chop-chop, bring your suitcase and let's get you up to the house and have you scrubbed before tea."

She marched off, leaving Danny to rub his eyes and follow her out of the hall.

The journey to their destination was very steep. Miss Trimble set off at a furious rate and Danny, though not unfit, was overcome by fatigue after the first mile and lagging behind. He paused to take in the countryside. The road was all uphill, so when he turned around the view almost brought a smile to his face. The bay in the distance was surrounded by hills that swept down to the sea. A long promenade curved around to a far-off cliff that jutted out into the ocean as if cutting the area off from the rest of the world. In the middle of the curving promenade stood a pier, like a sword against the elements, brilliant white and fascinating to a lad who had never left his home city.

The town of Old Colwyn sat on the outskirts of the larger Colwyn Bay, but they seemed to merge into one big sprawl. Danny could make out a couple of church spires and towers in the distance, but not much else. The view looked untouched and calm, a direct contrast to the devastation he was used to in Liverpool. For the first time since the loss of his mother, Danny felt a quiet contentment. The feeling made him wonder if there was a heaven and if his mum was there now looking down on him. Recognising the vista was so calming. He pondered joining the army when he was old enough, saving money, and then after they'd beaten the Jerries, come back to live there.

His reverie was broken by a stone bouncing nearby and ricocheting off into the hedge, followed quickly by another that edged a little closer but still missed hitting him. The hedge rustled up ahead and four lads and a girl stepped out into the road. One of the boys towered above the others, but it was a dark-haired middle-sized one who spoke first.

"Pwy wyt ti felly? Ffoadur o Loegr sy'n mynd i fyw yn yr hen ficerdy. Ti'n gwybod ei fod yn gadiffan, yn dwyt?"

(Who are you, then? An English refugee going to live in the old vicarage, is it? You know he's a poof, don't you?)

Not understanding what was being said, Danny tried to weigh the situation up. One was younger than the rest - about twelve, he reckoned - holding a loaded catapult in his hands. Another was red-haired and looked about Danny's age. His malicious grin warned of the trouble ahead.

The girl stepped forward, eyeing Danny up and down as if inspecting an animal. "Sais ydio, un o'r hogiau o'r ddinas. Efallai bod ganddo bres?" (He's English - one of those boys from the cities. He might have money.)

"Look, I'm sorry, I don't understand what you're saying. My name's Danny Kelly, from Liverpool," he smiled, hoping to curry favour. Danny wasn't afraid of a scrap, but four against one was stupid in anyone's books, and besides, he didn't want to mess up his jacket.

The lad who had spoken first stepped forward. "Now listen Englishman, we own this area and it's our patch right here. You want to go through on our road, you'll have to pay." He looked around to the big lad behind him and then back to Danny. "Or Bryn here will kill you."

The girl giggled at Danny's look of dismay and the ginger-haired lad laughed openly. For some reason the laughing redhead didn't bother him but the thought of being beaten in front of the girl was a sickener, and there didn't seem there was anything he could do about it. Fight and she'd laugh at him, running would mean he was a coward. At that moment, his predicament and his available choices made Danny loathe them all and he could feel the slow rise of vexed hatred boiling up within.

"I haven't got any money," he declared, fearing for his pride and jacket.

"Then Bryn will just have to beat you until you can find something."

The dark haired lad smiled and the girl became visibly animated as the lads strung out to bar his escape. As he dropped his suitcase to defend himself, the young lad fired his catapult and the stone hit Danny in the leg. He cried out and bent down to rub his leg when suddenly the giant charged, landing on Danny like a ton of bricks.

Falling back on to the road, Danny could hear his trousers rip at the back, which sent the girl into squeals of delight. Helpless under the big lad's weight, Danny could only try to sit up, to protect his face from the punches that were raining down on him.

Suddenly the laughing and shouting stopped, as did the punches.

"What on earth is going on here?" It was Miss Trimble. "Daniel Kelly, you stand up and get over here right now! And as for you gang of young reprobates, I'll be having words with all your mothers!"

As Danny stood, he noticed the belligerent looks the five gave him. He knew they'd blame him if Miss Trimble did tell their parents, and they'd be back for him.

"Edrych ar ei drowsus, wedi rhwygo o gwmpas ei din," (Look at his trousers, they're split up the arse) the girl giggled in Welsh.

The laughing stopped abruptly when Miss Trimble turned to her. "Go and wash that filthy Welsh mouth out with soap this instant, Elizabeth Thomas. I'll be having extra words with your mother about this!"

*What a start,* Danny thought to himself. *What a bloody awful start.*


The house stood to the side of an old church, which clearly was abandoned to the elements and out of use. A massive oak tree had taken over one side of the building and it almost seemed to be leaning on the ancient roof.

Miss Trimble caught his look of disdain and swiftly admonished him for it. "Just because a building looks rundown doesn't mean it isn't still a holy place. You, young man, will have to learn to curb your temper and hide your condescension. Not everyone was brought up in a big city. We don't fight everyone we meet and we don't pour scorn on anything that doesn't meet our expectations."

Danny knew it was pointless to argue. For the rest of the walk he'd tried to tell her what had happened on the road, but Miss Trimble simply wouldn't hear his side of it.

"I don't care who started what. All I know is on your first day here you have managed to start a fight and ruin your trousers in the bargain. I fear the Reverend will be most annoyed by your rudeness."

So he followed meekly on, saying nothing and taking in the scenery.

They reached the main gate of the grounds, and though the church may have been derelict the house next to it was still impressive, surrounded by a high wall with a large wrought iron gate. He walked up the long path which ran between a large orchard on the one side and the graves of the dearly departed on the other. Just beyond was the vicarage.

"The ground is still consecrated and will be while there's a war on as the graves will have to stay here until the Council has someone to move them to the village," the housekeeper pointed out. "The orchard is strictly out of bounds, so don't harbour any ideas of stealing the fruit, do you understand?"

Without waiting for an answer, she turned away to pull out a key for the front door.

Danny paused to take in the building while Miss Trimble fiddled with the ancient lock. Old, two storeys high, with a roof that sagged with age and moss, its stained-glass windows looked like they'd once belonged in the ruins next door. Ivy clung to the walls like scar tissue and the faint tang of mildew seeped from rotting timbers.

The door creaked open, and above the sound of the tortured hinges Danny heard the low growl of a very large dog.

The housekeeper stood aside as an Irish wolfhound stalked slowly towards him, the constant rumble of its anger revving between snarls. Danny was used to dogs, Liverpool was full of them, but this black shaggy-headed monster resembled a small horse. Its eyes were as black as its nose and its lips were pulled back, trembling over a double row of fangs. The beast drooled freely as it growled. It stopped advancing and the snarling grew in intensity, as if it was winding up to pounce, and Danny, already retreating slowly, pushed his hands up to fend off attack.

"Well Mister Kelly, I do believe you're afraid," the housekeeper sniggered.

Danny let his focus move away from the dog and gasped at her sardonic smile.

"Such a big man like you, a fighting man like yourself, afraid of a little dog? Well, I'm shocked."

As if in answer, the snarling notched up a gear.

"Astaroth!" she snapped, and the dog stopped as if she had flicked a switch, turning away from Danny and back to her.

"Go inside now, there's a good boy. The young man will be staying with us for awhile, so you're not to harm him, do you hear?"

The beast turned to give him one last warning

growl and then padded inside. Had it not been so terrifying it would have been funny.

"Do not get on the wrong side of Astaroth, Mister Kelly. I don't think he likes you. As it is so, I'd be on my best behaviour if I were you."

"Yes, Miss Trimble," Danny intoned, breathing deeply in fear, numbly following her inside.

A cluttered corridor led past two rooms - one the study, strictly out of bounds, the other the main living room - out of bounds between 8 a.m and 7 p.m. Next to the unlit fire Danny noticed Astaroth watching as he trudged past.

Next, they passed the kitchen with a glossy buffed flagstone floor and a huge fireplace. The wooden tables were scrubbed.

Highly polished pans and utensils glistened from the walls, and the whole room seemed in direct contrast to the rundown exterior. "This is where you will spend your day until I can arrange for you to go to the local school." Miss Trimble's stern direction interrupted his observations. "The other children here in Peulwys are all younger than you, so I don't know how we're going to continue your studies. Perhaps the Reverend will teach you, I'm not sure."

Danny's heart sank at the thought, along with hopes of attending the school, and then his mind clicked into gear. "What about the other kids here, the ones who attacked –?"

The housekeeper angrily stopped him short, "Don't you dare backchat me, boy!"

"But all I said was –" Danny stopped when he

saw Astaroth standing in the doorway, growling again.

"If I say there is no school here that will have you, then there is no school here that will have you. Do I make myself clear?" Trimble elucidated in a hissed tone, the low growl of the dog in the background emphasising the point.

"Yes."

"Yes what? Show some respect, boy!"

"Yes, Miss Trimble."

A silence spanned between them, with only Astaroth's displeasure making any sound. Danny broke his stare and looked away, ignoring the hiss of triumph.

"Astaroth, back to where you were. Daniel, pull the bath tub out of the back room there, fill it up and scrub yourself. You're filthy. I'll give you a sewing kit. You can mend your trousers yourself."

Wordlessly Danny went to the door the housekeeper was pointing to, opened the door and pulled out the bath.

After he filled the tub Miss Trimble perched herself on a stool, watching him boiling the water without saying a word. Out of the corner of his eye he could see her monitoring his progress until he finished.

When she made no move to leave, he decided to tell her he was ready. "It's full."

"So get in, then," she said, shifting her weight forward as if to watch.

"But I've still got my clothes on. They'll get wet," he stammered.

"Take them off, then, you stupid boy," she scolded, loud enough to initiate a growl from the living room.

"But you're still here," Danny almost pleaded, looking once more to the living room door to see if Astaroth was there.

"Do you think I've not seen a little boy like you in his birthday suit before? Now stop being silly and get in the bath, before the water gets cold."

Danny's cheeks burned in unqualified shame and he contemplated refusing her demand, to simply run out of the back door and away, until the feral rumble of Astaroth's warning made him think again.

Would she set the dog on him if he did run? *Yes, she would.*

Miss Trimble now sat forward, eagerly watching. The fire of malice twinkled in her eyes as she goaded him to undress. "I know what you're thinking Daniel, and I can tell you, yes, I would send him after you if you ran."

His shock was complete. How could she have known what he was thinking? A trickle of piss almost seeped out as the housekeeper cackled her glee. "Now get in the bath before the Reverend returns," she hissed.

Slowly, as if in a walking dream, he took off his jacket and shirt. The housekeeper surveyed him, a half-smile playing on her lips, and once again it was Danny who broke the stare to look away. He untied his shoes and slipped them off with his socks. Daring to glance up, he nearly gasped when she slowly licked her lips. As he undid his belt she audibly sighed. And then he dropped his trousers.

"There now, that wasn't so hard, was it, you silly boy. Now off with those underpants and into the bath with you," Trimble said, as if nothing had happened.

His shame now lost to shock, he mutely took off this last garment and stepped into the lukewarm water. She stood up to fetch soap and a large wooden scrubbing brush, which she chucked into the water between his legs.

"Now scrub," she demanded, "scrub yourself until you're red all over, and I will be checking."

As if reading his mind, the dog in the front room growled a warning at any thought of rebellion he may have held, so he lathered himself and started to scrub with the brush.

"No, no, you're not doing it right," Trimble admonished. "Stand up and really scrub, scrub to cleanse your wicked soul, boy. Or I'll do it for you."

So he did. Swallowing the last remnants of pride he might have otherwise kept hidden, he stood up in front of her and scoured his body with the stiff bristles. His skin burned from the action of the brush, but worse, far worse, was the slow rise between his legs.

He closed his eyes and willed it to go away, but the more he thought about it, the bigger it grew. He opened his eyes again to see the housekeeper eyeing up his tumescence as it guiltily stood out from his body. Her chest rose in great heaves, a deep blush painting her school mistress cheeks, the flames of excitement dancing in her eyes.

"Oh you wicked, wicked, boy," she breathed, smiling lasciviously. Taking a step forward, she peered down at it. "Make it go away," she commanded. Astaroth barked from the living room, making him jump, but the housekeeper steadfastly looked him in the eye as she demanded, "Make it go away, now!" Then she left him alone, her last directive cast over her shoulder, to pour the bath water away when he was finished.

The dog stopped barking as soon as she came into its line of sight, which struck Danny as very strange. He knew there and then he had to get away - this woman was mad. However, he also knew he had no chance of outrunning the dog, so he was stuck until something came up.


By the time the Reverend returned, the bath was packed away and it was dark outside. Danny heard him enter the house shortly after Miss Trimble began rattling off a lecture of the list of things he was allowed to do (work), and not to do (everything that meant fun or rest).

Then the housekeeper escorted Danny to his room, a bare dusty cell with one threadbare carpet over the boards, a closet for his clothes, and a bed that creaked when he put his suitcase on it. As with the rest of the house, it had no electricity and relied on a cheap sputtering candle for light. The housekeeper made it quite plain the bed was out of bounds during the day, and any spare time he had would be spent either working in the kitchen or the garden. She gave him a brush to clean the dirt off his trousers and instructions to unpack, clean his clothes, and come downstairs when he was ready.

Then the Reverend's loud booming voice called her name and she was gone. Opening the case he pulled out his frayed spare clothes and laid them on the bed. His second jacket and trousers he hung on a hanger. It was dark inside and without the candle he could hardly see at all. Groping with his free arm to find the hanger rail, he sliced nicely through a thick tangle of spider webs and onto the damp wall. Deciding it might be a good idea to clean the closet first, he returned the clothes to the bed and retrieved the candle.

Peering inside, he gasped in shock at what the candle illuminated. Amid the cobwebs, damp and grime on the walls of the closet, was writing, a couple of sentences and one long passage, all written in a foreign language. He first busied himself with the cobwebs and then gave up on the idea when he realised the job was too big and he needed a cloth to do it properly.

Closing the door, he pondered what the writing could mean. He suspected it was Welsh but didn't know for sure, and he wasn't about to ask Miss Trimble or the Reverend either.

Perhaps he could copy some of the passages down on paper and ask one of the locals.

Those thoughts were interrupted by the Reverend shouting for him to come downstairs.

Reaching the threshold of the living room, he wasn't sure whether to enter or not. The Reverend was sitting in a chair with a Bible on his lap, reading. Miss Trimble stood next to him patting the dog.

Danny decided to ask for a cloth and some water to clean the closet, to give a good impression and maybe find the first rung on the ladder to their approval.

He coughed lightly and was about to ask when the Reverend looked up and roared, "You wicked, evil, vile specimen!"

The vehemence of the attack rocked him and his jaw dropped as the Reverend stood and advanced on him, shaking a walking stick in anger.

"I brought you into my house as a haven from the German bombers and you treat it like a Sodom and Gomorrah! This is a house of God, a holy place. How dare you play with yourself in my house you piece of filth!" As his voice crescendoed, the stick waved dangerously in his hand.

The blow was coming, Danny just had to get the timing right so he could dodge it. He cast a glance at Miss Trimble to see her gleefully smiling at him, patting Astaroth. She slowly closed her eyes and wrinkled her nose at him in mock pleasure, and then the older man, still shouting his rage, swung with all his considerable might.

Danny stood back and let the stick rush past

him, causing the Reverend to stumble slightly, but not enough to stop his advance. Danny saw Astaroth stand and growl, and his mistress nod in caution. He realised she wanted him to take a blow; she wanted to see him hurt.

He felt sickened that any attempt at retaliation would end with a mauling, with him as villain, so as the next blow from the stick came down, he stepped forward and into it, catching it on the fleshy part of his forearm so it connected but without any real power. The years at Fazakerley Boxing Club for Boys trained him to take a punch on the arms, and though the old man's swing had been arrested, it still hurt like hell. He stepped back to rub where it connected and mentally decided he'd take the dog on if he had to, but he wasn't going to take another one from the stick, but there was no need.

The Reverend merely pointed to the stairs and said, "Go, go now to your room. There'll be no tea for you tonight. You can dwell on your sin with an empty stomach."

Pausing to look at both the old man and his housekeeper, he contemplated telling them he didn't want to stay here - he'd sooner go back to the German bombs than live in their madhouse - then decided against it. Miss Trimble's smirk of victory and the Reverend's anger-creased face would brook no quarrel on this day. So, shaking his head in the only show of defiance he could muster, he walked back upstairs.

A feline growl of annoyance greeted him as he opened the door to his room. On the bed curled up next to his pillow was a large ginger cat, one ear almost missing, fur as ragged as the carpet in his room, a large scar over one eye. Though no expert in such things, Danny judged him to be at least fifteen years old. It lifted a massive head and yawned widely, showing a set of broken teeth and fangs that had the appearance of a battered, curved saw blade.

Danny put his hand out towards the creature and approached the bed carefully, "Hello there, old boy. What's your name then, eh?"

Instantly the cat sprung up on all fours, arching its back while hissing outrage at being disturbed.

Danny backed off and moved to his case, chiding the cat as he did so. "Alright, have it your way, you bad tempered old goat. I only wanted to be friends but if you don't want to be, then fine …"

A cold blast of air from the closet stopped his muttering dead and he turned to see what had caused it.

Nothing.

There was nothing to be seen, although he noticed the door had moved with the gust. Shrugging the incident off, he turned back to the bed to see the cat was now gone.

"Suits me fine," he muttered to himself.

A longer blast of cold air blew the candle out and suddenly he was in darkness. He hadn't thought about matches and didn't want to go back downstairs, so he simply decided to leave everything in his case and go to sleep.

The draft coming from the closet grew colder, so by the light of a three-quarter moon he quickly shut the door with a bit more force than intended and jumped into bed. He cursed as he realised he'd left the case on the bed, but he pushed it to the far end with his foot amid a choir of squeaking springs, and closed his eyes.

Turning over the day's events in his head, he wondered about Sandra and where she was. Remembering her smile, he grinned to recall those crystal blue eyes and the flick of her long blonde hair. If only it had been Sandra there today in the kitchen and not that dreadful hag Trimble.

The grin faded as he recalled the look of excited fascination as she stared, the slightly open mouth, cheeks a high blush and the glee, that awful glee in her eyes.

As sleep wrapped its solemn arms around him, he heard her words in his head, repeatedly. *Oh, you wicked, wicked boy. You wicked, wicked, wicked, boy ...*

# 2

Danny had never woken up to the sound of a cockerel before. He'd heard they crowed early in the morning but to actually hear one brought a smile to his face. The smile soon faded when he thought back to the shame and terror of the day before.

Rubbing his eyes, he sat up and gasped. The entire contents of his case were strewn around the room; the case itself was still on the bed. Springing out of bed he saw the closet door was open as well.

"What on earth …?" he whispered.

Treading slowly towards the closet, he wondered who had opened it, and why. Did the Reverend and Miss Trimble do this? It didn't make sense. They had no reason. Was the dog being curious, or maybe even the cat? He doubted it.

Reaching the door, he looked inside, shocked at what lay on the floor. Amid the dust and old cobwebs, the dead flies and dried husks of long gone spiders, was the picture of his mother, taken from his jacket and thrown to the floor like waste.

Lovingly he picked it up, blew the dirt off and held it to his chest. In a flash it hit him. He was alone, so very alone. If she was still alive, if those bloody bombers hadn't obliterated their home, he would not be here.

Tears flowed without shame at the memory of her laugh, the way she sang, how she rubbed his head when he was cheeky ... there seemed to be a million other recollections that flooded his memory.

At that moment grief and humiliation slowly turned to rage, and he decided to leave.

Marching wordlessly into the kitchen he took out the biggest knife he could find. The Reverend and Trimble were in the living room, but more importantly so was Astaroth, so he turned for the back door.

"Where are you going Daniel?" the housekeeper asked in her best address-the-class voice from the other room. Danny decided not to answer and made for the door.

The now-familiar low growl stopped him in his tracks, so dropping his case he hefted the knife and turned to face it.

"I'm going out, away from this mad house," he shouted. "And if that fucking dog comes near me, I'll gut the fucker. Now leave me alone!"

By this time both the Reverend and the housekeeper were standing at the kitchen door, the Reverend shocked, not quite knowing what to say,

Trimble was calm, so infuriatingly calm.

"Well, Reverend, we'd better let him go, then," she drawled as if already bored by the confrontation.

Danny turned, opened the door with one hand, then holding it open with his foot he picked up his case and ran out. The click of the latch falling back into place was sheer music and he set off at a jaunty pace, leaving the horror, antagonism and degradation of the house behind him. He didn't have a plan other than to get away from there and go back to Liverpool by any means necessary.

The back door led into the orchard, so he doubled back past the house to the main gate. There was a brief panic at the thought of meeting them again at the front door, but there was no one there and the path was clear. The morning sun mirrored the freedom in his heart, and as he turned to look one last time at the vicarage and derelict church, his heart stopped in his mouth. At the front door stood Trimble with Astaroth by her side, the ginger cat from the night before rubbing itself against her legs.

"You'll be back Daniel Kelly, you'll be back, and we'll be here, we'll be here waiting for you."

He turned and started to walk again. Running was out of the question but he upped the pace and set off down the road to the town, her words ringing in his head like echoes of a bad dream.


He hadn't walked five minutes when his stomach started to rumble. Provisions and funds for the journey hadn't been high on the agenda when he made his break, and now he regretted being so impetuous. Turning a corner, he spotted an orchard he hadn't noticed on the way up and he took that as a sign his mother was watching over him.

Daniel dropped his case at the wall that stood between him and the trees, jumped up, and pulled himself over.

He landed as lightly on the other side and stood, to be greeted by the five kids who attacked him the day before. Once again it was the middle-sized darkhaired lad who spoke first.

"Well, well, what have we here?" He grinned broadly, though Danny saw no affability in his smile. The other four dropped what they were doing and turned to face him.

Danny took heart from the large kitchen knife he'd tucked into the back of his belt, but decided to leave it there for the time-being.

"Look, I don't want no trouble. There's four of you, so that'd be unfair ..."

"Five of us," the girl butted in aggressively. "There's five of us."

Danny nodded and held his hand up to placate her, but the ginger-haired lad broke in. "Shut up. Since when do you ever fight? You only ever start them. It's always Bryn who has to fight for you."

"Talk in Welsh, Geraint. He doesn't understand that," the leader directed him, and a light-bulb went on in Danny's head. Perhaps they could read the writing. If only he'd written it down ...

"Have any of you ever been up to the old vicarage by the church?" he interrupted. "Any of you ever stayed the night there?"

"No," the dark-haired lad answered. "We're not poofs like you."

Danny ignored the jibe, "I don't blame you. I'm running away from there. It's too weird. That's why I came here. I'm starving and I want some apples."

"Well, it'll cost you," the smallest of them said, slotting a stone into his catapult.

Danny saw a spark of interest in their leader who had half-turned to raise his hand, as if to stop him firing any stones, and said, "Why, what happened? Is the old goat really a poof after all?"

The five moved in to hear him but what would he tell them? Why did he suddenly feel the need to understand the writing in the closet when he was set on going home anyway? He didn't know but they seemed friendlier now, so he'd talk with them for a while and then go.

"No, he isn't. Far from it, I think." He smiled when they collectively let their shoulders fall in disappointment, but swiftly moved on. "But the thing is, in my room there, there was a closet, and I opened it to hang my stuff up and it was full of writing, I think it was in Welsh. And that housekeeper, she's strange, I had to get away from there."

The girl, Elizabeth, had her fingers to her mouth in rapt attention, but the others didn't look so interested.

"So," the red-haired lad, called Geraint, asked, "what's that meant to mean? We are in Wales, you know."

"I don't know what it's meant to mean, but I think she's a witch and that bloody dog of hers is dangerous. Do you know if anyone's been killed around here?"

Now they were interested and started to babble to each other in Welsh. Danny suspected they had similar suspicions about Trimble and the monster dog, so he let them talk while he ate an apple he found on the ground.

Finally the spokesman of the gang turned to him. "We think she's a witch too. You'd better come with us to the village and tell Sergeant Evans about what you've seen there."

"What am I going to say? She looks like a witch, the dog's dangerous, and I found some writing I think is Welsh? He'll laugh at me and they'll send me to the loony bin."

The girl giggled and the others joined in. "Well, we'll walk with you to the village anyway if you want. My name's Huw, by the way." The dark haired leader smiled. "Bryn, you know, that's Geraint, and the youngest is Dafydd. I think you know Beth as well."

They shook hands and Danny felt very solemn doing it.

The cheerful impact of the moment was cracked by the voice of an adult. "O'r gorau, gollyngwch yr afal, a dewch yn eich blaenau!" (Right, you lot, drop the apples and let's be having you!) a stern voice called out in Welsh from the other side of the wall.

"Who's that?" Danny asked, wide-eyed in panic.

"Sergeant Evans," Huw said resignedly.

Sergeant Evans turned out to be the kindly-looking man who had taken Sandra and the two other kids in on their first day in the church, though he looked far more severe in his uniform.

"Look, lad," he said matter-of-factly after Danny had told him why he had to leave the vicarage, albeit in a very watered-down version of the events. "I know the Reverend is a bit loud now and then, and Miss Trimble is a bit old-fashioned when it comes to discipline, but I can't have you running around the country on your own. You'll have to go back, I'm sorry but them's the rules."

Danny's desperation swiftly turned to panic. "I can't go back. They'll kill me!"

"Don't be so bloody daft. Now, are you going to come with me or do I have to make you?"

Danny sized the man up. Though he looked amiable enough, he was a very big man and he doubted very much he could best him. He could run though …

"And don't even think about running away, because when we catch you, and we will, you'll have me to deal with, and I hate being made to look stupid by young lads." Then in a more sympathetic tone, "Look, lad, I'll take you up there and I'll see what's what, but you'll have to go back and that's final. Now, are you going to make this easier on both of us?"

And that was how he found himself back at the front door of the old vicarage, facing a very angry priest.

The policeman's persuasion, his lack of preparation, and the fact he didn't even know where he was going had made up his mind for him, he'd have to return.

"Ah, Constable Evans. I see you've brought our Jonah back to the fold."

"That's Sergeant Evans, Reverend, and I believe his name is Daniel."

The Reverend nodded sagely. "It is, Sergeant, but Jonah was the man who tried to run away from God and was swallowed by a whale."

Danny looked up to the policeman with a see-what-I-mean look on his face, but Evans ignored him. "Well, Reverend, from what the young man tells me, it's more like Daniel being pushed into the lion's den."

As he spoke, Astaroth poked his head out from behind the Reverend and panted in an almost friendly manner. Danny took a step back but the Sergeant placed a hand on his shoulder.

"Easy now, lad, it's only Astor. He may be big but he's as daft as a brush is that one."

"He's a killer, Sarge. She was going to set him on me!"

As if on cue, Miss Trimble came to the front door in a waft of perfume and smiled at the policeman. "Good morning, Sergeant. So glad you found our runaway, and we didn't even have to telephone you to tell you. How very efficient you are."

Danny noticed she had taken her glasses off and her hair was let down, which had an obvious effect on the Sergeant.

""Well thank you Miss, but it was pure luck really. I caught him scrumping up by Jones Milk's orchard, and well it was no bother."

Closing his eyes in despair at the Sergeant's embarrassed, almost teenage twaddle, Danny decided to try once more.

"Look, Sarge, that dog's a killer. She was going to set it on me. Last night the Reverend beat me with a stick and I was sent to my ..."

"But why were you sent to your room?" the Reverend exploded. "You dare to lay accusations at my door? Shall I tell the good constable what you did to be sent to your room or what you put poor Miss Trimble through? Shall I? Shall I?" Without waiting for an answer, he turned to Sergeant Evans and spluttered his indignation, "Playing with himself, in full view of Miss Trimble, Sergeant. Playing with himself. So what do you think of that, then?"

Danny gasped in horror and quickly rallied, "She was staring at me, I swear! She was staring at me!"

Sergeant Evans, now fully out of his depth, looked aghast at Danny. "I have never, in all my years in the Force, heard of such a thing."

"And there's more, Sergeant," Trimble added. "Ask him who was threatening whom with a knife this morning. Who wanted to stab poor old Astor. I bet he still has the knife on him."

Danny deflated into submission. He knew he was beaten by circumstance, his own stupidity, and the workings of a woman's wiles on a middle-aged policeman.

"If you still have it on you I suggest you take it out now, lad," Evans said in a threateningly low tone, all trace of his earlier good nature gone.

From behind his back Danny pulled out the knife, eliciting an audible gasp from the policeman. "Lad, I know you do things different in Liverpool, but here in Old Colwyn we don't tell lies, threaten old people with knives, or play with ourselves in front of the ladies. Now I'm going to hand you back to the Reverend, who's a man of good standing in the village. If you run away again I'll have you arrested for theft, threatening behaviour and public indecency. You'll go to prison for that and I don't need to tell you what happens in prison to boys like you."

Danny couldn't bring himself to speak. His humiliation was complete, so he merely shook his head.

"I didn't think so," Evans admonished. Handing the knife back to Miss Trimble, who held it as if she were holding a dead rat by its tail, he gave Danny one last look of disdain and politely nodded to the

Reverend. "I'll leave you all to it, then, Reverend. Good day to you both." With a lingering smile at Miss Trimble the policeman was gone, and with him any hope Danny had for escape.

He watched Evans go and turned back to the door. The Reverend was already inside. The boy had been dealt with and for him the matter was over. However, his housekeeper stood waiting to meet Danny's eye.

Gloating like a cat with a cornered mouse, she smiled and rubbed her tongue over her lips. "Don't try that ever again, Danny Kelly. You belong to me now and there's nothing you can do about it."

As if to underline his mistress's words, Astaroth gave a quiet growl and eyed him as he trudged back into the house.

# 3

Sandra listened at the door and couldn't believe her ears at what was being said. She knew some boys were strange and liked to show themselves, but she had never thought of Danny as being one of the weird ones. He seemed so nice, a quiet strong type. It couldn't be true.

Ear-wigging was not her normal routine but she had stolen downstairs for a glass of water and heard Danny's name being mentioned. Mister Evans, normally so pleasant and composed, was beside himself in outrage at what had happened, and Sandra had to know more. Standing in a thin beam of light from the nearly-closed door, she gasped aloud when he heard about him playing with himself and was only saved by the even louder exclamation of shock by Mrs Evans.

"In front of Miss Trimble!" she exclaimed, and Sandra wondered if Miss Trimble was young or old, pretty or ugly.

She stole back upstairs and thought over what

she heard the Sergeant telling his wife, and still couldn't believe he was speaking about the same boy. She knelt by her bed to say her prayers, much to the delight of the two young boys who shared her room, and then lay down to sleep.

Beth Thomas, one of the friendlier girls in her new school, could maybe corroborate some of the story tomorrow in class. She liked Beth, though it was a little disturbing the way she always tried to provoke boys into fighting each other, taking an almost impish delight when they actually did. Sandra reckoned it was because her father had left her when she was a baby and she didn't like men. She never mentioned her father, but some of the other girls had told her the story.

As she dozed off quietly into sleep, she mused over whether Danny showed himself to all the girls, or only to older women.

# 4
## THE VICARAGE

This time Danny had thought to bring matches, and a paper and pencil. He was determined to copy down the tracts to find out what they meant.

He waited until all were in bed and crept over to the closet. Lighting the candle, he set it on the floor and opened the door to look inside.

Expecting a draft he cupped the flame, but nothing happened, so he inspected the inside properly. Using the candle he burnt away the cobwebs and illuminated each of the corners to see if he could discover where that draft came from. But there was nothing to see. He checked the floorboards but all he saw were husked out insects, arachnids of various sizes, and a lot of grime.

Next he checked the writing to make sure it wasn't English after all. It wasn't neat by any means and perhaps he'd mistaken the spidery script for something else. There was no way on this earth it could be English, so he copied it down as best he could.

He used the only book in his room to rest the paper on to write. Leather-bound and mildewed, it held the aroma of old paperbacks and libraries, and once again his mind wandered to times of old, when at age ten he used to wait in the local library for his mam to finish work in the cloth factory so they could drive home on the tram together. He smiled fondly at the recollection but forced himself to push on with the copying.

There was an awful lot to write, and because he wasn't familiar with the language, he had to check every word two or three times to be sure of the spelling. His eyes started to tire and he contemplated leaving it for the next day, but his determination to see what it meant kept him at it.

Mentally he made a pact with himself to finish the large block of writing tonight and do the rest tomorrow. It had to be done. Trimble and her Hound of Hell were up to no good, to put it mildly, and he was sure the writing meant something.

He grinned at his subconscious use of the phrase Hound of Hell, and how he'd dramatised the situation to himself. It was unbelievable, everything in the last forty-eight hours was like a nightmare to be found somewhere in a story book - the journey away from Liverpool, coming to Wales and everything since then. It all seemed so unreal, and yet he was dealing with it. He *was* dealing with it, he had it under control, and he felt quite proud of that fact.

Today had not been as bad as he thought it

would be. The Reverend had shouted, called him an ungrateful sinner, an Irish thief who'd come to a bad end if he carried on, but all in all he had been rather subdued.

Miss Trimble, after the initial glory of her triumph, had also seemed a withdrawn and he wondered if it had anything to do with his show of aggression that morning. Only the damned dog persisted in hating him, oh and the bloody cat who had shat on his bed. Having a purpose boosted his mood, but he'd still sooner be away from the place.

"Take every day as it comes, Danny boy," he muttered to himself, shrugging off his troubles.

The last word was copied and checked, and he looked at the text by the light of the candle. It was gibberish to him, but he was sure it was Welsh. Slipping the folded sheet between the pages of the book, he suddenly heard the door squeal slowly open.

He quickly blew the flame out as a deep growl permeated through the room. He peeked through the crack in the door between the hinges to see Astaroth standing motionless in the doorway. A dark shadow in the moonlight, he stood shoulders hunched, head hung low and legs splayed. Danny was terrified. The growl sounded again, deep and rumbling, and Danny knew if he attacked he had nothing to defend himself with but a book. His mind raced over possible scenarios. Maybe he could bat at the dog with it. No, he'd ram it in its mouth. Dogs aren't tigers. They bite things, and without their teeth they're powerless, well sort of ...

He clutched the book close to him. He knew he couldn't stay crouched behind the door forever, so emboldened by his plan to impede those massive jaws, he stood up and walked into the dog's view.

Danny saw the dog's hackles rise and the growl moved up a notch. He knew there was no use trying to pacify it, so Danny decided to let it make the first move. He pushed the book out in front of him, side-on, ready to wedge it into Astaroth's gaping mouth. He'd learned long ago one of the golden rules in any fight was belief in one's own abilities; to go into a fight with any doubts was a mistake.

Astaroth took one step forward, then another. His movements seemed jerky, tense, and Danny made ready for the attack. Mentally he envisaged the book sliding into the dog's mouth, then holding its mouth shut and trying to strangle it. He was so confident now he wanted it to happen.

"Come on, you bloody mutt," he hissed through gritted teeth. "You want me? Come and get me."

And before he knew what he was doing, he took a step forward. The growl turned into a snarl but Astaroth moved one leg stiffly back and Danny almost cheered in triumph.

Then, as if on cue, Miss Trimble appeared. Her hair was tied back and she wore a dressing gown, Danny had the distinct impression she had been watching from the shadows in the corridor, and she, much to his pleasure, looked decidedly disappointed.

"Astaroth, come now, the young man needs his

sleep. He has a long day tomorrow."

Obediently the dog stepped back and padded out, panting and tongue lolling as if nothing had happened.

"Sweet dreams, Daniel. Don't stay up too long."

Miss Trimble gave him a scowl and was gone.

Realising he'd been holding his breath, Danny exhaled and inhaled. Finding the matches with trembling hands, he lit the candle, considering what had just happened. Did the dog retreat a step? Had Danny really made him do that?

Sitting down heavily on the bed, he remembered the sheet of paper. Had she seen it?

Fumbling with the book, it opened, and the sheet fell out onto the bed, giving him a glimpse of a picture of Noah's Ark.

Bringing the candle closer to read the ancient cover, he saw though the writing had worn off, the furrow of the script could still just barely be read. Pressed into the black leather cover were the words, Holy Bible.

# 5

Danny woke up to the hot stench of old meat. Pulling his head back from the fetid blast, he opened his eyes to see Astaroth's cruel open jaws not six inches ways from his face.

At first the dog stared, its fangs glistening in the moonlight, drool falling onto his pillow. Then the growling really started, from deep within its massive chest, growing in volume.

Danny, too fear-crazed to intentionally move, instinctively jumped when Astaroth finally barked, a sound so loud, so full of hatred and rage, it triggered a primeval fear so deep he was frozen in terror. Still it continued, a sound too ferocious to call a bark, a mindless canine fury only inches from his head, pushing Danny backwards until he could mentally shrink no more.

His arms crossed over his head in a last-ditch defence while he waited for the onslaught to end. Terror overrode every instinct; every physical movement was locked into submission as he almost willed death to take him.

And then it stopped. From Hell's fury to silence in the blink of an eye, Astaroth wasn't even breathing heavily.

Peering from behind his crossed arms, the dog looked as if it wanted him to throw a stick or a ball, with its tongue comically lolling out. Astaroth turned its head quizzically and peered down as if nothing had happened. Then in a flash it was gone, out through the door and away into the corridor.

He stood up and cursed his pissed pyjamas. He'd wash them and say nothing. The whole house would have heard what happened.

Danny now knew this war would never be won on moral victories. This was real. Either he would die, or they would.

# 6

As he ate his toast, Danny took stock of what had happened. He had a passage of writing copied from the wall in the closet. He didn't understand what was on it but he reckoned it was written in Welsh. And that was it. He knew Miss Trimble was evil, her dog and cat were somehow in league with her, and the Reverend thought she was a saint. Other than that he had nothing.

He couldn't run away because the police would be involved, and he'd more than likely end up in prison. Killing Trimble without proof of her criminal persuasion would mean a one-way ticket to the hangman, and his only defence was a passage of writing he didn't even understand.

Taking another glance, he surreptitiously hidit under the table in case the housekeeper decided to check up on him.

It made absolutely no sense whatsoever.

Ein Tad yn y nefoedd,sancteiddier dy enw;
deled dy deyrnas;
gwneler dy ewyllys,
ar y ddaear fel yn y nef.
Dyro inni heddiw ein bara beunyddiol;
a maddau inni ein troseddau,
fel yr ym ni wedi maddau i'r rhai a droseddodd i'n herbyn;
a phaid â'n dwyn i brawf,
ond gwared ni rhag yr Un drwg.
Oherwydd eiddot ti yw'r deyrnas a'r gallu
a'rgogoniant
am byth. Achlad Rhydderch

He sighed, popped the last piece of toast in his mouth, and started to put the things in the basin to wash. Trimble had given him a list which at first glance didn't seem like much.

However, after seeing what the jobs involved, they now looked more like the labours of Hercules: clean the kitchen, sweep the house, dust the house, pick up the fallen apples in the orchard, and finally clear up any dog muck - Danny had smirked at this term until he realised what was meant – not just from the grounds but the graveyard as well.

Shaking his head at the injustice of having to shovel the shit of his tormentor, Danny decided to start the list with the nastiest task and headed for the orchard.

She watched him from her bedroom window and smiled as he retched while picking up the dog shit. He was perfect for what they needed: an orphan with no known family ties, introverted, with very low self-esteem. Perfect.

Last night could have been a terrible defeat. They had returned to her room angry and disappointed at how things had turned out. However Astaroth, Prince of Thrones and servant of Hell, had shown his cunning. Now the boy was back where he belonged, crushed and scared, ripe to be worked into meat.

She sighed to herself. Being a servant of Hell had its trials, but it was necessary and had to be done. In these hard times they needed protection, and the Beast only gave that in exchange for souls. Since Gwyn had been nearly stripped of his priesthood by the Bishop, it had all fallen to her to see things through.

She thanked the nine rings of Hades the church had agreed any scandal would be bad for all concerned. The Bishop, a kindly man who always tried to see the best side of everyone, had arranged for them to live in the vicarage on the explicit condition nobody will ever know about his dalliance in the dark arts. Otherwise the church would be closed, the congregation moved, Gwyn would be pensioned and no one would be any the wiser. If only he had known what that 'dalliance' entailed.

Yet though he escaped investigation and

punishment to live a free man, Gwyn was not the man she had formerly known. The near-disgrace seemed to have quenched his fire and he was satisfied to let her lead. Despite size and vigour, he was a broken man, his urges and passions now all but dead, and she had long since realised the best years were behind him.

No, it was up to her now; and Danny would be her first real offering. She'd overdone the guilt and bullying on the last boy, and he'd killed himself before they could arrange everything. Gwyn had been livid, but what did he expect? She had to do everything while he languished in his well of self-pity. If it wasn't that the vicarage and church were so ideal for her plans, she would have done away with him long ago.

No, this one she'd do right. She'd feed him, emotionally fatten him up like a calf, and then like the countless others Gwyn sacrificed before, they'd kill him. She was determined it should be done correctly. No more plying tramps with alcohol until they passed out - then strangling them. This time they'd bleed him on the altar and offer him to first to Astaroth and then Satan. And this time it would be her slitting his throat into a bucket.

How life had changed. What would father think of her now? Middle-class, snobbish, impatient and overbearing, he had been absolutely furious when she broke off her engagement to the young cavalry officer he'd lined up for her; and shocked beyond words when she declared she was leaving Sutton

Coldfield to move to Wales and live in a vicarage.

"Wales?" he'd exploded. "Have you gone completely insane? What's in Wales except sheep and bloody Presbyterians? You'll do no such thing, girl. What do I tell everyone at the club?"

Her mind was made up and the delight of rebelling against her father, a feat never before accomplished, gave her the drive to see it through. His social embarrassment meant nothing to her. She knew what she wanted to do, and be; and his laughable qualms about what the neighbours might say and its effect on the family name were no more important to her than the dead insects in her closet.

Astaroth joined her at the window and she patted his head lightly, chanting the names of the seven Princes of Hell and making the sign of the upturned cross on her chest to please him.

"Belphegor, Mammon, Asmodeus, Leviathan, Beelzebub, Lucifer and Satan ..."


An apple hit him with a bit more force than if it had simply fallen.

"Ow!" he complained, rubbing his head and looking up to see who had thrown it.

It was the little lad Huw had called Dafydd, sitting on the orchard wall. Danny smiled. The kid was unusually aggressive when it came to throwing things, but for some reason he radiated a vulnerability Danny found disarming.

"Hello Dafydd, what are you doing mate?" he

smiled.

"Scrumping," he answered seriously, and smiled back. "And throwing things at you. Be glad it wasn't from my catty," he said, pulling out a catapult from his back pocket.

"Well, don't let the dog see you. He's a nasty piece of work when he gets going."

"I know, he's massive. He killed Mrs Weather's dog, Spot. I didn't see it happen but Tommy Lang said Astaroth chased it all over the village until he caught it, and then ate it in one go. I still reckon my catty would take him though, like John and Goliath. I'm going to kill that cat of hers as well. It's evil, that one is."

Danny agreed about the cat and was about to correct him on the John and Goliath when a brain wave hit him. "Dafydd, can you do me a favour? Do you speak Welsh?"

"Of course I do," he said, affronted. "We all do here in Peulwys."

Pulling the sheet out and unfolding it, Danny said, "Can you read this for me and tell me what it means, please?"

A cloud of doubt crossed the young lad's features as he took the paper and screwed his face up to read it. After a while he announced, "Well, I can't actually read Welsh, but I do speak it, all the time."

Danny nodded understandingly. "Could you take it to Huw and ask him to tell me what it is, then, please?"

Dafydd nodded and continued to rattle on about

his reading problems. "I can't read English either. Mrs Trelawney, from the school, called me an idiot in front of the whole class, but I'm not. I can do my maths easy-peasy, but the reading just jumbles up in front of my eyes."

Nodding as he listened, not wanting to upset the lad so he would throw the paper away without first showing it to someone, Danny broke in, "Don't forget now, it's very important." And then to put a dramatic edge to it. "It could be about a murder."

The effect on the young lad was instant. Eyes wide in shock, he breathed the word in awe at the gravity of his task. "A murder? You mean the boy last year? I liked him. He was big like Bryn, but nice. Nobody found him. They found the others on the beach, but not him. Can't remember his name. There was an orphan, stayed at Jones the Milk's farm. The police took him away for two days. They thought he was the killer but they let him go, released him. He didn't do it. He's too kind. He let me ride one of his cows once, me and –"

"Dafydd, what murders? What other boy? They found bodies on the beach?" interruptedDanny.

Dafydd's eyes widened in fright as he looked over the older boy's shoulder. Danny turned to look.

Fearing the worst, his blood froze in his veins. Astaroth, like a maddened wolf, was galloping towards him and there was nowhere to run. Danny looked back to the boy but he was gone, which was a relief because he didn't know what might have happened if they'd both been caught with the passage of writing. In a flash the big dog was in front of him, barking at full volume, and it was all he could do not to cower in raw fear at the assault. Behind the dog Miss Trimble casually approached them, seemingly oblivious to the racket her pet was making.

"Who was that boy, Danny? What did you give him?"

Danny swallowed hard, trying to gather his thoughts, but the unholy baying of the hound made it almost impossible to think.

"Astaroth be quiet now, there's a good boy," Trimble scolded, and the dog snapped its jaws shut like a bear trap and stood mute guard over its prisoner.

"Now, Daniel, I'll ask you once more. Who was that boy and what did you give him? I saw it all from the window, so don't lie to me."

The bravado he knew he was going to have to affect made him feel like he was laughing at his own hanging, but he'd be damned before he gave her the pleasure of seeing him scared. Lifting his chin in defiance, he said, "If you saw it all, Miss Trimble, then why are you asking?"

She snorted impatiently and Astaroth menacingly growled. Danny's mind raced and then, Eureka, a flash of inspiration hit him.

"I just gave the lad his paper aeroplane. It flew over the wall."

"Who was he? Don't tell me you don't know who he is."

The confidence gained by his successful lie

emboldened him and he felt cocky as he said, "How would I know? He was just a boy from the village who lost his plane, that's all." He decided to qualify his innocence with an audacious statement, Astaroth's fang filled mouth now a million miles away. "I've never seen the boy before in my life."

The steadfastness of her gaze, the slow and controlled nod of her head spoke volumes, and Danny knew he'd gone too far.

"So you didn't recognise him from the other day, then? Dafydd Owen, one of the boys you attacked on your first day, one of the children Sergeant Evans found you with yesterday? You've never seen him before, is that what you're saying to me?"

There was no need for an answer. She already knew. He had nothing to say that could help, so he stayed quiet.

"Finish your chores out here. You still have the kitchen and the rest of the house to do, which means no more aeroplanes with strange boys you've never met before. I'll have words with the Reverend about your lies. Let's see what he has to say about it."

She turned to leave but froze when Danny asked in a loud fragile voice, "What are you hiding? You call me a liar but the kids I met all go to school here, when you said there isn't one. Why are you so worried if I give a kid anything? What do you know about the lad who was murdered here last year or the bodies on the beach? Are you going to kill me?"

Turning very slowly, Trimble cracked a false

smile that didn't quite make it to her eyes, an act that only managed to make her look hateful. "Why, Daniel, I believe you've quite an imagination. Nobody wants to kill you and that poor boy probably ran away. That awful dairy farmer is well known for beating the children they send to him. Now finish your chores and we'll talk about this later."

# 7

Gwynfor Davies rested his weary bones in the only place he knew he'd be left alone, the old church - *his* old church. He was now feeling all of his fifty-five years, and though he put on a good front, inside he was breaking up.

The church had been gutted when it closed, everything removed. Only the stone pews on the sides and to the rear of the church remained because they'd been too heavy to lift, and it was on one of those he was sitting, at the back, facing where once the altar stood.

They'd had some great times in this building, this House of God, as he sarcastically liked to call it. He'd held masses here that would have given the Bishop a heart attack if he'd have known. It had all been such a great laugh. The biggest laugh of all was he wasn't even a real priest. Using forged papers and references he'd blustered his way into the post, and that blithering idiot Bishop had naively accepted his word. His true occupation was anything that made an easy penny and the Church had fit the bill just right.

Ever one to see an angle for a profit, he'd started the devil worship two years after the Great War, purely for money, the sex being a pleasurable by-product. After seeing how much money the pious poor put in the collection box each week, he had wondered at how much the sinful rich would be willing to give once a month.

After biding his time and scouring the North Wales gentry for suitable candidates, he quietly invited the best prospect to an evening at the church. On the invitation he wrote something laughable about entertaining some nuns from St. Catherine's Convent in Bootle, a name he'd made up on the spur of the moment. Privately he dropped veiled promises and hints the nuns were young and full of the lusts of the inexperienced that need quenching, and so may not prove to be so pious after all.

He invited six young gentlemen he thought most susceptible to the idea of sin for the soirée - wild young men who had lost their fear of society in the trenches of Belgium and were constantly on the lookout for the next thrill, the next chance to dice with danger. Unfortunately, one of the guests brought a young lady with him, but seeing as Davies couldn't very well just shoo her away, he simply hoped it would all go well and she'd play along.

For the first Black Mass he'd hired an actor and six prostitutes from the Liverpool dockland. "Make it convincing," he told the actor. "Wait until they're all drunk and just start right in with some kind of mumbo jumbo about a ceremony or a bet! Make a bet you can summon the devil. I'll soon have the whores nude and that'll get their attention." And so it did.

The girls, coarse but appealing, were the nuns - and the evening started off low key and proper.

But Davies had mixed vodka into the sherry and as soon as the tongues were wagging in hearty abandon, the Reverend left the room so the hypnotist could suggest the wager. "Is anyone willing to bet against me if I said I could raise the devil in Reverend Davies' church?"

A stunned silence greeted his words, and Gwynfor listening from behind the door cursed to himself, thinking he'd mistimed the announcement. The actor, like the Reverend, was also sure they were ready, and yet the doubt etched on everyone's face told a different story.

Then Giles Erskine, from the Liverpool Erskine family who'd made their millions on the docks during World War One and went on to lose it all in the Crash of '29, stepped forward and pronounced with a flashing a smile, "I'll be damned if you can!" and the whole room erupted into laughter.

After that it couldn't have been easier. They'd filed into the church and stood at the altar. The actor, who was now thoroughly into the role, donned a black cassock and commanded everyone to stand in a circle. After intoning for a while, he pointed to one of the prostitutes and solemnly ordered her to, "Show yourself for Satan," which she promptly did.

Pulling off her habit she stood naked in front of everyone, to the astonishment of all. How she'd hidden her smile even Gwynfor didn't know, but she managed it and one after the other the nun-prostitutes undressed in front of the men.

Then it was the turn of the male guests who readily abandoned their clothing as the actor ordered them, to stand bare and ready in the circle. The only independent female of the group, the lady invited by one of the male guests, had initially been shocked by the proceedings. Yet now she looked on in fascination as one by one the men dropped their clothes on command.

Fiona Trimble, a businessman's daughter from Sutton Coldfield, worked voluntarily at the local library and had only agreed to come to Wales because she had wanted to impress her cavalry officer fiancé, blushed deeply and started to breathe heavily in visible excitement. Before the master of ceremonies commanded her to undress, she was already tugging at her blouse.

So there they stood, six men, seven women, naked and devoid of all inhibitions, waiting for a thespian priest to lead them in what they thought would be an archaic demon-raising ceremony. However, he simply clasped his hands before him in mock humility and said, "Now fuck for Satan!"

Gwynfor's first plan had been blackmail, his idea being he'd storm into the church, demand to know what was going on, and extort money from his shamed victims. However, another idea hit him. As he watched the bodies writhing in ecstasy, it dawned on him he could make this a regular thing, maybe build a following of sex-starved young male Satanists using whores, lies and ceremony to extort money from them. They may have been hard up in their own eyes, but to the common man these people were rich beyond their wildest dreams.

Walking up the aisle towards the fornicating assembly, he nodded to the actor to follow him out. He had plans and he reckoned the actor could do with a bit of extra money.

"The next time we do this, let's really put on a show. We'll use fire and brimstone, costumes and a couple more whores. Think up some sort of ritual ceremony type of thing to say to everyone. Tonight was good but let's make the next time even better."

The actor, out of work and hungry, nodded eagerly at the idea. "It'll cost a bit more, mind."

"If all goes well that won't be a problem. Just do as I say, put on a good show, and we'll try to recruit as many followers as possible. Then we'll milk them for tribute. We should all come out good from this."

Smiling at the memory of that first night almost twenty years ago, he remembered when Fiona had caught his eye. After he'd made his plans with the actor, he stopped to gaze at the lightning flashes in the autumn sky. As they rumbled menacingly a brain wave hit him. Going back inside to stand among the copulating pairs, he lifted his arms as if in praise and boomed in a strong baritone, "Hail Satan, hail the King of Hell and all his black-hearted minions.

Come to us, show us your sign, show us you are here among us, your naked acolytes."

And by a pure fluke of chance he was answered by a resounding clap of thunder, freezing all in shock. The rumbling heavens acted as a catalyst for everyone to pause. Couples stopped in their sex act as if waking from a dream. Gwynfor panicked. If the mood was broken, if they suddenly became scared, then all was lost and he really would have to resort to blackmail to recoup his losses.

"No, don't stop, continue, continue in your fucking, for he is here among us. No harm will come to you, no danger lurks, for he sees what you do and approves. Worship him with your bodies, venerate him with your pleasures, for he is of a time when love was pure, not dirty. Do this for him and all will be well. Leave now and all is lost."

He mentally patted himself on the back for the speech. How on earth had he come up with that codswallop? Nevertheless it had the desired effect: the lovers continued until gasps of climaxes and strains of orgasms rang through the church.

Fiona Trimble lay under the hammering body of her young cavalry officer, her legs wrapped around his waist, looking over his shoulder. She stared fixedly at Gwynfor until he noticed her. Raking her nails on the young man's shoulders and back as he rammed himself into her, she gazed at him, mouth half-open in passion and eyes alight in desire, her message clear.

Gwynfor, though excited by the activity around

him, wasn't sure he wanted to go seconds after the soldier was finished with her, so he nodded to her wisely and turned to leave the church, taking one of the undressed whores with him. After all he had paid them, so why not?

He knew the signs, he knew women, and she'd come to him when it suited her. Back at the vicarage he finished with the girl, sent her packing, and delighted by what had happened he poured a Scotch.

He'd told the actor to wrap up the ceremony when they were sated and to say they should keep in touch if they wanted to do this again. He wasn't exactly sure how he'd angle this into a profit but he did know that any church, of any kind, always made money with the minimum of work involved. Faith and sex, the biggest money makers of all, and he now had a hand in both of them.

A timid knock on the door stirred him from his reverie. "Come in!" he thundered, suspecting it to be one of the Liverpool prostitutes demanding more money for the play acting. But it wasn't.

Coughing demurely Fiona Trimble entered the room. Now properly attired and looking as if she'd just left a tea and cake afternoon at the Mother's Union, she smiled at the Reverend and said, "I just wanted to say thank you for the evening, Reverend Davies. I must confess at first I was a little shocked, but I enjoyed it greatly and hope you'll think of me next time you decide to hold another soirée."

The Reverend stood up and smiled wolfishly, "So it was to your taste, then, Miss Trimble?"

Batting her eyes and chastely looking to the floor, she nodded and smiled secretively. "Yes, very much so."

"Then I hope to see more of you in the coming months as I intend to hold regular meetings, for a select crowd, of course."

Trimble looked up and stared straight into his eyes. "I'll look forward to our next meeting Reverend, and I hope next time you'll also play a more active role in the proceedings."

"You can count on it, my dear."

The Reverend smiled at the memory. Fiona had been so much easier to handle in those days. Compliant and curious, she had let him take the lead and willingly immersed herself in everything he suggested, be it carnal or spiritual. Now she was different.

Ever since that infernal dog invaded his home she had changed, and Gwyn Davies foresaw a bad ending on the horizon; a very bad ending indeed.

# 8

Danny played back the events of the day in his mind, reliving Trimble's reaction to his questions. If he'd been worried before, he was terrified now. The cold smile, the smooth lies, he knew she was going to hurt him, maybe even kill him, and he didn't know what to do about it. Thanks to the Reverend telling Sergeant Evans about the bath tub incident and finding the knife on him, he had nowhere to go, nobody he could trust.

The rest of the day he spent cleaning. The house was spotless and even the housekeeper had expressed her satisfaction at his efforts. Now tired and depressed, he lay in his creaking bed and contemplated the hopelessness of his position. Even if he did manage to overpower Astaroth and kill Trimble and the Reverend, he'd still have the police on his tail, and a penniless Scouser tramping around North Wales would be easy to pick up. He wondered if they hung seventeen year olds, or would they wait until he was eighteen to execute him?

Would anyone be able to make anything of the sheet of paper he'd given Dafydd? Surely it had to be of some relevance. Or was that just wishful thinking? If only he could decipher it. He hadn't managed to snaffle more paper yet, but finding some was a priority by tomorrow so the rest could be copied. There were only a couple of sentences left, but he hadn't looked at them properly yet.

From outside a low moan sounded in the darkness. "Cats!" Danny cursed. Every night had been the same up to now. "That ginger beast must have more enemies than Adolf Hitler," he mused. It fought all night and slept all day, no doubt due to major character defects only an extra-strong dose of arsenic would be able to cure.

After bearing the caterwauling for five minutes, he stood up to close the window. It was stifling hot in the room but he needed his sleep as Trimble had already told him tomorrow would be a hard day of cutting and stacking firewood. As he walked back towards the bed he heard the slow creak of the closet door opening. Puzzled, he turned and pushed it shut with a bang that made him wince. After listening for a while until he was satisfied no one woke up, he went back to bed. No sooner was he under the covers than the door to the closet opened again. This time he knew there was no reason why it should open on its own. The first time he'd put down to movement of air as he closed the windows, but now? There was absolutely no reason why it should do that.

A blast of cold air shot out from the darkness

and Danny found himself shrinking under his bed covers. The room temperature had dropped noticeably and he could not fathom why. He hadn't found anything that might have caused such a frosty draft. Was this Trimble and the Reverend's doing? Were they playing a trick on him? He wouldn't have put it past them, and though he couldn't quite shake off his doubts about this theory he grasped at it with both hands. "I know what you're doing; you're trying to scare me," he spoke quietly into the shadows.

An almost audible puff of wind blew something out of the closet and into the moonlight. Peering down to see what it was, his heart fluttered as he recognised the photo of his mother. All fear left him as he threw the covers back and dashed towards the open closet door. But there was nothing there, only the cold blackness inside. Incredibly, he found himself talking to the empty space. "I don't know what you want from me but leave the picture of my mother alone." Other than the muted screaming of the cats outside, nothing answered, nothing moved.

Danny felt the cold slowly drawing out of the room, pulling past him and into the blackness of the closet beyond. Walking slowly backwards without taking his eyes off the door, he scooped down and picked up the photo, his fingers fumbling on the floor until he found it.

The room felt normal now, all trace of the earlier chill was gone. Slowly his heart wound down to a normal beat and the tension in his shoulders relaxed. Had the experience been a dream? Had he actually spoken to an empty closet? He shook his head and looked at the picture in his hand. The cat fight outside started anew and Danny rolled his eyes in exasperation. Crawling into bed and lying on his back, he studied the ceiling and tried to conjure up an image of his mother doing her chores around their small terraced house, singing one of her favourite hymns as she always did when she worked. He stroked the face in the picture briefly and closed his eyes, hoping for sleep to claim him.

He woke up with a start. A draft of cold air buffeted his face and rattled him rudely from sleep. The picture was gone and he scrabbled around the bed clothes searching. Illuminated by moonlight, his gaze found it on the floor next to the open closet door, and he was about to jump out of bed to grab it when soft as wind through branches the sound came.

Someone, a boy by the sound of it, was crying in despair and yet singing at the same time. The voice, as pure and high as that of a soprano choirboy, gradually grew in volume until he could clearly make out words through the sobs.

*"Heb wrido wrth fy ngweled i? Pa le mae'r wên oedd ar dy wefus. Fu'n cynnau 'nghariad ffyddlon ffôl?"*

Danny couldn't understand what was being sung, but the slow haunting melody struck like a dagger of ice through his heart. Fear made him forget the picture and he pulled the sheets over his head and pressed fingers into ears, attempting to block the sound. But the unearthly singing droned on, interspersed with weeping, overpowering him with terror. Then, in a flash of guilt-inspired lightning, he remembered the abandoned moonlit picture on the floor. He must retrieve it.

Steeling himself against dread he threw back the sheets and sat bolt upright. Instantly the voice stopped and the closet door closed with a bang. Whatever caused it was now gone, leaving him again to the sounds of battling felines outside. Cautiously he stood up and walked towards the picture on the floor. Eyes still fixed on the closet door, he bent down and picked it up, checking it for damage.

Danny sharply inhaled.

Instead of the smiling woman who had so carefully nurtured him through his early years, he saw a wailing gnashing soul surrounded by fire. Naked, its eyes and mouth gushing blood, two open wounds where breasts might have once been and skin blistering from heat, it seemed to see him and screamed like a Banshee, a shriek that pierced his skull and exploded inside like a thousand daggers.

Then it was gone. Once again silence ruled and even the cats were quiet. The picture returned to normal - his mother smiling at the camera. At the bottom right corner there was something he'd not seen before. A brown stain had eaten into the white border, a scorch mark, and Danny knew it hadn't been there earlier in the evening. Somehow he slept soundly after that. Taking the picture and placing it in the breast pocket of his pyjama top, he lay down and pulled the covers over him.

He woke up to the gentle sound of a bird singing, and as the cobwebs of sleep slowly withdrew, wondered about what had happened the night before. It didn't seem possible he'd simply fallen asleep, and considered the whole episode was a very realistic dream. It was either that, or he was going mad; or his room really was haunted. He washed in cold water, threw his clothes on and opened the closet to inspect the walls again. Considering the writing, the large passage dominated the wall, but the others which hadn't seemed so important before now took up his interest. He still had no paper to write them down on, so with a sigh he closed the door and turned to leave.

The sight of the waiting figure of Miss Trimble by the bedroom door stopped him in his tracks. Immaculately dressed in a white blouse and black skirt, her hair was pinned high, and without her glasses on Danny could see what Sergeant Evans found so interesting. He subconsciously checked for Astaroth, but she was alone.

"You're going to have to do some washing today. Your clothes are starting to reek, I can smell you from here. Do your chores and then I want you to wash your clothes and have a bath."

Danny's eyes widened. "Will I be allowed to bathe on my own? I don't want to get in trouble again."

A sly smile crept onto the housekeeper's face,

"Do you want me to be there?"

"No!" he exclaimed, then more calmly so as not to cause offence, "I'd rather bathe alone, if you don't mind Miss Trimble."

She entered the room and stood before him. Slightly taller than he was in her heels, she reached up and stroked the side of his face. "You do really want me to be there, I know you do. I can feel it," she said in a soft husky voice that sent a thousand fireworks off down his spine. "Perhaps if the Reverend leaves us alone for a few hours, I might come and help you wash."

The tip of her tongue slipped briefly over her top lip and Danny swore she could feel the heat from his loins and face. His heart in overdrive and knees dissolving to water where he stood, Danny realised he did want her there, did want her to see him naked, and the thought of breaking the taboo sent a dizzy wave through his mind. He blinked twice, stuttering, "I just don't want to get into any more trouble."

"I'm sure you don't," she said, her hand drifting down towards his groin to hover on his erection, "but we're all naughty at heart Daniel, you wicked, wicked boy."

She was so close he could smell her perfume and it overwhelmed him with desire. The moment lingered: him standing before her in his pyjamas, she with her hand resting lightly on his manhood, rubbing its head between her finger and thumb. Then with a squeeze, she turned and walked out of the room, calling briskly over her shoulder, "Do your chores and wash your clothes, and have a bath for God's sake!"

A gust of cold hair hit him from behind and Danny turned to see what was there, automatically reaching for the picture in his breast pocket. There was something in the closet, he knew it. He hadn't seen anything, but on a base instinctive level he knew he wasn't alone in this room.

"Who are you?" he whispered. "What do you want?"

# 9

Sandra liked Beth. She was talkative, outgoing and friendly, and if it wasn't for her pathological hatred of boys, she'd have probably been an ideal best friend.

Up to now their short but intense friendship had only been marred by two minor incidents, one when Sandra caught Beth looking at her in the changing rooms after PE. It wasn't so much the fact that Sandra had caught her staring at her body as if in a trance. Anyone can stare off into space while concentrating and not see what's in front of them. No, it was the embarrassment afterwards when she realised Sandra had noticed her gaze, as if caught doing something dirty. Sandra didn't quite understand what was wrong but it opened up a gap between them that afternoon that took a whole day to close. The other time was when they were sitting in the school yard at dinner break. Beth, in a fit of giggles, had told Sandra about the time she had watched Huw and Bryn peeing on the railway embankment. They'd crossed their streams, as if sword fighting, and were laughing like little children.

"Boys are so stupid!" she exclaimed, and Sandra, who knew what boys had to pee with but had only ever seen her younger cousin doing it when he was little, laughed along with her.

"Do you like boys, Sand?" Beth asked, suddenly serious.

"Promise not to tell?" Sandra whispered.

Beth nodded and they moved their heads closer together. "I sort of like the boy I came on the train with. Daniel, Daniel Kelly."

"Him?" Beth exclaimed, and then quietly, "He was caught playing with himself. I heard my dad talking to the Reverend about it. And anyway, he's rubbish at fighting. I saw Bryn make him cry on the road up to Peulwys the other day."

Sandra was mildly annoyed with this instant denigration of Danny. "Boys don't have to be good fighters to be nice, Beth. He's just nice, that's all I said."

"I know Sand, I'm just telling you what I heard and saw. I don't like any of the boys around here. They're all stupid. Bryn can't even read and Geraint thinks the Welsh were in Britain before the English, and the English are really German and French!" Beth laughed riotously but Sandra found she could only smile along with her. "Your Danny gave Dafydd a letter the other day and Dafydd couldn't read it, so he threw it away. That's typical of him.

All he ever wants to do is go scrumping, shoot stones at things and play war. Well, he is only twelve," Beth reasoned.

"A letter?" Sandra's ears perked up. "For who? What did it say?"

Beth smiled slyly. "Dav couldn't read it. He speaks Welsh but he can't read it. I told you, he's stupid."

"Why would he give anyone a letter in Welsh? I don't think he speaks it," Sandra puzzled.

"He doesn't," Beth answered. "When Bryn beat him up and made him cry, we were talking to him in Welsh and he didn't understand us. And he ripped his trousers and I saw his bum because he wasn't wearing any underpants."

Beth exploded into fits of giggles but Sandra fell deeper into contemplation. "I wonder if the letter was for me?"

"It was in Welsh, and anyway, why would he write to you? You only met him the one time on the train, you told me yourself."

Ignoring the question, Sandra stood up. "Where's Dav? I want to know where he threw the letter. It might be important."

"Why?"

"It just might be. Why would he write a letter? Perhaps he's in danger or, oh I don't know, it just seems strange to write a letter for no reason. Let's go and see where Dafydd is."

Beth looked doubtful but stood up to go with her. "I think he's playing football in the other yard.

I'll come with you."

"What did you do with the letter Danny gave you the other day?" Sandra asked straightaway.

Dafydd was tying his shoe laces on the side of the game and he answered without looking up. "Threw it away."

"Why? It might have been important. Who was it for?" Sandra asked, annoyed at his flippancy.

Dafydd stood up. He was a small lad for his age but extremely aggressive. Huw, Geraint, and Bryn saw him as a sort of mascot for their gang. Beth thought him retarded, as did Sandra to a certain degree.

"Because I couldn't read it, he couldn't read it, nobody could. So I threw it." He shrugged, nonplussed at her annoyance.

"Where did you throw it?"

"Up by the orchard, on the way to Jones the Milk's place. I scrunched it into a ball to play footy with it but it was too small. Then I tried to shoot it with my catty but it wouldn't fly, so I left it."

"Can you show me where after school?"

Dafydd looked affronted, "No, there's footy practice after school."

"I'll show you where the orchard is," said Beth. "It isn't far away."


The rest of the afternoon passed at a snail's pace for Sandra. She couldn't wait to see what he'd written.

Perhaps it was for her. She doubted very much he'd written something in Welsh, and reckoned it had probably more to do with Dafydd's lack of reading prowess than anything else.

As the wall of the orchard came in to view, she picked up the pace a little. "Did Dafydd say exactly where he threw it?" Beth asked.

"No, he just scrunched it up and tried to play football with it," Sandra said, slowing down as she reached the corner of the wall surrounding the apple trees. They sauntered up the road, eyes to the ground, until Beth squealed, "I've found it. Over here"

It was dirty and crumpled into a tiny conker-sized ball. Beth picked it up and solemnly gave it to Sandra. Carefully opening it as if it were antique, Sandra straightened it out and palmed it flat on her thigh. Her heart dropped when she realised it was in Welsh, or some foreign language she didn't yet recognise. Handing it to Beth, she asked, "What does it say? Can you read it?"

Beth scanned the first two lines and started to laugh.

Sandra smiled at first then grew slightly annoyed. "Don't just laugh. What does it mean?"

"He's gone all religious. It's Our Father in Welsh."

"The Lord's Prayer?" She asked, puzzled. "Why would he write that down?"

"Perhaps he's practising his Welsh and that was what the Reverend gave him to learn."

Sandra contemplated her next move. She felt sure there was a reason why Danny had written it but couldn't for the life of her think why.

Then an idea hit her. "Fancy walking with me to the vicarage to see if he's there? We can ask him."

Beth pulled a face, "Why, do you fancy him or something?"

The tone of the question put Sandra on the defensive. "I told you I liked him, but I'd like to know why he wrote this and why he's not at our school."

"Because he's probably too old for school."

"Well, I still want to go and ask him about the paper. Coming or not?"

Beth shrugged, "Okay."

And off they went.


Miss Fiona Trimble looked down from her bedroom window at the two girls walking towards the house, and smiled. Astaroth padded into the bedroom to sit next to her and she idly stroked his head.

"I wonder what those two want here," she asked. "That's Elizabeth Thomas, the little lesbian from the village. I caught her looking at me at the beach last summer. How she squirmed when I smiled at her and patted the towel next to me." She laughed at the memory. "But I don't know the other one. I bet she came with our guest, another orphan perhaps. Let's go and intercept them before Danny sees them."

Sandra was just about to knock on the door when it opened.

"Yes?" said Trimble with a plastic smile. "Can I help you?"

Sandra, who thought this idea had gone from bad to worse as they approached the ancient building with its graves on one side of the path and its dark foreboding orchard on the other, cleared her throat and said in a trembling voice, "Hello. We're from the village and we were wondering if we could talk to Daniel Kelly. I know him from the orphanage in Liverpool."

"Yeeees ... Daniel." Trimble drew out the yes as if weighing the name up. "I'm afraid he isn't here right now. Can I give him a message?"

Looking doubtful at the answer, Sandra shook her head and was about to say no when Beth cut in. "Is it okay if we wait, Miss Trimble? We'll be quiet. We just need to talk to him."


Trimble really didn't need this. Danny was upstairs clearing the attic out and she was hoping to corner him and play a little. He was a good looking lad for his age and so deliciously innocent - well for a city boy anyway.

Then she had an idea. "If you want to, ladies, you can come inside and wait if you wish. I made some lemonade this morning."

Beth practically squealed in delight but Sandra wasn't so sure. She couldn't put her finger on why, but this woman gave her the creeps and she just wanted to go. They could come back tomorrow. "Thank you but I think we have to go now. We'll call back another time."

Beth pouted in disappointment. "Sand, why? It's early yet. We can stay for a little while. Perhaps he'll come?"

Sandra struggled for an excuse but lying had never been her strong point, "I have to...er... do my homework," she exclaimed in a rush.

Beth looked puzzled and Sandra hoped against hope she wouldn't let on they had no homework.

To her immense relief she clicked on, "Oh, okay then. I forgot about that." She turned to the housekeeper. "Goodbye Miss Trimble, and thank you," she said, smiling and holding out her hand to shake hers.

"Yes, pity, Elizabeth. I would have loved the pleasure of your company, but if you have homework that must come first. If you're ever in the area, do pop in and say hello." She took the proffered hand and stroked Beth's palm with her index finger, smiling at the look of shock on the girl's face as her finger traced a small circle, relishing the feeling of power when the girl smiled up at her and blushed.

Sandra looked on, puzzled that the act of departure seemed to be taking such a remarkably long time, but said nothing.

Finally Trimble dropped Beth's hand and turned to Sandra. "And the same goes for you. Any time you're around here, pop in and say hello. Perhaps you'll catch your friend."

Sandra smiled weakly. "Thank you, I will. Bye-bye now." She turned to leave.

Beth, who'd stayed back, looked up at the housekeeper and whispered thickly, with her heart in her mouth, "I will come around again if you want me to."

Trimble checked briefly to see if Beth's friend was looking and then whispered back, "Oh but I do, sweet Elizabeth, I do," stroking the side of her face before turning to go inside.

She closed the door, leant back on it and smothered the laugh that was bursting to escape.

That child was sweet, so sweet. She wondered what she'd do to her if and when she did come on her own. Astaroth will know, he always does.


"What was that about? We should have waited for him to come back," Beth complained.

"I had to get away from there," Sandra hastily answered. "That place, she was giving me the creeps. What was with the handshake? You never do that normally."

It was Beth's turn to be defensive. "I just thought it proper, that's all."

"There's nothing proper about that woman."

"She isn't that bad," Beth said sharply, and they walked home in silence.

# 10

Danny lay in his bed watching the closet door. His whole day revolved around what happened the night before. He had thought of nearly nothing else. Not until Trimble ambushed him in the attic did his thoughts of the closet and its black mysterious corners disperse into the background.

She had sent him up to move boxes around and create some space in its cramped confines. Danny knew she was going to come up after him, had expected it and wasn't sure if he was dreading it or not. He saw her now in a different light; did she love him? Would she be nice to him from now on? The way she ordered him around during the day didn't seem to say much for her devotions, which confused him because he'd always thought women only did things like that, sexual things, when they absolutely loved someone. Pushing the closet to the back of his mind, his thoughts dawdled upon Miss Trimble. It was amazing how many different looks she could put on just by pinning her hair a certain way. She always wore the same white blouse, black skirt, stockings and high heeled shoes, but her hair changed her appearance and, it would seem, her mood, almost uncannily. By the time he'd finished the chore he was hoping she'd come up. When she finally did, he wanted to ask about the delay.

Her hair was down around her shoulders, and as she slowly ascended the stairs to the attic Danny swallowed audibly in confused thought-fogging desire. Finally she reached the top and looked around her, her hands on her hips, legs astride. "Well, you've been busy Daniel. I should really reward you with something, shouldn't I?"

Danny laughed, high pitched and nervous, and cursed himself for the reaction. She approached him slowly, hips swinging, her heels the only sound he could hear over the roar of blood in his ears. "Now what would you have me do to reward you for your efforts, hmm?" she whispered, inches away from him.

"I don't …" he stammered and then cleared his throat. "I don't know, Miss Trimble."

He felt her hand against his crotch and involuntarily closed his eyes and moaned. "You like that, don't you?" she asked silkily. "I can smell you, your sweat from working so hard to please me and I'm grateful, Daniel, I really am." She continued massaging him through the cloth of his trousers. "I want to reward you with something, something we'll both like, but …" From behind her a low growl rumbled and brought him back to the present.

"But Astaroth gets so jealous, it wouldn't be wise to indulge." She smiled as she spoke and then stepped back, her hand lingering on his groin until finally falling away. The huge dog stalked around her, growling and snarling, slaver now dropping from exposed fangs and pooling on the floor by his massive paws. Danny's eyes widened as Astaroth dipped its head and took a step forward, its ears slicked back in a way that made its head look almost snake-like. Somehow coming to his senses he twisted and grabbed the broom he'd been using to sweep. As he brought it around the immense hound sprang at him. The broom caught it cleanly on the snout, but the momentum of the dog's pounce carried him forward and it juggernauted into him, pinning him to the ground. The broom flew out of his grip and suddenly the dog's fangs were on his throat, paused, waiting. Time froze with Danny sprawled on his back and Astaroth on his chest, sharp yellow incisors around his windpipe, the stench of its breath overpowering everything.

"One word, Daniel. I just need to give him one word and you'll be meat. I know you want to be with me, a big strong boy like you would want to fuck everything that moves. But Astaroth won't let us." She turned to leave and at the top of the stairs, as if as an afterthought, she called back, "Astaroth, leave him be now." The massive jaws opened and the dog stepped off him, trotting over to where she stood.

"Get off the floor, Daniel, you're ruining your clothes," she said, descending the steps. "Better clean them before the Reverend comes back." Then she left.

Lying on the floor, the dog's drool growing slowly cold on his throat and his heart in overdrive, Danny focused his terror-struck mind on escape. Escape or death, it didn't matter, he simply had to get away. In that moment he felt worthless and powerless, and a vague sense of betrayal to his mother's memory made death seem like a viable route out of this misery.

Later on in bed, rehashing what happened in the attic and his thoughts at the time, he shook his head in disbelief; he could never kill himself, could he? He was a fighter who never gave in, so why should he let her win now?

A slow creak from the closet brought him back to the present. Slowly the door opened and a cold draft skirted the room again, radically dropping the temperature. Burrowing down into the bed clothes, he felt for the picture of his mother and to his horror couldn't find it. All fear now secondary to the apparent loss of the photo, he sat up in bed and reached to the matches for the candle.

The room was now icy cold and by the time the wick was finally lit he could see his breath in its feeble light. With one eye on the door he searched the sheets for the picture. He was about to get out of the bed to pull the covers back properly when in his periphery he saw something fall like a leaf in front of him. In the split second it took for him to register the picture he also noticed a human shape at the end of his bed. Danny snatched up the picture and gazed at the figure properly.

Silhouetted against the light of the waning moon, it stood motionless and silent. Danny's mouth dried in a heartbeat and drops of cold sweat broke on his brow. He'd known all along there was something in the closet. Radiating terrible sadness the spectre remained mute before him, and studying it compassion welled up in Danny.

Obviously male and very large, about six feet Danny reckoned, his aura of sorrow caused Danny to wonder if he was also an orphan with tender feelings for a lost mother. Was that why he kept stealing the photo? Now, as Danny faced the unknown presence from the closet, he found he wasn't as shocked as he would have thought. He wondered idly if he was from now or sometime in the distant past; the house and church were very old, so why not?

Clearing his voice, Danny asked, "Who are you? Do you live here?"

The silence that greeted him was burdened with misery and yet Danny couldn't fathom how he could sense it. An overwhelming sense of betrayal smothered him, betrayal and sorrow, and then a waft of a fragrance assaulted his senses.

He recognised the smell but before he could identify it, the figure turned and moved silently to the closet. "No, wait, tell me what you want, don't go, perhaps I can help," Danny whispered as loudly as he dared, but the figure simply walked into the closet and the door closed.

The temperature in the room gradually warmed up and Danny wiped the sweat off his forehead, shaking his head in astonishment at what just happened. A gear clicked into place: was the perfume a hint or a message? Maybe it belonged to the ghost's mother. Was she still alive? Was he trying to find her and asking for his help? The lad had lost his mother and was looking for her. It made perfect sense, if you accepted the reality of ghosts that is.

He realised abruptly he wasn't afraid of whomever the spirit might have been; and it was a ghost. There was no other answer; the drop in temperature, the draft, the picture missing all the time. It could only be some kind of haunting and he thrilled he was in the centre of it. Was it the ghost who had emptied his suitcase the other day?

Another thought came to him in the darkness. If there were spirits, and this experience seemed to prove it, then could his own mother visit him? Stunned at the idea and yet elated beyond words, he clutched the photo to his heart and wished she would come to him. After a few moments Danny felt an ember of warmth at the thought that maybe, just maybe, his mother was waiting for him on another plane; that there was an afterlife.

Curiosity now overshadowed any fear he once had and decided to inspect the closet again. Picking up the candle, he walked over to the closet door and opened it up.

Poking the candle in first he saw nothing except

for the cobwebs, the grime and the writing. The air was the same temperature as the bedroom and Danny reckoned whoever the figure was had now departed to whatever other place he inhabited. "Is anyone there?" he asked in a low voice. Nothing stirred except for the dancing flame on the candle wick.

Looking down at the writing on the walls, he made a mental note to steal paper tomorrow and finish copying what was written. He wondered briefly if Dafydd had given the writing to anyone to decipher, and then discounted the thought entirely. What would he have done at that age? Throw it away more likely.

He decided to speak to his mother again; perhaps he'd have more luck in the closet. He pulled the picture out and looked at it in the candle light. "Mam, can you hear me wherever you are?" he breathed. "If you can, please give me a sign." He waited, tenser now than when he'd first seen the figure at the bottom of his bed. One sign, that's all he needed, just one sign.

Without warning the temperature dropped in the closet. A small gust blew the candle out and Danny stepped involuntarily backwards. From the bottom right corner of the closet a fragile glow erupted in the wall. Plaster and brick fell back and away to reveal more light, then more and more. Rapidly the back wall of the closet disintegrated until the wall was completely gone, revealing a landscape of green fields and blue sky.

Danny stepped forward to look down on the vista, and smiled. He saw figures in the distance, dressed in white, unhurriedly working in the field. One looked up and waved, but Danny was too stunned to move. His mouth was agape; was this heaven? Was this where his mother was now?

On the horizon he noticed a distant glow, a radiance that soon burst into flames. To his horror, a huge all-consuming fire swept up from behind the unknowing people in the fields, roaring like the apocalypse, blasting all it touched and incinerating everything to ash.

He screamed at the people to run but they carried on working, seemingly unaware of the rampant inferno until the blaze was upon them. He could hear their screams as the heat scorched first their backs and then as it caught up with them, engulfing them completely in fiery death. One last person ran towards him, a woman, the one who had waved to him, hysterical in fear, her white dress riding up her legs as she ran. He looked more closely and saw to his utter despair it was a younger version of his mother. "Run, Mam, run, please run!" he shouted, but the flames caught her and stripped her bones clean of flesh in a flash of heat.

Danny screamed at the sight and moved forward, but a blistering pain in his hand stopped him. The picture of his mother spontaneously ignited and he threw the burning image to the floor. He heard a bleating sound and looked back to the panorama of fire and burning bodies. Standing among the flames and yet untouched by the heat was a goat. It stared steadily at Danny and then changed shape to an Irish wolfhound.

"Astaroth!" Danny shouted, but a blast of heat blew him back. His clothes caught fire and he beat furiously at the flames, but they wouldn't go out. Fighting panic he stripped off his pyjamas.

Glancing back to the hole in the closet he saw the face of the goat again, now taking up the whole of the closet's back wall, etched in flames, somehow speaking. "Your mother's in hell, boy, for all the whoring tricks she pulled to feed you you fucking worm. She's burning in agony because she was fucking for money so you could eat, you cunt!"

Wretched grief swamped him as he felt his heart tear in two. From the depths of his soul he cried out anguish, not caring that the flames were now voraciously consuming the whole room. The pain and heat became unbearable and he looked down to see to his utter horror his flesh was now burning. Falling to the floor in agony, his skin blistered and crackled. He knew now a horrible death was imminent and he gave up his last breath to shout in defiance. "No!" over and over, until his vocal chords could only screech pitifully as the heat melted his body.

"What on earth is this noise?"

Danny looked up from where he splayed on the floor. The closet door was closed and everything was as it should be. In the early morning light Miss Trimble stood above him, hands on hips again, but this time her hair was pinned back and her stance was not exciting in any way whatsoever.

He looked down and was mortified to see he was nude, his clothes strewn on the floor next to the bed. Hastily covering himself he tried to stand, but his legs seemed weak and he staggered backwards, embarrassingly needing both hands to steady himself.

Trimble smirked at his discomfort, saying, "Mister Kelly, are you drunk? I'm afraid if this goes on I will have to tell the Reverend. Please put some clothes on and have a wash. I'll be downstairs. You have chores to do."

"Yes, Miss Trimble," he muttered, studying the closet.

# 11

She showed him the page but the Reverend was still unimpressed. "You've had this book now for nigh on ten years, Fiona, and nothing in it adds up. It was obviously written by a crackpot who has absolutely no idea about the ceremonies and rites we use."

"It must have been some sort of omen or sign. I mean, we found it the same time Astaroth found us, Gwynfor. Doesn't that tell you something?"

Gwynfor raised his gaze, "Frankly, no. Nothing in here corresponds with anything we've looked up in the library, or any of the books our friends have brought around."

Ever since she found this book in the orchard next to the suicide it had been a growing source of conflict in the house. He thought back to how it had entered their lives, well, Trimble's; he didn't give a fig about it if truth be known. The suicide was a tragic affair and could have brought far too much publicity to the church, and consequently to his scam. It could have been very damaging if he hadn't made an arrangement with the local constabulary. Sergeant Evans, or as he was then, Constable Evans, being the devout Christian he was, had helped keep the death out of the papers. Things had blown over, but it 'd been a close call.

It started in the summer of 1930 with a knock on the door. Miss Trimble answered it to see a dishevelled man with a Labrador/Alsatian cross by his side. While the large eyed huged pawed mongrel whimpered, the young man began his story.

Told in a practised monotone, he related how he'd come back after the war to find his wife gone, leaving him with the kids, who had all subsequently died of the Spanish Flu. After which he'd lost his job. All he had were the clothes on his back, some books in his bag, and his dog.

The Reverend sitting in the front room reading the paper heard everything, and gritted his teeth in annoyance at the man's awful Birmingham accent. Slamming the paper down, he decided to send the tramp on his way before he lost his mind in anger at the man's trifling, counterfeit story and Black Country dialect.

He picked up his stick and mentally rehearsed what he was about to say as he strode down the hall. Opening the door wider to speak his mind - a sort of prepared sermon about how a lot of people had a hard time after the war but everyone simply had to get on with life - not that he had suffered but that was by the by - when he spotted Jones Milk's wife in the background.

"Hello, Reverend," she said, waving at him and indicating the vagabond on their doorstep. "I sent this young man to you. He's in need of help and I thought if the church can't help him, then no one can. I do hope that was alright."

Gwynfor gave his most pious smile and boomed, "But of course Mrs. Jones, of course," a little too heartily to have any integrity, but it satisfied the dairy farmer's wife and that was all that mattered.

Mrs. Jones held a lot of sway on the church roof committee and he didn't want her looking at the finances too closely.

Rolling his eyes at his housekeeper, he said, "Well, you'd better come in young man. Let's see what we can do for you."

Touching his forelock like a serf, the man followed the Reverend, and Trimble noticed how his eyes darted everywhere, as if casing the house for a robbery. The dog followed him, panting and whining continuously, and she was on the verge of telling the vagrant to quiet the mutt down when the Reverend stopped in his tracks and turned to speak.

"Now listen, lad, I don't know what scam you think you're up to but it won't work here. You can stay the night but then you're off."

The tramp looked truly shocked. "I'm not up to any scam, Rev, honest. I'll gladly work for my keep, I just need a few days to rest. I've been on the road for the last eight months, sleeping rough, begging for food. I just need a chance to work for my food, maybe get my life in order."

The Reverend, a tall man of very powerful build, looked down at the slight emaciated person in front of him, and said in slow deliberate words, "One day and then you're gone. Do you hear?"

Trimble, who had gone to stand behind the Reverend as he spoke to their guest, saw the raw hatred in the tramp's eyes and shuddered. As if a switch had been flicked he pointed at Gwynfor. "You think you're so fucking special, dontcha? You and your stupid fucking church think you're better than the likes of me. Well, I'll tell you what, you ain't. None of you are."

The Reverend decided to answer anger with anger and shouted forcefully at the man, "How dare you spread your filth in my house, the House of God!" But the tramp, aided by the dog's growling, fiercely faced him down despite the difference in their sizes.

"How dare you shout at me! I fought for my country, did you? I bet you didn't. None of you snotty-nosed pastors were at Flanders until it was over. I spit on your shitty church, your stupid Welsh sheep-shagging –"

Suddenly the man stopped talking as Trimble, who realised a slanging match would be most unfitting for a vicarage in the eyes of anyone who might be passing, pushed past the Reverend and said soothingly, "Look, you've obviously had a terrible time of it. The Reverend has had a few bad experiences these last couple of years and is only trying to put up a brave front. Some people have taken advantage of our hospitality to the church's and our parish's cost. Let me take you to your room. You can have a wash, I'll make some food, and we can discuss things like civilised people. Is that alright?"

The rage melted like ice on hot coals and the ex-soldier almost smiled in gratitude. "You mean it, really?" And then to the Reverend, "I'm sorry your honour, I've had such a time of it these last years it all gets on top of me. My name's Dave, Dave Price. I'm sorry I got all upset there."

Baffled but impressed by Trimble's handling of the situation, the Reverend smiled and nodded. "It's okay my son, I was a bit too heavy-handed in my actions. It's just so many people come and seem to do what they want with us. Miss Trimble will show you the way. Please follow her."

Nodding obsequiously, Dave the tramp followed Miss Trimble upstairs. The dog sat where he'd landed, and Gwynfor smiled and bent down to pat it.

Three minutes later his housekeeper came back downstairs. "He's having a wash right now, Reverend. Shall I go make something for him to eat?"

Gwynfor nodded. "Yes, do that. He can stay for a couple of days. It would look bad if we sent him away straight after he got here. Give his dog something as well, would you?"

Trimble smiled and bent down to pet the mongrel, but just as her hand hovered over its head it snapped and started to growl at her. "Oh, I think you've made a friend, Miss Trimble," the Reverend said, smiling.

"Hateful beast!" she cursed, and busied herself off to the kitchen.

As it turned out, Dave was a dab hand at woodwork and fixed no end of jobs Gwynfor had started but never finished. All he asked for was a bed, food in his stomach, and the chance to be treated as a man. As the couple of days turned into weeks, the Reverend and his housekeeper found themselves increasingly reliant on him. Dave's dog also found a place in Gwynfor's heart and would regularly lie with his head on the Reverend's lap in the evenings. It was a great source of amusement to Gwynfor that the hound, Sailor, (a most unfortunate name Gwyn had thought), didn't like Miss Trimble.

She only had to enter the room and a quiet yet angry growl would rattle from him, which was invariably met by a huffed, "Hateful beast!" The pair of them began a silent war for Gwyn's affections and slowly the deplorably named canine started to win the race.

"I don't mind the man, he works hard and is an asset to the house, but the dog has to go," she'd complained one morning.

"You're only saying that because he hates you. It's only a pup Miss Trimble, it can't harm you," he jocularly answered, but he knew the dog's days were numbered.

And then it came to pass.

Trimble had gone to Dave's room to give him an early call - well, that's what she told the Reverend - but he was nowhere to be seen. On the bedside table lay a note, which she read.

Ten seconds later she screamed down the stairs to the kitchen where Gwynfor was drinking his first cup of tea. "Where is he?" she gasped. "He's going to kill himself!"

"What?" the Reverend exclaimed, spreading tea and toast over the table. "How do you know?"

Without a word she ran down the stairs, threw the note down on the table and ran outside to see if she could find him. A horrified scream confirmed she had. Gwynfor looked at the spidery handwriting and read the note.

*Dear Reverend Davies,*

*What I now do is a mortal sin and will see me burn for all eternity, but I was bound for hell anyway so it doesn't matter. In your house I have finally found the peace I needed. I was an animal and a thief, I was a fighter and a killer, but your friendship healed me.*

*Your kindness to me and Sailor showed me the error of my ways and turning my back on God was wrong. Now I can only hope he saves me from*

*Satan's fiery pit.*

*In my bag is a book. I bought it in a London market not long after being demobbed from the army.*

*In Flanders it struck me there wasn't a God and I found myself drawing nearer to the black arts. It took me five years from leaving the church to attending my first Black mass, and since that time I never looked back.*

*Now I know it was wrong and there is a God.*

*I thank you and Miss Trimble from the bottom of my heart for all you've done for me. You showed me the church is a power for good.*

*Reverend, please pray for me, give all my possessions to charity, destroy the book and look after Sailor.*

*David Price.*

He put the note softly down and walked outside. His housekeeper stood in the orchard, and as he approached he saw what she was looking at.

David Price, one time soldier and now penniless vagabond, had hung himself from the old pear tree. His clothes neatly folded and left by its roots next to his kitbag; his naked body turned slowly in the soft summer breeze. His eyes bulged hideously and his tongue, engorged and turning black at the tip, poked out horribly from his mouth.

The Reverend noticed a large pentagram tattooed onto his heart and wondered at its meaning and what he had written about turning from God. The warm thick smell of faeces from the dangling corpse hung in the air and made him gag involuntarily, so he decided to move things on.

"Why do suicides insist on taking all their clothes off?" he asked nobody in particular.

"He wanted to give everything to the poor," Trimble answered quietly.

"Well, who'd want his underpants?" he asked incredulously. It made no sense to him, other than the fact Price must have been stark raving mad.

He followed Trimble's gaze and saw she was looking at his manhood, engorged and unsightly to his eyes, yet his housekeeper stared transfixed as it stood out and pointed its anger at the world. He thought briefly about telling Trimble that was one of the reasons why old women used to enjoy public executions, but decided against it, and merely sighed in amused surprise at the thought processes of his very prim-looking housekeeper.

He took her shoulders from behind and turned her to the house. "Come inside, Miss Trimble. I'll go find Constable Evans, He can deal with this."

Trimble nodded and turned to leave. "But the dog?" she asked suddenly.

Looking back, Gwyn saw the dog next to the tramp's sack. "Take him inside and give him something to eat. I don't know what we're going to do with him. I have no time for a hound."

Moving towards Sailor, she bent down and put her hand out to coax him to her. "Here, Sailor, there's a good boy. I bet you're hungry now ..."

Sailor sprang forward and bit her on the hand, cutting her coaxing mantra off in mid-flow. Trimble jumped back and automatically nursed her hand. "You ungrateful, horrible, fucking hound!" she cried, bringing another amused smile to the Reverend's face. "He bit me!"

"Go inside, Miss Trimble. I'll deal with him and then fetch the police."

She left for the house, nursing her wound and cursing the dog.

Gwynfor moved towards Sailor but the unhappy low growl the dog made told him he'd better leave it for now. He edged further to the bag and snatched it away, eliciting a barrage of canine snarls and growls. Backing away, he sat at the base of another tree and went through the contents.

Inside was a diary, a couple of tarnished medals, a broken pencil and a book. He'd never forget the feeling of wonder when he pulled out that ancient tome. It was an old leather bound volume titled, 'The Devyl and his Hellifh familiars'.

The cover was age-cracked and curling, the pages mildewed but legible, and he pondered briefly on what adventure Price had had in his life and on how this landed in his hands. The pages were thin, brittle almost, and though it meant nothing to him he still felt the need to handle it carefully. The writing was legible but the language, though English, was the old type he envisaged Shakespeare might have used. The pictures and diagrams were two dimensional and almost childlike, depicting scenes with tortured and mutilated bodies, various demons and lots of fire.

Gwynfor dated it around 1700 and congratulated himself when he read the date 1721 on the back leaf. The book would be worth a mint he guessed, and he ran down a list of suitable buyers of risky goods who would be able to take it off his hands.

His deliberations were interrupted by Sailor.

The dog, now slowly approaching him, was menacingly growling. Although he had always seen Sailor as a friendly pet, the Reverend noticed for the first time how sharp and long his fangs were, and from his place sitting on the ground how his face was at the right level for Sailor to bite.

He placed the book back in the bag and tried to soothe the dog's anger. "Now, Sailor, come on boy. It's me, Gwynfor. There's a good chap …"

However it was of no use and soon the dog stood before him, front legs splayed, head down and snarling.

From out of nowhere a massive bulk slammed into the side of the growling dog and bowled him over. Gwynfor jumped in shock at the thud of the impact and watched in fascinated horror as another dog, twice the size of Sailor, ripped into the mongrel's throat.

Blood spattered everywhere as they tussled, with each beast vying to get a bite of the other. But power, weight and surprise were with the attacker, and soon Sailor started to yowl in pain and fear, hoping for mercy. It was not to be. The yelping and snarling continued until the bigger hound crunched into Sailor's neck, and all sound died from the Reverend's erstwhile attacker.

The dog worried a bit more on Sailor's neck and looked up at the Reverend. Gwynfor pushed himself back against the tree in panic as it padded over and calmly sat in front of him, panting as if nothing had happened and the blood and gristle on his snout weren't there at all.

It took a while for Gwyn's panicked mind to latch onto the idea the dog was waiting for praise. Scared after the show of brute force, he carefully nodded to the dog and said in a hushed voice, "Hello boy, you're a good dog, aren't you?" The dog's tail wagged in recognition and Gwyn, emboldened by the show of friendliness, reached forward to stroke it. The dog moved forward and Gwyn knew then, like it or not, the dog was here to stay.


Trimble found the pair outside and went into near hysterics at the sight of the nearly decapitated Sailor. However, something almost magical happened that the Reverend found hard to believe even though he witnessed it. The dog moved away from Gwyn and dragged Sailor's carcass towards the shocked housekeeper, who looked down in mute disbelief. Then the dog sat back and nodded, as if to say, "It's alright, he's gone now."

Gwynfor swore he heard those words in his head but discounted them as being in his imagination, until Trimble bent forward, and smiling said, "Yes, he is, thank you." Looking up towards her employer, she laughed and said, "What's that book in your hand? Was it his? Give me the book Gwynfor, I want to read it. You go get Constable Evans."

Which he did.

John Evans shook his head and tutted sagely at the sight of the hanged man, giving a world-weary sigh only an experienced policeman can manage. No stranger to death, he had fought on the Somme and been the only survivor in his section of a flame-thrower attack that scorched up his trench like a lit gas leak through a row of scarecrows, which was his favourite simile to explain what happened. Death in all its hideous forms didn't really bother him.

"Why did he take his clothes off, though?" he asked the Reverend.

"Miss Trimble thinks it was because he wanted to give everything to the poor."

Satisfied by the answer and by the suicide note he'd read, he seemed more worried about the Reverend's housekeeper than as to whether any foul play was involved. "Has she seen this?"

"She found him."

"Poor woman," he said, frowning. "I hope she

can get over it."

Nodding sagely, Gwynfor inquired as to what would happen next.

"Well, I'll have to write a report of course. But I think if we take the body down, and if you can give him a Christian burial, we might be able to keep this out of the limelight. If anyone asks about him, tell them he simply left. There are so many tramps nowadays, nobody will know he was here, or if he even existed at all, Reverend," the policeman explained.

And that's what they did.

Three days later the soul of David Price was sent on to meet his maker, or his tormentor, and it was as if he had never existed - until Fiona Trimble finished reading his book.

For some time Gwyn had been happy with the way things had progressed with the devil worship. To him it was down to a bit of ritual dressing up, chanting, "Hail Satan" a couple of times, and then sex, but Fiona, ever the pedantic librarian she had once been, now wanted to do it properly.

"What do you mean 'properly'? Do you think I've been making this up as I go along?" he choked when she confronted him. "I've been involved in ceremonies since before the war. I know what I'm doing and I don't need some old book to tell me what to do."

Miss Trimble was not to be moved on this one. In her mind, if it was written black on white, it was gospel; be it heavenly, worldly, or in this case, hellishly gospel.

"Reverend, we've been doing this wrong for too long and the Great Beast won't be happy with us if we carry on as we are. Instead of granting us power and wealth, he'll punish us."

Gwynfor knew women and he knew when he was beaten. "Right, Miss Trimble," he said formally. He insisted on titles and hierarchy in the house when they disagreed on something in those days, regardless of what they'd indulged in during the ceremonies. "I'll have a read of it and see if we can use it in the next ceremony."

Eyes alight with anticipation she nearly clapped at his words, and despite himself the Reverend had to smile. He had never seen her so bubbly.

The book itself was as confusing as it was old, but it was fascinating reading. Though he didn't personally believe in the rubbish he preached during the Christian services in the church, and the satanic ceremonies at night, he was still interested by it all. The power of persuasion was a profitable vehicle to ride if one used the right platform, and religion was definitely the express train.

The collection box in the church served up a pretty penny or two, but the devil worshippers paid hundreds to partake in the Black Masses, a phrase he'd found in a book in the library, and all of it went into his pocket.

Apart from a list of demons he could use in the chants and a few trinkets - black crosses, goat horns, etc - he'd found nothing in the book he could use.

However, his housekeeper was of a different mind. She read it from cover to cover, studied it and learnt from its ancient passages.

And that's how they'd decided, or how Miss Trimble decided, to use human sacrifice to appease the demons they'd worshipped so wrongly for so long.

# 12

After he'd woken naked on the floor, Danny spent about ten minutes contemplating what had happened. Had he dreamt it? Was the stress of everything playing games with his mind, or was he already mad?

Sleepwalking had never been a problem before and it was pretty safe to say taking his clothes off in his sleep must be a sign something bad was happening to him. There was an urgency to get out of the house but his chores kept him on the go all day. He couldn't run away as Evans had promised to have the whole of the police force on him, and he was no longer of school age so he couldn't go to school. He decided to ask what was expected of him.

Was he here to work? If so, would he receive a wage or would he be allowed to go back to Liverpool? He wasn't a prisoner; he hadn't done anything wrong, so why couldn't he just go?

The Reverend was in the front room, out of bounds to Danny, but he felt the situation warranted his being taken seriously, so he knocked politely and walked straight in.

"I'm pretty sure Miss Trimble told you the living room is out of bounds for you, lad," the Reverend said without taking his eyes off the newspaper he was reading.

Danny stood before him and wondered if he should dare to sit on one of the chairs. He decided against it, thinking that might be one step too far.

Swallowing his nervousness, he took the bull by the horns. "And why is that, Reverend? Why am I not allowed in the front room? Why am I not allowed to lie on my bed during the day? Why am I not allowed to eat my food in the dining room? I work here for no pay, you keep me here, feed me scraps and don't allow me to go out. Your lunatic housekeeper keeps sexually assaulting me and yet I'm the one made to feel a criminal. I want answers Reverend, and I want them from you."

From behind him the accustomed low growl of Astaroth sounded and Danny's eyes darted to the poker at the fire place. The Reverend saw his focus and smiled. "Do you really think that poker would save your life if Astaroth attacked?"

"I know you want to kill me, so I thought I might get it over with now. I'll simply hammer you with it and then Astaroth can do his worst as I'd be for the hangman anyway." A small glimmer of triumph flared at the back of his mind when he saw the façade of coolness fall from the Reverend's face.

"And why would I want to kill you?"

"I don't know," Danny shrugged. "But there's something going on here and this constant threatening with your dog makes me think I'm not the first victim who's ever lived under your roof."

The paper thin smile and an open-palmed gesture made Danny all the more convinced they were up to something. But he couldn't for the life of him think what that might be. He had no money, no rich family to be ransomed to, so why did he feel constantly threatened?

"Listen, my boy," the Reverend said, standing up. "I don't know what's got into you but I have no wish to harm you. If you remember correctly, it was you who threatened us with a stolen knife." The Reverend's voice, so smooth and unruffled, mixed in with his doubts to create a calming effect on the young man. "I agree Astaroth can be intimidating sometimes, but so is a young man holding a knife to my throat and running away."

Danny inwardly shook himself.

He was forgetting why he came downstairs, and stepping back from the Reverend he asked, "Okay, if I'm to work here, how much do I get paid?"

The veil of bonhomie dropped like a weighted curtain as the Reverend's indignation soared. "You what? You insolent little tyke! We take you in, we feed you, and then you expect it all for free?"

Danny blasted back at him, "I don't expect to work fourteen hours a days for a bit of dried bread for breakfast and gruel at night!"

From behind Astaroth barked once as if to calm

the situation, and the Reverend looked physically slapped by Danny's words.

Danny took the large man in, shocked to see he had seemed to be afraid for a split second. The flash of fear vanished as suddenly as it appeared, but Danny was sure it had momentarily betrayed his captor. The Reverend wasn't quite the man of the house he pretended to be. Danny smirked to himself.

"Is something the matter, Reverend?" It was Trimble.

Danny turned to look at her in the doorway, watched her idly stroking Astaroth's head.

"No, nothing Miss Trimble, but I think you're right. Mister Kelly here is unhappy and wants to leave us. I'll contact Sergeant Evans in the morning and he can take him away."

Now it was Danny's turn to look scared. "What do you mean *take me away*? Where to?"

The Reverend lifted one hand in mock resignation and half-turned to go back to his chair. "You obviously want to go to prison as the good Sergeant warned, so tomorrow I'll tell him to come and get you."

Danny's mind spun out of control. His first reaction was to run but the older man cut this thought off with, "Or you could do me a favour and simply run away. Then I don't have to go to the police tomorrow, I can delay it until I've finished my things. I'm meant to be giving a sermon in the village and it won't write itself, you know. They'll simply start a manhunt when I tell them the dangerous sexual predator who steals knives to threaten old vicars has run away and is on the loose. I can get on with writing my sermon and report your absence at my leisure, with all the paperwork it entails. It's better for you too as you'll have a couple of days head start; a couple of days to steal food to survive and thus add to your crimes."

Danny's triumph wilted like a slice of wet bread and he realised he was beaten, again.

Intuitively reading his defeat, Miss Trimble asked, "What are you doing in here anyway, young man?"

"I think he was just going to finish off his chores Miss Trimble, weren't you Daniel? And if you do that like a good boy, perhaps I'll forfeit my chat with Sergeant Evans tomorrow, eh?"

The line about being a good boy stung. They had him with nowhere to go, and there was nothing outside of murder he could do about it. His shoulders drooped in resignation and he left the room, ignoring the snarling Astaroth and his gloating mistress as he pushed past.

"He's nearly ready," Trimble mouthed as he trudged up the stairs.

Raising his eyebrows in question, the Reverend asked, "Already?"

"I think a couple more days and it'll be like the book says. He has to wish for death, to be utterly defeated so when he enters the Great Beast's realm he's totally miserable. That's how that one wants it, not as we've been doing all these years with drunken vagabonds. This time we'll do it right."

"Just make sure you don't overdo it on the misery this time. We don't want him doing anything stupid like that last one."

She looked up the stairs, "No, this one is different. He really is trapped and he knows it. Sergeant Evans played nicely into our hands, and when he does disappear he'll probably think he's run away, same as they thought about that idiot who was staying at the dairy farmer's place; Achlad, or whatever his name was."

"Just bear it in mind, that's all I'm saying," Gwynfor warned. "You went too far with the last one and we disappointed a lot of guests."

Shaking her head in disgust, Trimble snorted, "This goes further than money, Gwynfor. This will mean power, real power. We'll be untouchable, all our wishes will be granted and our thrones will be made in his kingdom. Fuck the guests. If we do this right the beast will be forever in our debt, don't you see that?"

The Reverend approached her, arms up in reconciliation, "Yes, yes, of course I can see that. I just want to be sure we'll be alright if something goes wrong."

"Nothing can go wrong. The boy is nearly ready now –"

"Yes, my dear, but if you make a mistake, or cut him too deeply so he doesn't die at the right moment, what then? That's all I'm saying. Trust in what we're doing but make plans in case it goes wrong." He placed his hands on her shoulders and looked into her eyes. "Fiona trust me, I have our best interests at heart."

Astaroth watched them from the doorway and growled in disgust. Trimble sensed the dog's dislike and agreed. The Reverend wasn't a true believer and never had been. He might have to go as well.

She decided to test his mettle. "We're going to have to hobble him when the time arrives. We can't afford to have him run away. He needs to be hobbled, and properly."

He dropped his hands from her shoulders and looked puzzled, "You mean tie him up, surely?"

"No Gwynfor, I mean break his legs so he can't walk, on the thighbone where it hurts the most. He'll be helpless from the pain and easier to drag into position. It's all in the book you so deride."

"You don't want to drug him?" his voice rose in shock, and he ducked his head as she put a finger to her lips.

"No, he has to be conscious and wretched, preferably in pain, but drugs and alcohol won't be playing a role in this anymore. We're doing this one right, Gwyn and you'll thank me for it after."

Gwyn looked over her shoulder to see Astaroth wagging his tail, ears perked and panting happily. It was the dog, he wanted them to do it this way, and almost fainted when a voice in his head said, "I do."

# 13

That night, with a candle, the broken pencil and some paper he'd scavenged during the day, Danny copied down the rest of the writings on the wall.

It had taken all his nerve to open the closet door again, but this time nothing happened. Keeping one eye on the corner where the bricks fell away previously, he crouched down and laid the paper on the book to write. As before it was painfully slow as the language was so alien, and he was forced to write it down letter for letter.

He still hadn't heard from Dafydd and guessed the lad had lost interest in his transcription and simply thrown it away. Over the last two days he'd wondered again at the passages meaning. Perhaps it was a list of all the bad things they'd done to whomever had written it. That idea, and the fact he'd smuggled it out of the grounds, offered a bit of hope.

There were four other passages, one a little longer than the other, the other three mere sentences. Danny had never been in a situation where he'd felt the need to write something down for someone else to find.

When he contemplated his situation, even now he didn't feel particularly endangered. Perhaps he should have. But he'd put a look of fear on the Reverend's face and he'd fended Astaroth off. These things emboldened him even though the Reverend regained the upper hand.

There was no way he could run now, and if he did and it came to court, who would believe him? The judge would weigh his words as a Scouser orphan with allegations of indecency hanging around him, against those of the vicar and his housekeeper, throw him into nick, and there was nothing he could do about it. No, he'd stick it out, but first he had to know what the passages on the wall said.

The candle's spluttering flame danced in the corner where the first bricks fell away in his dream. He noticed the corner bricks had a lighter mortar around them than the ones surrounding. Out of curiosity he prodded the back of his pencil into the grooves between the stone and was mildly surprised when it sank easily into the cement. On closer inspection he saw the cement wasn't actually solid but seemed to have been hooked out of the groove whole, and then pushed back in.

Was there something behind the brick?

The writing quickly forgotten; he started to lever out the mortar around it. When it was free, he pushed the pencil in as far as possible to try and hook the brick out, but the pencil snapped. Danny pulled at the stone with the tips of his fingers but it wouldn't budge, cursing when the nail on his index finger broke. What was behind it, if anything at all? He'd have to steal a knife or some kind of tool tomorrow. He didn't want to risk walking around the house on his own at night. Considering a number of possibilities, he reluctantly left it for another day and turned back to the writing.

When all four passages were down, he checked them through again and decided they were copied correctly. If he didn't hear from Dafydd, Huw, or anyone in the next few days, he'd have to think of some other way to decipher their meaning, it was as simple as that. Actually, he thought glumly, not really so simple at all. Sighing at his predicament, he leaned forward to pick up the candle from the corner.

A small gust of wind puffed the candle out and left him in darkness. The rational part of his brain jumped straight onto the fact he'd just cleared a brick free of mortar and the draft probably came from there. But on a deeper more spiritual level, he knew why the candle blew out.

The temperature dropped rapidly in the room, and in growing fear he couldn't find it within himself to move. Eyes becoming more accustomed to the gloom, he mentally took hold of himself and stood up, to turn and look around.

From his place in the closet doorway the room looked empty. The pale shade of his sheets and pillowcase stood in stark contrast to the forbidding dark of the corners, and he couldn't ever remember wanting to be under blankets more in his entire life. In the austere light of the moon he saw his matches on the bedside table and turned to pick up his candle from the floor.

A shadow stood behind him, and jumping back in shock Danny involuntarily screamed. Slowly the shadow formed into a person, though only half visible. The rational mind told him he was seeing a ghost, the irrational part yelled at him to run away. For a moment curiosity prevailed and he studied the form in front of him.

It was tall, muscular and definitely male. Its clothes were nondescript and ordinary, its hair short with a long fringe that hung over its eyes due its chin being lowered. The smell of manure assailed his nose and he somehow caught an impression of working on a farm.

Danny swallowed hard, "Who are you?"

No answer, and the silence only implied an air of malice. Above the hammering of his own heart, Danny could hear the figure breathing and a slow pat, pat, pat of liquid falling to the ground. A distant part of his mind wondered which tap was left on, when suddenly the form moved. Lifting up its forearms, it turned its wrists outward and Danny saw the long cuts slashed into its arms, seeping blood onto the floor.

Eyes wide in shock, Danny looked back up to the face and was about to ask why, when with breath catching he gasped in horror. The figure was now looking at him, face-to-face. A black mark ringed its neck, thick and oily, like a burn turned bad. The face itself grinned in a mirthless caricature of a smile, the lips rotted away to expose horribly blackened teeth, the nose a mere hole in the middle of its face and the skin papery thin, almost mummified. Only the eyes looked untouched, alive, fresh even. They burned hatred and anger, and the force of emotions stunned Danny as if he'd been physically punched.

The mouth opened and words sounded inside Danny's head like a scream. "She is mine! She's not yours, she's mine!"

The malevolence in the voice was plain and yet Danny couldn't quite escape a feeling of sadness, of insecurity behind those words. His every molecule bellowed to run away, yet he fought it and stood firm. With throat and mouth drier than sand, he said in a voice choked by fear, "I don't understand. What are you saying?" And then, "Did you write those words on the wall?"

The figure let his arms drop and Danny heard the voice in his head. Slowly, as if talking to a child, the figure said, "Oh your poor precious mother, what sort of son were you to her? She worshipped you and you made her turn tricks. She fucked so you could eat, you ungrateful bastard! I would never have done that to my mother. I never had the chance! So I'm going to have your mother fucked by a bull and torn to shreds for my delight! And why? Because I can. I have her now in my power and you can't do a fucking thing about it. **Why are you even here?**

**This is my place. She belongs to me! She's mine!**"

Confused and distraught by the outburst, Danny gasped again as the figure suddenly ignited in front of him, continuing the litany of abuse and threats.

"Oh your poor, poor mother. We'll break every bone in her body with a hammer and slit her open like the pig she is! We'll smear her innards like grease and spike her head on a shit pile!" The figure burned brighter and brighter, threatening to torch everything, and yet touching nothing. Danny saw the fire but felt no heat, and as suddenly and as quietly as the dark figure came, he was gone.

The room darkened, the memory of what he'd just witnessed still fresh yet already starting to fade with disbelief. Danny stepped back and turned to go to bed. The thoughts and images the spectre had put into his mind were too monstrous to contemplate and he felt his sanity starting to unravel.

Crawling into bed he pulled the covers over his head. As the first tears welled up to run down the sides of his face, he reached into his breast pocket of his pyjamas for the picture of his mother.

He knew she wasn't in Hell, she was too good for that, and yet the images he'd seen, the scenes of horrific torture and mutilation that played out in his mind were telling a different story. Tears of fresh grief flowed freely onto his pillow as his doubts grew like the waxing moon.

# 14

Their first victim was the easiest, and yet somehow the worst. October 1931 had been a cold winter, and the poor had a difficult time finding food, and firewood to keep warm. Coal was at an absolute premium and beggars were out in force. Trimble always gave them short shrift when they came to their door, which annoyed Gwyn since they were meant to be a centre of charity for the community. However, this was the least of their quarrels.

Miss Trimble was badgering him about a sacrifice; she wanted to kill something for The Beast. The Reverend, who up to that point had never really taken her or the book seriously, asked "What? A chicken, a goat, a cow?"

"No, no, a chicken's too small and a goat - never! Sacrifice a goat to the devil? That's unheard of!" she exclaimed, and Gwynfor had to hide his smirk.

"Well, what then? A cow, that'd be far too much work and think of the cleaning after. And it would be too expensive. They cost money, cows do, and if we bought one people might talk. Even a sheep would have its problems."

"People buy cows to slaughter all the time."

"Not in churches, they don't my dear," Gwynfor smiled benignly.

"A lamb, then? Small enough to conceal, easy to clean, and innocent enough to please him," Trimble suggested.

Gwynfor didn't like the idea but he knew a bit of blood-letting would give a certain integrity to the ceremonies that had been sadly missing. As unbelievable as it was to him, the congregation was slowly tiring of the sex; it needed something more. A few had all but told him they wanted to take it further, but a lamb?

"I don't know. Wouldn't that put the people off? Some of the ladies might be squeamish about bleeding a lamb," he'd told Trimble, much to her annoyance. "Let's see what turns up. Perhaps something will fall into our lap."

"The people are already being put off by only being offered the same old thing. It's not all sex, Gwyn, it's black magic, the pursuit of power, of favour," she scolded. "You'll soon be losing your precious tribute, so give the worshippers what they want - blood."

"Let me ponder on it, Fiona. Something might turn up." Six weeks later, something did turn up.

His name was Mark, he was homeless, penniless, and in Trimble's words, 'Perfect'.

"You cannot be serious?" the Reverend exploded. "Murdering a tramp? I'm not sure if you realise this Fiona my dear, but the last time I looked, murder was a capital offence. We'll be hung if we're caught!"

Trimble, who knew his weakness wasn't just money, approached him with that hip swinging gait she knew sent the right signals. "He's a drunk, Gwyn, he has no contact with his family and he's here. He'll disappear just like the suicide last year, and nobody will ever know." Standing a couple of inches away from him, she looked up into his eyes and whispered, "If you do this, I'll be forever grateful. I'll let you into my room again."

The hushed promise evaporated his resistance and he nodded, muted and ardent. The fact was since the arrival of Astaroth he'd suddenly found himself on the outside of her desires. He'd entered her room one night with the plan of joining her, and without ceremony or concern for his feelings was coldly told to leave.

"It's over for now, Gwyn," she'd told him. "You just use me, you never listen to my ideas. Just leave me be. Perhaps if you start treating me properly we can resume our trysts."

Enraged by the humiliation he'd advanced on her bed, determined to show her who the boss was, and then suddenly froze in his tracks when a warning growl sounded from the side of her bed and Astaroth lithely jumped up from his place on the floor in a show of protective defiance.

"Astar, now calm down boy," he'd said, confused by the turn of events and still mildly angry at the rebuke. He backed to the door, and in a last show of bluster, said, "If that's the case, Miss Trimble, feel free to pack your case and go, and take your hound with you."

Her laugh his threat elicited shocked him, as did her reply. "I'm not going anywhere, Reverend, as we both know what will happen if you try to throw me out. The whole village will be talking about the evil vicar who wasn't even a real priest and how he raped poor Miss Trimble, held her captive and made her perform in black masses. And I won't even mention what Astaroth might want to do with you if he finds himself on the streets again. No, I'm staying right where I am Reverend. We'll live together, side-by-side. I'll comfort you when the mood takes me, pleasure you even, but I am not going anywhere."

Beaten, the Reverend left her room and they had continued, since that day, as if nothing happened. Sometimes she deigned to pleasure him when the mood took her and she needed a man, but it was all on her terms, to be used when she wanted something from him. Now was such an occasion.

"How do you want to do it?" he asked, trying to control his need for her.

"I'll leave the details to you. Do it and you can visit me in my room again. Well, until I tire of you, anyway." She laughed.

Mirthlessly he smiled and left the room to contemplate the pact he'd just entered into.

Whiskey was the answer. Mark was a hardened drinker. Gwyn decided to render him unconscious and strangle him, so he almost laughed out loud when Trimble suggested ordering more wine.

"Wine, wine …?" he asked, a grin twitching his lips. "He drinks wine for breakfast. The whole of Christendom hasn't enough wine to knock this man out." He stopped his mocking when he caught her frown.

"Well, I don't know. I never drink, so how would I know?" she said, sounding hurt.

"Yes, yes," he nodded, smiling to mollify her hurt feelings, "I know you don't drink. I was just pointing it out to you. No, what we need is whiskey, and lots of it, and I know just the source. Bryn Parry, the cobbler in Abergele, makes his own and he's often offered to sell me some. I think I'll take him up on his offer."

Three days later a very happy traveller sat at the kitchen table, beaming at the Reverend and his normally aloof housekeeper. Today she seemed of a better mood.

"It's good stuff, Reverend. Don't you want any?" he'd asked.

"No, my son, I try not to partake of the hard stuff. I like a sherry now and then but that's as far as I go. You drink it, it'd be a shame to throw it away, and as you're obviously an expert I see no reason why you shouldn't enjoy it."

Hardly believing his luck, the young man set about quaffing the home-made whiskey as if it were milk. He passed through the different phases of insobriety with ease, and loud-mouthed bonhomie soon turned to whining self-pity at his situation. There were a couple of songs, which the Reverend gamely joined in to the amusement of his housekeeper, and then after three bottles of what tasted to Gwynfor like 110% proof whiskey, came unconsciousness.

The congregation was waiting for the sign, and as soon as Gwyn gave the nod they rushed into the kitchen and carried him to the church. Gwynfor had thought up a kind of ritual for the sacrifice but he'd baulked at the idea of bleeding his victim. He'd decided to tie a rope around the prone tramp's neck and suffocate him in his sleep.

They stripped him naked and laid him out in the middle of a pentagram. Gwynfor had sacked the actor for being too amorous with Miss Trimble and now took on the mantle of Chief Goat, as he called it, himself. Wearing a black cassock and a mask he'd made out of a carnival goat's head, he intoned a couple of Hail Satan prayers he'd made up and slowly approached the sleeping, and now snoring, drunk.

He reached for a black rope, and chanting in a low voice about the fires of hell, the taking of a soul and whatever else he could contrive on the moment, he tied the rope around the man's neck and pulled it tight. He looked up to Trimble who had opened her robe and stood in the circle in front of him, semi-naked. Her eyes afire with the power she held over him, she nodded her approval as he pulled the cord tighter. Suddenly the naked man sat up, and gasping for air tried to fight the Reverend off. Gwynfor pushed his knee down onto the man's chest and pulled the bindings with all his might. The tramp swung and landed a punch on the side of the Reverend's head, knocking the goat's head mask clean off. But Gwynfor, ignoring the fact the tramp could now see his face, only pulled harder.

The assembly stood immobile, watching the struggle in fascinated horror as the two men fought their one-sided battle. Gwynfor, far heavier and stronger than the smaller emaciated traveller, soon took the upper hand.

Choking horribly as he tried to pull the cord away, Mark's eyes bulged and then rolled back in his head as he gradually lost the brawl. His tongue lolled out and the smell of defecation filled the air as his lifeless body voided its bowels.

Gwynfor jumped back from the stream of urine that soiled his cassock and looked down at the dead man as his nerves gave their last shudder. Breathing heavily from the exertion, he stood and staggered backwards from the corpse. Its face now blue, the eyes and tongue hideously swollen, it reminded Gwyn of a broken mannequin dummy with a badly painted head.

After the fight, the violence and death, he'd expected everyone to leave rapidly but that was not the case.

Trimble approached him, stepping over the body as if it were a piece of wood, and dropped her robe. She fell on her knees in front of him and unbuttoned his cassock. Looking up when his covering was fully opened, she proclaimed to all from where she kneeled, "You have the power, you are the one, you are beloved of the Great Beast! Hail Satan!" Then she dipped her head and took his now semi-engorged organ in her mouth.

Shell-shocked and trembling with adrenalin, Gwynfor Davies looked around as the congregation, all eighteen of them, intoned the last words Fiona Trimble had spoken three times in a flurry of undressing. As if an unspoken dam had been broken by Trimble's words and deed, the worshippers turned to each other to consummate the ceremony.

As he looked around at his fellow acolytes now writhing in passion around the slain victim, with his housekeeper's head working furiously between his legs, Gwynfor had an inkling of what Trimble meant by the word 'power'. They were following his lead, they would do whatever he said, he was their leader.

This was the first time they hadn't used whores. All the women present were just like the men, willing and looking for adventure. It was their first true black mass and it felt good. It felt really good.

The horror of the struggle to kill their victim was for the time-being forgotten, cast aside by the dizzying pleasure of power and the physical rewards it brought.

He knew they couldn't stop now.

# 15

Sandra wanted to go with Beth up to the house but she'd promised Mrs Evans she'd help with the carpet beating. "Wait until tomorrow Beth, we can go up together."

Standing outside the school gates at the bike sheds, they were on their own as the rest of the students were already on their way home. Beth shared a story about a girl in her class whose father had been captured by the Germans before she dropped the bombshell about going up to the house by herself.

"I want to go today to see if he's there. If I do see him, I'll tell him to be at home tomorrow afternoon, so we can talk to him."

Sandra begged her not to go. "Please Beth, wait for me, don't go up there alone. I have a terrible feeling about that woman, and her dog scares me half to death."

And that was what she didn't understand. They'd both agreed on the way home the other day that

Astra, or Astar, or whatever it was called, was dangerous. However, they'd disagreed on Miss Trimble

"She's creepy as well," Sandra mentioned in passing after discussing the dog and all the local anecdotes about it at length.

"Oh, she isn't, she's nice. She reminds me of a lady, though I know she isn't," Beth giggled. "I've heard all sorts of tales about what goes on in that church, but it's probably only gossip."

"What sort of tales?" Sandra asked, curious.

"Oh, just stuff. Do you know what an orgy is?"

Sandra knew what it was, sort of. She had visions of Romans eating grapes and drinking wine but she knew there was another side to it she didn't really know about. "Yes, it's where they all get drunk and do things to each other," she'd ventured, not wanting to sound unworldly for her sixteen years.

Beth didn't notice her ignorance and whispered, "Well, they have them in the old church apparently. Everyone knows about it, though I'm not sure who has seen it. Anyway, that's what they do. I don't think the Reverend has anything to do with it though."

Sandra raised her eyebrows in mock surprise.

Beth said, "So, if I see him, should I give a special message to him from you?"

"Beth, please don't go on your own, I have a terrible feeling about it. Please. I'll do whatever you want but just wait for me to come with you. Go tomorrow," she pleaded, but her friend wouldn't take her seriously.

"You're just jealous in case I end up alone with him, aren't you?" Beth laughed as she spoke, prodding Sandra lightly on the arm, but Sandra wasn't in the mood for games.

"I don't care if you're alone with him. I don't like him like that. I just think he's nice," she answered. "I just want you to go with me tomorrow, that's all. Please, Beth, for me, wait until tomorrow."

A calculating look crossed Beth's face and she looked around her to check no one was listening. "You don't like him like that? You said you did."

"I said I like him, he's nice, because he is. That's all."

"Oh," Beth murmured and smiled at her. "And you'll do anything if I wait for you to go tomorrow?"

Sandra smiled. "Yes, of course. Please don't go. Wait for me and we'll face her and her dog together."

Beth's face turned serious and she looked around once more to see if anyone was eavesdropping. "And you'll do anything I say?" she asked, leaning back with her hands behind her, pushing her hips forward. Confused but not alarmed, Sandra nodded.

"Then kiss me," Beth whispered.

Sandra swallowed hard. She had almost known this was coming and she'd been a fool to have brought it on. Suddenly she was nervous. It was as if those three words had turned their relationship on its head, and though Beth was pretty, she was still a girl. "On your cheek?" she ventured hopefully.

Beth stared at her, not saying a word, and Sandra knew she didn't mean on the cheek.

"Beth …" she started to say but her friend cut her off.

"I knew you wouldn't. It was a test. Don't worry about it but I am going to the house now, with or without you." Beth laughed, though it was forced and brittle.

"Beth, don't go, I'll do it, I will, just don't go, please."

The girl paused. "You'd do it, you'd kiss me? On the lips?"

Sandra swallowed hard again and nodded.

"No, I don't think so. I'm going up there now. I'll tell you what happened with your fancy boy tomorrow," Beth answered.

Sandra, downhearted and scared for her friend, could only offer a strained parody of a smile and tried to mask her all-too-visible disappointment.


Trimble watched Beth approaching from the bedroom window. Idly stroking Astaroth's massive head, she chuckled to herself as the girl stopped to pick a flower on the roadside.

"So innocent, so confused and so very silly." And then to the dog, "With the boy's sacrifice so close and the protection of our master more or less secure, we might be able to play today, if she hasn't told anyone she's coming, that is. You stay here for now. I'll call you if the game is on."

Astaroth whined and wagged his tail.

Beth looked up, seeing the housekeeper in the window, and Trimble smiled, giving a small wave of recognition. The grin on the girl's face, one of unfettered happiness, lifted Trimble's heart and she hissed between her teeth, "Oh, I can't wait to see you crying for your life."

Trimble let her hair down and hurriedly put lipstick on before answering the door.

"Elizabeth, how lovely. I'm afraid Daniel isn't here but do come in," Trimble purred, raising the hairs on Beth's neck.

"Thank you," she answered, nearly curtsying. "I picked these for you." She held out a small posy of wildflowers and Trimble smiled warmly at the gesture. "You are so sweet, my dear. Don't stand there, now, come inside. I'll make us some tea and we can talk."

As Beth moved past her, Trimble quickly checked to see if anyone had seen her arrive. Turning back inside, she ushered Beth into the living room. "Now, dear, tea? I have some very nice fruit tea, if you like that sort of thing. "

"I don't mind," she shrugged.

Trimble wrinkled her nose, saying, "I'll make us nice fruit tea, then. I'm afraid Daniel is with the Reverend today, cutting wood up Colwyn Heights, so it'll be a girl's afternoon. We can do whatever you wish."

Letting her suggestion hang in the air, she left the girl and walked to the kitchen, saying over her shoulder, "Now don't be shy, Elizabeth - or can I call you Lizzy? Sit down, make yourself at home and I'll be right there."

Beth, her heart now pounding, sat on the edge of one of the overstuffed chairs and looked around the room until Trimble returned bearing a tray with tea cups, a sugar bowl and a teapot.

"So, Lizzy, I made us some apple and strawberry tea. It's very good with sugar. Don't worry about the rationing. The Reverend never uses sugar, so I save his." Trimble sat on the sofa and patted the place next to her. "Now, don't sit over there, dear. Come and sit by me, then I don't have to reach over with your tea."

Beth nodded, her excitement mounting.

Trimble leaned forward and stirred the teapot. "Smells good, I do so prefer fruit tea to normal tea, don't you, dear?"

Beth, caught off guard by the line of questioning, nodded readily. "Oh yes, it's a lot better. My mother makes nettle tea all the time."

"Really, how quaint." Pouring from the teapot, the housekeeper grimaced. "Now, drink it while it's hot, dear, and do try it with sugar. You'll taste a whole world of difference."

Their knees touched accidentally and Beth felt an electric tingle run through her.

Trimble left her leg touching Beth's and sat back, looking over her cup at her. "So, what did you want to talk about? Was it something important or is this a courtesy call? Is this a secret rendezvous? Does anyone know you're here, my dear?"

Beth thought about telling Miss Trimble about Sandra, but decided against it. It was nice here, alongside the woman she had longed to be alone with for a long time. If she mentioned Sandra's name it might spoil the atmosphere.

"No, I came here on my own. Nobody knows. I just wanted to tell Daniel we wanted to come around tomorrow to talk to him. Sandra, my friend, likes him. I can't really say I do. Boys all seem so silly," Beth said, testing the waters, her heart beating so loudly she was sure it was audible to her hostess.

"I know what you mean, dear, boys are so …" Trimble searched for the right word and her eyes flashed when she found it, "… rough."

Beth drank some of her tea to hide her excitement. The hot fluid skimmed over her tongue, numbing it on touch and she nearly pulled a face at how bitter it tasted.

"Take some sugar, dear. I know you're sweet enough to do without, but the tea can be very bitter." Trimble said. She leaned forward, putting her hand on the girl's knee to steady herself and started to spoon sugar into Beth's cup.

"Now then, try it now," she ordered kindly.

The tea numbed the rest of her mouth and Beth's head started to spin. Putting the teacup clumsily down, she sat back in her dizziness and Trimble moved in closer, as if to comfort her.

"Oh, my poor dear, I think the tea was a bit too strong for you. Are you alright?"

Beth, sweating in panic at the giddiness, couldn't answer as her tongue seemed paralysed, as was the rest of her mouth. She vaguely heard Trimble cooing something comforting to her, and blacked out.

She woke up on in a strange bed with Trimble holding her hand. As she came slowly to, she felt the coarse bed sheets against her body and realised she was naked under the covers. She tried and failed to move her limbs. To her astonishment, she noticed Trimble was in a silk bath robe.

"Where am I? Is this your room?"

"You're alright, dear. You had a turn and a small accident. I had to undress you to clean your clothes. Yes, this is my room. Now, how do you feel, dear?" Trimble asked, smiling.

"I'm cold," Beth said, puzzled. "What happened to me? Why do I feel so cold?"

Wordlessly Trimble stood and slipped off her bath robe. Beth gasped to see she was naked, but smiled in pleasure as the housekeeper slipped into the bed beside her.

Cuddling up to her, Trimble asked, "Is that better now, Liz. Am I warming you up, dear?"

Beth could feel the stiff hairs of Trimble's sex against the side of her thigh and the warm squash of the woman's breasts on her arm. Slowly Trimble stroked her forehead and then tenderly kissed her cheek. Frozen by nerves, by passion, by indecision, Beth lay stiff as a board, not really knowing if she wanted it after all. She had always felt drawn towards women, but now presented with the reality she wasn't so sure what she wanted.

As if reading her mood Fiona Trimble whispered softly into her ear, "Make love to me Elizabeth, or I'll feed you to Astar and your soul to Satan."

The door opened and Astaroth prowled into the room, growling quietly in warning. Beth stiffened and opened her mouth to scream, but Trimble, with a strength that shocked the young girl, clamped a hand over her mouth.

Her eyes furious and staring, she hissed between clenched teeth, "Don't you dare scream, girl, don't you dare. Now you are going to play with me you little bitch. And then you're going to play with Astaroth. We'll see how well you perform and whether you survive this day, hm?"

As Trimble roughly probed her hands into the girl's body, a current of cold air circulated the room. As if it was a physical entity it paused over the bed, laying like a thin hint of frost on the blankets until Astaroth growled for it to move on. The dog knew who it was, Trimble knew too, and it was only Beth, wrapped up in her own terror, who didn't feel its presence.

•

"Come on, lad. It isn't that heavy, surely?" the Reverend chastised testily from his place on the woodpile.

He was right, it wasn't heavy, however Danny had been chopping wood all day for the church to donate to certain older members of the community, and it was early evening now. He was bone tired.

He didn't mind doing it for the old folk, in fact he was happy to. It was the first charitable act he'd seen the Reverend do since his arrival, and the grateful looks he'd received as he chopped and bundled the firewood to dry out for winter were worth the back ache. However, now he was forced to chop for the vicarage, and it seemed a bit unfair, especially as the Reverend insisted on watching him work.

To make matters worse the Reverend had been given a pint of whiskey by one of the people he'd chopped wood for and was steadily making his way through it.

"Put your back into it, lad. I'm not paying your food and board for nothing you know!"

Danny held his tongue and pounded his anger into the timber as the Reverend carried on his cajoling and denigration. "When I was your age I chopped wood for the whole village. Tonypandy, do you know it, lad? Down South Wales, in the Rhondda. I chopped the wood and my dad sold it, the old tyrant. He'd beat me with his belt if I didn't chop fast enough. I forgave him though …" He stood up. "Hit it, man. What's wrong with you? It'll never split properly if you don't put enough weight behind it."

And so it continued, a constant barrage of half anecdotes about his life and directives to work harder.

Danny had only been at the house for two weeks but this was the first time he'd seen the Reverend behaving like this. It seemed as if the older man was unhappy about something, and that something was slowly surfacing under the influence of the whiskey, of which a good two-thirds was now gone.

At length, the Reverend told him to stop. "Come here, lad. I want to tell you something."

Rolling his eyes, Danny put down the axe down - an axe he'd already decided to hide in case he needed it one day - and wiping his brow walked over. He didn't know what the Reverend wanted but he guessed it would be some drunken yarn or piece of advice for life, as it always was with inebriated men, maudlin in their cups.

"Sit down, lad. Have a drink. It'll do you good," he offered, holding the bottle up.

Eyebrows raised in surprise, Danny took it and swigged from the bottle, coughing as it burnt into his throat.

The Reverend laughed and clapped him on the back. "You did well today, Daniel. Oh, I know I go on a bit but you worked well. You deserve that."

Danny didn't know what to say to this; one minute he was the worst wood chopper in the world, the next he was swigging whiskey.

They sat in affable silence, sharing and swigging from the bottle. The Reverend didn't seem like a bad sort. He wondered why he put on the gruff act. The last dregs were swilling around the bottom as a short cry of shock turned their heads. The sight of Miss Trimble marching towards them sank his heart.

"Daniel Kelly, you are not old enough to be drinking hard spirits young man. You will go to your room this minute!" she scolded, shaking in anger. "There'll be no tea for you again today."

Danny didn't actually mind. He was tired and he knew the pleasant buzz would mean a good night's sleep. Forgetting to hide the axe, he sauntered off and went to his room to sleep the sleep of the righteous, and drunk.

Trimble looked down at the Reverend in disgust. "You couldn't leave it, could you? You had to spoil everything and get drunk!"

Gwynfor said nothing. Casually putting the bottle to his lips, he drained the last dregs and let it fall. "Shut up, woman. Have you any idea how much you annoy me at times?"

Crossing her arms and putting her weight on one leg, Trimble cocked her head and raised her eyebrows in annoyance. "So, the whiskey has finally found your backbone for you, then? I wondered when it was going to show, how long you've been harbouring your resentment about how things have turned out. A year? Two years ago, after the last sacrifice? You started this Gwyn, I just carried it on and I want to do it properly."

"Do what properly, Fiona?" he snarled. "All I wanted was to make a nice pile on the side. An easy life, some laughs, fuck some whores. But that wasn't enough for you, was it? You had to try and make it proper, accurate." He stood up and held her shoulders. "We've killed a lot of people, Fiona. Killed them! It has to stop."

Trimble stared into his face as if reading his soul through his eyes. "No Gwynfor, you killed people, you were the one who dosed them with whiskey and opium. You were the one who tied the knot around their throats as they slept on the church floor. I watched you do it. We all watched you do it. But they died for nothing because we were doing it wrong."

Sitting back down on the woodpile, Gwynfor put his head in his hands, whispering, "Don't you understand, Fiona. I did it for you. It started out for the money but I carried it on for you. It was always for you."

"Well, Gwynfor, you were doing it wrong, and if there's one thing I can't stand it's sloppiness. Now pull yourself together. In two days the guests are coming and we have a lot to do."

He looked up, wretched and blurry-eyed, "I don't want to do it. He's a good lad. I can't do it, Fiona, I just can't."

Disgusted, Trimble sneered, "You'll have to, Gwynfor, and if you can't do it, I will, with Astaroth. There's no turning back now Gwyn. We're in this for the whole run. Now stand up and be a man, not a whining little girl. We've got work to do upstairs."

Gwynfor gasped in horror at the blood. The bed seemed to be painted in it, an explosion of red, and at its epicentre lay the broken, twisted body of a young girl.

"You did this?" he exhaled, his mind grasping to comprehend the sickening scene before him.

"Astaroth did. I told her to please him but she wouldn't, so he became angry. He gets so jealous sometimes. If she had done as she was told, it would have all been alright."

Turning to her, now sober from the adrenaline and shock, he struggled for something to say. "You, you stupid psychotic bitch! Do you know what you've done here?"

His voice crescendoed and Trimble put a finger to her mouth and shushed him. "Daniel may be asleep now but we don't want to wake him. We need to get rid of the body. I'll clean the room tomorrow when you're both out chopping wood again."

"What? I don't care if he's awake or not. We'll be hanged if –!"

Trimble slapped him hard across the face. "Pull yourself together, man! We'll take the body out, bury it, and I'll clean and paint the walls tomorrow. The sheets I can wash, and if not, I'll simply burn them."

He rubbed the side of his face where she'd slapped him. "What, why did you do this Fiona?

Why? Isn't it enough we're making a sacrifice on Wednesday?"

"Thursday, Gwynfor, the guests are coming on Thursday, and this wasn't a sacrifice, it was a bit of fun that went …" She paused to search for the right word. "… awry."

"Awry." He tested the word as he looked at the atrocity before him. The girl's lifeless eyes searched the ceiling as if asking why had they done this to her. Her white body was splattered from head to toe in her own blood, that was obviously from the area where her throat should have been, but was now a ragged hole. "Fiona, tell me now, why did you do this? I still don't understand."

"The girl wanted me but I knew Astaroth wouldn't want to share me, so I told her in a very straightforward manner she'd have to be nice to Astaroth as well. She was scared but agreed, and then the Welsh bitch wouldn't do it, so Astaroth killed her," Trimble explained, as if recounting a picnic or a game of bowls.

"And now what do you expect me to do with the body?"

"Well, carry it downstairs and bury it, of course. I can't do it, she's far too heavy, and Astaroth hasn't any hands. So you'll have to."

She looked at him as if he was simple and Gwynfor shook his head at the situation. "I'm not doing your dirty work for you, Fiona. This is your mess. You sort it out."

From behind him an angry growl started up and

Gwynfor turned in shock.

"No, Gwynfor," Trimble said matter-of-factly. "This is your mess too. You're in this with us, whether you want it or not."

"You're mad!" he exploded, drawing an irate snarl from the dog behind him and a warning look from Trimble. Then, in a quieter tone, "You killed this girl for your pleasure and I'm supposed to clear the mess? That makes me culpable as well. I'll hang too. This can't go on, Fiona, you need help."

"Yes, I do, to clear this body away. Now, take it downstairs, bury it in the orchard and I'll cover this all up," she ordered. Then, in a more conciliatory tone, "Gwynfor, it'll be alright. When we do this sacrifice on Thursday we'll be able to do as we please. We'll have so much power we'll be unstoppable. Don't flake out on me now, Gwyn. I need you by my side to see this through. On Thursday we'll make our gift to the Great Beast and then nothing can touch us. Nothing!"

Gwynfor opened his mouth to say something but the growling Astaroth made him realise he couldn't win here. Not today. He'd bury the poor girl, help hide what had happened here, and leave. He thought of the boy and a flash of inspiration hit him regarding a way of disrupting the madness that had manifested itself in the vicarage. However, an increase in the volume of growling and Trimble's smile made him pause.

"Astaroth knows what you're thinking, Gwyn. He's just told me and, believe me, you can run from here if you want, but you will not let the boy go. Do you hear me? You want to leave, that's your choice, but you will not let him go. He stays and dies on Thursday."

Speechless she had read his mind before the thought had even crystallised, Gwynfor gaped like a gaffed fish. "He told you that?"

"He sees all, Gwyn, he knows your heart of hearts, he speaks to me of your cowardice, your cynical self-centred slant on life and your inability to see what we're doing here. He sees all. If you run I'll tell the police everything, which will be my word against yours, but seeing as you ran away I think I'll hold the upper hand, especially after I've finished with that sex-starved worm Evans. I'll have him kissing my feet and they'll hang you like the rubbish you are." Trimble moved closer and took his arm as if to comfort him, "Or you can stay here, witness something wonderful and we'll reap the benefits together. Gwynfor, the Beast will protect us. Astaroth has told me everything."

"How long have you lived in this church? If there's one thing I've learnt from the Bible, it's that the devil is a liar …"

Trimble cut him off sharply, "Oh, and the Christian Church doesn't lie? How many popes have achieved office through trickery, deceit and murder? How many poor people were trounced on by the Church? How many old women were burnt as witches on the say-so of the church? Don't come to me with your laughable pious shit, Gwynfor. You're the biggest liar of all. You're not even a priest."

"But I'm not the one who wants to commit murder!"

"But, Gwynfor, dear," Trimble chided, "are you telling me those tramps and vagabonds you drugged with whiskey and opium don't count? You are a murderer, and all those you killed know it. Their spirits wander the grounds, waiting for revenge, and your only hope of protection against them is to give yourself to the devil. Your soul belongs to him, you're a murderer. You can either go to his realm as a sinner or be treated as an ally, the choice is yours."

Gwynfor sat on the edge of the bed and waited for tears, but they didn't come. He was trapped, and for the first time in his life he actually thought of praying for forgiveness. Astaroth ambled over and licked the Reverend's hand, and a voice whispered from a dark corner in his mind, "Join us."

"Astaroth says even your God can't help you now. He wants to be friends. Join us Gwynfor, join us," Trimble said, her tone of understanding almost convincing him of her integrity, though he knew he was just a pawn in this. Somewhere, somehow, the student had become the master, and he was now on the outside.

He'd play along. He'd clean their mess up, bury the girl and help kill the boy, but after that he didn't know, he really didn't know.

# 16

The school hall was packed. The first lessons had been cancelled straight after school prayers and the children chatted freely, seated on the floor in ranks. Finally the guest of honour arrived and the headmaster clapped his hands for their attention.

"Now then, children, I've gathered you here today as I want you all to listen to Sergeant Evans. He has something very serious to say, so pay attention." Mr Gerrard, the school headmaster, turned and held out an arm for Sergeant Evans to take the podium.

Grim-faced and sweating in his uniform, he surveyed the assembled children before starting his address. "Now then, who of you here knows Elizabeth Thomas?"

Sandra heard the words and fainted.

She came to with what seemed to be the whole school surrounding her. A low throb on her forehead told her she must have fallen forwards and landed on it, and the school nurse had placed a cold towel over where it hurt.

"Sandra, are you alright?" Sergeant Evans asked over the nurse's shoulder. "Have you seen Elizabeth?"

"You can ask her in a minute, Sergeant. The poor girl's only just come around," the nurse chastised him. "Come on, Sandra, let's have you. We'll take you to my room and the Sergeant can have a chat with you," she said, hauling Sandra up onto her feet.

The school nurse's room was really only a storeroom that had once held cleaning material, the smell of which had never actually left. Sandra sat on the couch that served as a bed, holding the compress to her head.

Sergeant Evans, his note pad out and pencil licked, took his cue from the school nurse and asked in a kindly tone, "Now, Sandra, am I right in thinking you fainted because you know something of Elizabeth Thomas's whereabouts?" He nodded encouragingly for her to answer him.

Gathering her thoughts, she coughed to clear her throat and started in. "Mister Evans, I mean Sergeant... the last time I saw Beth ... Elizabeth ... was yesterday after school. She told me she wanted to go to the vicarage to see if she could see Danny Kelly. I told her to wait until today as I had to help Misses Evans with the carpets, but she wouldn't and she went up there. I knew she wouldn't come back, I just knew it. There's something happening up there. That housekeeper and her dog have her!" The outburst gradually gathered speed as she told it and ended up burying her face in her hands in tears.

"The vicarage? Why did she want to see Daniel Kelly?" the policeman asked ominously.

Sniffing loudly into a hanky the nurse had given her, Sandra said, "We wanted to ask about the prayer we found."

"What prayer? Sandra, start at the beginning. This isn't making much sense."

So she told him about the prayer Danny had given Dafydd, how he'd thrown it away and why they went up to the house.

"So, let me get this straight," Evans said, removing his helmet and scratching his head. "You think there's something going on up the vicarage because Miss Trimble gives you the creeps and Astor scares you? And you think that's where Elizabeth Thomas went to last?"

Realising her account sounded rather ludicrous and childish, Sandra decided against back tracking to explain it all better, as that would only make things more ridiculous. "Sergeant Evans, yesterday after school Beth told me she was going up to the house. When I heard you were looking for her, I thought the worst. I hope I'm wrong, but I think you should ask up at the vicarage."

She was satisfied with that; he'd have to check there now.

"Where's this piece of paper with the prayer on?" the Sergeant asked.

"At home, on the desk in our bedroom," Sandra

told him, half-excited he asked, but also feeling guilty he was taking it so seriously. Now she thought about it, the story did all seem a little unlikely.

"Show me it again tonight, Sandra, alright? I doubt it means anything but I'll have a look at it anyway." He winked at her and her heart dropped when she realised he was humouring her to be nice.

"So Miss Gerrard," he continued. "I won't take any more of your time. I'll be off now to the old vicarage to ask there. Work hard now Sandra, and I'll see you later for tea."

He ruffled her hair and walked out. Sandra watched him straddle his cycle and pedal away, wishing she hadn't come across as being such an excitable little girl.

•

"I know," Trimble said. "I saw him pedalling up the hill. He has so much stamina on that bike of his, he must have thighs like a bull."

Gwynfor was standing at the door, feeling foolish in the glow of his housekeeper's cool exterior. He'd seen the policeman from afar and run up the stairs to warn her, only to be rebuked before he'd said a word.

"Let me handle this, Gwynfor. Take Daniel out the back and go for a walk somewhere on the hills. I'll make sure Sergeant Evans goes away happy nothing untoward is going on here."

Gwyn nodded wordlessly and left. Danny was

brushing the backyard.

"Get your jacket, we're going for a walk lad," was all he said, and marched off up the road away from the house, leaving the boy to drop the broom and swipe his blazer.

Evans knocked on the door after arranging himself to look respectable. She was an odd sort, the housekeeper, and yet she held a strange fascination for the mild-mannered yet worldly sergeant.

Once, as a young constable, and when things hadn't been so good between himself and Mrs Evans, and the only thing holding them together was their fear of social disapproval, he had fantasised about the Reverend's housekeeper. Her long legs, spotless turnout and prim manner hid an energy he found irresistible, and it had taken all he had not to make a move on her at that time. Now, with the mellowing effect of age and habit, he would never dream of such a foray, but once, long ago, it had been an issue.

The door opened and Trimble stood in the doorway, her hair down, blouse open three buttons, and no shoes on, her black-stockinged feet almost immodest in a House of God, a small voice at the back of his mind sniggered.

"Sergeant Evans, how nice!" she exclaimed, smiling as if the Son of God himself had arrived. "What can I do for you?"

"Well, Miss Trimble, I'm here on official business, as always," he answered apologetically.

"Oh!" she said. "Oh silly me, where are my

manners? Would you like to come in for some tea, I can make a pot for us. We won't be disturbed as the Reverend is out looking for Daniel again. That tiresome lad is always running away."

Trimble nearly laughed aloud as the policeman's mind changed into overdrive at the potential meaning of the statement. "Run away? Does he always do this?"

Rolling her eyes, Trimble sighed, "All the time Sergeant, and we have no idea where he goes or what he does."

"Do you know where he has gone to now? I have some questions for him."

"For the Reverend?"

"Well, for both, actually, and you as well Miss. If you can tell me where they are I'll go and find them. It's very important."

"No, Sergeant, I'm afraid I don't. Daniel skips off without doing his chores and hikes around the hills. The Reverend will find him shortly and bring him back. In the meantime, do come in. I'd be so glad of some company."

Evans was about to cross the threshold when he paused and stood back. "Well, actually, before we do take tea Miss Trimble, I'm afraid I have to ask you a few questions."

Feigning disappointment and yet managing to convey a stoical sense of duty and respect for the law, Trimble smiled bravely, "Yes, of course, Sergeant, ask away."

Pulling out his pencil and notebook, he coughed

once to clear his throat and waded in. "Miss Trimble, did you see Elizabeth Thomas yesterday at any time whatsoever?"

"Elizabeth? The Thomas girl who lost her father in Belgium? Or did he just leave them? I don't remember. Whatever, no, she came around the day before with a delightful young lady. Very excitable if the truth be known, but still lovely. But yesterday, I'm afraid not. Why? Is something the matter?" she asked innocently.

"You're sure now, Miss Trimble? It's very important."

"Yes, Sergeant, I'm positive. I'd just finished cutting some wood. I was on my own as the Reverend was away that day on official business with the Bishop, I think."

"You were cutting wood?" Evans asked, surprised.

"Well, as I said, I was on my own and I thought I might as well do it as nobody else here does." She left her statement hanging in the air and Evans tutted, shocked a lady had to cut wood while there were two men in the house who could have done it. "Anyway, that was the last time I saw her, as both the Reverend and myself spent all day yesterday looking for Daniel again, so we weren't home. He's such a mischievous lad, but he is from the city so we shouldn't be surprised. Who knows what they get up to in their hovels?" She shuddered dramatically and then smiled again. "Now, Sergeant, may I offer you that tea?"

"So you have no idea where she could be at this moment?"

"I'm afraid not. Sorry."

Closing his notebook and slipping it and the pencil into his breast pocket, he removed his helmet and nodded, "A nice cup of tea would be welcome, Miss Trimble, thank you."


Danny thought about asking where they were going but it was obvious the Reverend had a lot on his mind, so he followed mutely behind and kept himself to himself. Trimble had been scarce today and he'd hardly seen her dog since the incident in the attic. However, he still had the feeling something was up.

The night before he'd been woken up by their arguing but had fallen straight back to sleep again, thankful it wasn't the thing in the closet that stirred him. The Reverend had thrown him a googly the day before with the whiskey. He seemed almost, Danny searched for the word in his mind - contrite, sorrowful, ashamed? He couldn't put his finger on it but he hadn't been the same authoritarian figure he'd been on his arrival.

Mr Pollock, his neighbour in Fazakerley when he'd lived with his mother, had said one day in a bout of one of his post-booze-up downers, "Whiskey can bring out the best and the worst in men." That saying had stuck in his mind and he figured the bottle had prised out the real Reverend, and Danny liked it.

"Let's have a rest, Daniel. My legs aren't what they used to be. Sit down here and we'll take some air," the older man ordered, not unkindly, so they sat on a bench that overlooked the bay the town of Colwyn had adopted for its name.

"I came here after the Great War and I don't think I'll ever tire of this view. Far better than the hills and slagheaps of the valleys in the South."

Danny nodded, not wanting to spoil the atmosphere. He had the feeling an unspoken bond was building itself between them and one word might break its gossamer strand.

"And it's probably a lot better than the factories and smog of Liverpool as well, eh?" the Reverend continued.

Danny nodded but stayed silent.

"Don't you miss your home town, Daniel?"

Unconsciously the answer blurted itself out on its own. "I miss my mother. I wouldn't care where I was as long as I was with my mam."

"I see," he nodded. "I suppose that does make things easier ..."

Danny looked across at him, alarmed, but the Reverend smiled tiredly. "In that you took comfort from your mother and not your surroundings. I have no mother. She passed away at my birth. My father raised me with a belt across my back and a hole in my stomach from his drinking." Another puzzled look from Danny elicited an explanation. "He drank too much and we never had money for food. He couldn't work in the mines because he had to look after me, so he chopped firewood, and so did I when I was old enough. Hard times but they put some shoulders on me," he said with a laugh.

Danny pushed a non-committal laugh out but the talk had taken him back to thinking of his mother, and it sounded hollow.

"What would you do if you ran away, Daniel?"

Shocked by the question, Danny swivelled to face the Reverend. "How do you mean, Reverend?"

"I mean, if you were to run away now, where would you go to?"

"I wouldn't run away, I wouldn't stand a chance," Danny said honestly.

The Reverend nodded. "Why? You're young, you have youth on your side. If you were to up sticks now and simply run away, I wouldn't have a chance to catch you, so what's stopping you?"

What was stopping him? The older man was right; if he ran away now there'd be nothing he could do to stop him, but perhaps that was his plan. But what would that bring? Then the closet reared its indistinct head. He was scared of what was in the closet, but he was more worried about the fact it wanted his mother. How had it fixated on his mother? He had to find out or he'd never rest again.

"Well?" prompted the older man.

"If I ran away, Sergeant Evans would have the whole of the police onto me. A Liverpool lad in Wales, every village would report me. I wouldn't stand a chance."

The Reverend nodded sagely. "Yes, she's stitched that up pretty well, hasn't she?"

Danny knew whom he meant, and before he even thought about it he was nodding his head remorsefully. "Yes," he said, "she has."

Backtracking a bit, the Reverend said, "But you didn't do yourself any favours, Daniel, running away, taking the knife."

Danny thought about his answer before saying anything. He had the feeling the Reverend wanted to communicate with him, to try and find some common ground, and as honesty seemed a good baseline to go from he ploughed right in. "It's just that I've been so scared. Of the dog, of the ghost and of Miss Trimble. She was the one who made me do that in the bath tub, honestly!" He turned to face the older man. "I swear it, she made me do it, her and that dog. She does it all the time to me, rubbing me and stuff …"

The Reverend held up his hands to stop him. "Whoa, stop now. Ghost, what ghost?"

"In my room, there's a ghost, a young man I think. He keeps waking me up at night. He's in the closet."

"The closet?" the Reverend exclaimed, and then more calmly, "He's in the closet, you say?"

"I've seen him a few times. Have you seen him?" Danny was delighted at the reaction, especially when he mentioned the closet.

A dark cloud of foreboding gathered in his head when he realised something must have happened there and the Reverend knew about it.

"You know about it, don't you?" he said accusingly and pressed the question when the Reverend's face turned from feigned innocence to shock. "What was it? What happened to him?"

"I don't know what you mean, Daniel. I ..." He paused to gather his thoughts. "I think it's time we went back now. I don't want to hear any more nonsense about ghosts in the closet, or Miss Trimble making you play with yourself. Let bygones be bygones - a clean slate." He stood up. "Come on, let's go back." And then he strode off down the hill.

Danny paused to look at the view. As the Reverend marched off, he pondered over his reaction.

What the hell is going on here?

# 17

Sandra wiped the tears away when someone knocked on the door and she sat up on her bed. "Come in."

It was Mrs Evans with a cup of tea. "I thought you could do with this. You've had an awful shock, my dear," she said, smiling kindly. "Mister Evans is up the vicarage now, asking about your friend. I shouldn't worry, she'll probably turn up."

Sandra nodded and took the tea. She had nothing to add to what Mrs Evans said, so she blew on the hot brew and sipped it. From downstairs they heard the sound of the front door opening and both their eyes lit up.

"That's him now," Mrs Evans said, "Let's go see what he has to say."

The Sergeant had taken his helmet off and was busying himself with his boots when they both joined him in the kitchen. Hardly able to contain herself, Sandra asked straight away, "Did you find her? Was she there?"

Shaking his head as he undid his laces, he sat

back and smiled ruefully, "No, I'm afraid not Sandra, and it seems like your friend might have a hand in her disappearance as well."

Sandra gasped and put a hand to her mouth in shock. "That can't be true!"

Shrugging, the policeman said, "Well, she's not there and he's disappeared. Apparently he always disappears, just goes off. It's all very strange. Anyway, I've been to her mother's, who's taking this all very stoically indeed."

"She's a tough woman, bringing her girl up all by herself," Mrs Evans interjected.

"Aye, well, like I say, she's taking it very bravely. As for where she is though, I haven't a clue. I spoke with Miss Trimble who swears she hasn't seen her since the day you two went up there."

"She's lying!" Sandra exclaimed. "She knows exactly where she is."

"Well, we can't go jumping to conclusions now. This is in fact a missing person, but they're not officially missing until they've been gone over twenty-four hours," he answered Sandra's outburst as kindly as he could.

The fact was his afternoon with Miss Trimble had altered his perception of her entirely. He'd always felt a little protective towards her in the past.

She was an attractive woman who'd devoted herself to the church and looking after the Reverend, or that was how he had seen her.

Today she had directed him to one of the large overstuffed chairs, served him tea and made polite conversation. She asked how things were in the new church in the village, explaining her absence there as it not being fitting for her to simply leave the church she had come to call home, regardless of the fact it had been closed down for nigh on three years.

"Well, the Reverend Hughes does a lovely sermon and the Mother's Union is very involved with all the functions," he'd answered matter-of-factly.

Trimble reflected on how Gwyn had always been at loggerheads with the MU. For one reason or another, they'd never actually felt welcome there, and by about the fifth year of Gwynfor's tenure they'd given up entirely on their functions.

"The Reverend Davies never saw eye-to-eye with the Mother's Union," Trimble observed dryly. "I never understood why, but each to their own I suppose."

Evans nodded and sipped his tea. He had no real time for village squabbles unless they disrupted the peace.

"And Mrs Evans, how is she these days?" Trimble asked from her place opposite him on the sofa. She sat back and crossed her legs, giving the police sergeant an eyeful of her long black-stockinged legs.

Prising his gaze away, he said, "Oh fine. She's enjoying having children in the house but it's very tiring, you understand. But nice. I'll be sorry when they go back to their parents if the truth be told." The Evans family had never had their own children and the sound of their playing had lit up the house like never before. They were even seriously considering adopting a child.

Trimble nodded sympathetically. "I can imagine. Children are such a handful nowadays, and three of them all at once, I bet she hardly has anytime for herself." She leaned forward to put her teacup on the table. "Or her husband."

Slightly confused by the suggestion, Evans raised his eyebrows and half-laughed, "Well, she's never really had time for me. Too many church functions to go to, you know how she is." He smiled, hoping Trimble would see it as a light-hearted observation and not a criticism of their marriage, which it secretly was.

"Oh, you poor man, Sergeant." She put her hand on his knee. "If you were my husband I'd have all the time in the world for you. I would make time."

Evans looked down at her hand and back to Trimble's face. "Yes, well, that's nice of you," he stuttered, a warm blush rising to his cheeks.

"Are you blushing, Sergeant? There's no need to. I know you have a lonely life as a policeman, I'm a grown woman and I know what grown men need."

Her hand moved higher, from his knee to his thigh, as she stood up and leaned forward, allowing the policeman to see down the front of her open blouse. Her perfume played havoc with his senses and it fogged his mind as desire took control.

Finally, after what felt like an eternity for Evans, she put her hand on his crotch.

"Sergeant, you're so big," she purred into his ear, sending tingles down his spine. As she began to massage him through the stiff material of his trousers, he came to his senses.

"Miss Trimble," he whispered awkwardly, coughing to clear his throat. "Miss Trimble, I really think I should go now, before something happens we might both regret."

"I won't regret it, John," she breathed, her fingers moving to the buttons on his fly.

Forcefully he stood up, brushing the clinging Trimble off him. "No, really Miss Trimble. I'm flattered, and if circumstances had been different I'd be more than happy to have obliged." He swallowed hard and looked around for his helmet. "I really must be going."

Trimble stood back and buttoned up her blouse. "Well, yes, Sergeant, I understand," she said, smoothing down her skirt. "I'll see you to the door, then."

She turned and quickly left the room, and Evans suffered a slight pang of conscience. Yes, he was married but how long had the poor woman felt like that for him? And his wife had long given up on the physical side of marriage. No, he'd leave here and not return unaccompanied again; it was better for all concerned. She stood at the door, her face a mask of embarrassed hurt and his heart went out to her.

"Miss Trimble ... Fiona ... please understand, I'm a married man. I can't, I just can't."

She nodded imperceptibly and closed her eyes

briefly. "I would appreciate it if you didn't tell anyone, please, Sergeant Evans," she whispered.

"Of course, that goes without saying. Let's just forget the whole incident and move on, eh?" He smiled at her warmly and she raised a brief smile in answer.

"Thank you, John. If you need me, I'll be here for you," she murmured bravely, and he raised a hand and stroked her cheek tenderly before turning to leave.

As he left, she closed the door and leant back on it, giggling into her hand at the memory of his face as she held his manhood. Sex-starved and callow, he would be putty in her hands from now on, she knew.

As he free-wheeled his cycle down the hill towards the village, his mind awhirl with regret and obligation, Sergeant John Evans thought back to the reason he had visited the vicarage and decided on the spot it must have been that lad from Liverpool who'd either kidnapped her, or worse.

Sandra listened to what Sergeant Evans had to say in silence. He'd made his mind up and she knew there was nothing she could say that would change his decision unless she somehow found concrete proof.

She knew Danny hadn't killed Beth. He might have run away from the place but he'd never kill.

As Sergeant Evans droned on about how some lads find it hard to adjust to the freedom of the countryside and simply go wild, she made a decision. At the next available opportunity she would go up to the vicarage herself and look for Danny, and maybe they could find Beth.

A horrible thought struck her: if the housekeeper had killed Beth, perhaps she also killed Danny and he hadn't run away after all …

"Are you alright, dear?" Mrs Evans asked.

"I'm fine. I'd like to go to my room now, if that's okay."

"But of course."

Bundling her out of the kitchen to the stairs, the policeman's wife cooed and clucked about her getting enough sleep and being in shock, and bed was just the right place for her.

# 18

Gwynfor couldn't believe his eyes as he looked down at the orchard in the church grounds from his place on the hill. It was full of people. He couldn't make faces out but it was clear there were a lot of people standing among the trees.

He turned to Danny, "Look at that. I wonder who those people are in the orchard."

Danny strained to see who he meant but all he could make out was the miserable bad-tempered cat that constantly fouled his bed. "I can't see anyone, Reverend."

Gwynfor turned and they were gone. He could have sworn he saw people. The orchard had been full and yet now there was no one to be seen. "Well, I'll be …" he puzzled. He must be either very tired or going mad, and he suspected the latter of the two.

They marched home in silence, Gwynfor spooked by the disappearing crowd he was sure he'd seen, Danny with his thoughts on what the night would bring.

A loud bark woke him from his reverie and the sight of Astaroth bounding up towards them was enough for Danny to stop walking and let the Reverend go before him.

Strangely, the Reverend slowed his pace down as well, and Danny was sure he detected a definite caution in his stride, but the dog ran up to him and welcomed him like any normal hound. Gwynfor exhaled audibly as he rubbed the dog's head and said by way of explanation, with a paper thin smile, "He's such a big brute, I'm always afraid if he jumps on me he'll knock me over."

Nodding curtly and skirting the pair, Danny walked off, fearing any minute he'd hear Astaroth pounding after him and feel his hot fetid breath on the back of his neck. It was all he could do to not start running towards the house, and when he arrived at the kitchen door he went straight to his room.

After kicking the cat out, he almost slammed the door. Gwynfor was puzzled at the way Astaroth gambolled around him like a happy puppy. All semblance of the old brooding wolfhound had seemingly gone, and for a spark of a second he wondered if Trimble had left. But he knew within his heart that would never be the case, not until they'd sacrificed the boy.

His thoughts flew back to Trimble's suggestion they hobble him by breaking his thighbones. The thought perturbed him as he weighed it in his mind. He had murdered in his past, but the only one that actually felt like murder was the first unfortunate who came to while being strangled.

The others had spent an ideal couple of days drinking the cheap whiskey and then slipped into a drug-induced coma to be strangled in the old church during ceremony. Aside from the first, none of them, not one, had known what was happening, and their deaths had been as painless as they had been merciful: painless due to the drugs; merciful owing to the mental demons that plagued each and every one of them; demons collected on the various battlefields around Belgium, France, Palestine, and any other hell hole they where they had served and lost their minds.

However, to knowingly break someone's legs to cause maximum pain, and then bleed them to death while they writhed in agony, seemed barbaric beyond comprehension. How on earth did she think they were going to do it? Granted, there were others in the congregation far more believing than he was.

A few of them unnerved him in their devotion to their belief, though he noted only one had ever come forward to tie the knot that killed their sacrificial victims - the mad butcher from Abergele who had wanted to strangle the victims with his hands, something Gwyn could never sanction. Gwyn forbade it in no uncertain terms, and though he was in charge, the man's sadism unnerved him.

As they approached the back gate to the church grounds, Astaroth suddenly froze in his step like a trained pointer. "What is it, boy?" he asked, almost waiting for the dog to reply, and was quietly relieved when it didn't. Suddenly Astaroth sped off around the wall and was gone. "A rabbit, probably," he said aloud in a lame attempt at explaining to himself why the dog acted like that.

He passed through the wrought iron gates and into the orchard, pausing briefly to look around and check if anyone was actually there. He scanned the trees and the corner beyond, but nothing stirred.

Then all at once the birds stopped chirping and an eerie silence descended on the scene as if a large predator was passing by. No insect droned, no leaf rustled. Utter calm hit the orchard like an unexpected change in air pressure, and Gwynfor, startled by the sudden vacuum, turned around expecting Astaroth to walk into view. But nothing came.

A cold sweat ran down his back and he was suddenly caught by the feeling someone was watching him. In fact, it felt like a lot of people were gazing at him, observing his reaction to the abrupt stillness, and judging him.

The gulp as he swallowed sounded perversely loud, but it acted like a catalyst for normality to resume and the silence suddenly lifted. The feeling of being watched didn't leave but the return of tangible sound did do something to prod him into motion, and without looking back he walked swiftly into the house, followed by the invisible eyes of his accusers.

Danny scraped hastily at the crumbling mortar

around the brick, every now and then pausing to see if it could be moved or pulled out.

The knife had found its way into his pocket at the evening meal, a surprising affair that consisted of meat, potatoes, carrots and gravy. It certainly looked to Danny that the Reverend and Trimble had taken his words to heart, which had done an awful lot for his brittle and battered pride.

After thanking them for his meal, he wordlessly cleaned the table and took everything into the kitchen to do the washing up, pocketing the knife as he dried everything. Now, in the dim light of the faltering candle he worked its fine blade into the crumbling cement. It quickly became apparent the mortar wasn't mortar at all, but dirt packed around the brick to give it some hold.

Wedging his fingertips into where he'd cleared, he pulled the stone out, rocking it jerkily in its place. It fell with an audible clump on the wooden floor and Danny froze until he was sure nobody had heard. Reluctant to simply stick his fingers into the hole, he leaned forward to see if he could see something with the candle. A corner of lace, dirty and no doubt mouldy could be seen, and he pinched and pulled it out. It was a handkerchief, and though fungus-flecked and grimy, it was folded with a precision that spoke of love.

Holding his breath, he laid it down to open it. Wrapped in its delicate folds was a piece of paper. The handkerchief itself was emblazoned with the initials 'F.T.' in one of the corners and Danny wondered who F.T. was? Was it Trimble? What was her first name? He didn't know, which seemed odd when he thought about it as he'd been there nigh on two weeks now. The paper was delicate and he was afraid of ruining it by opening it. After all, it might be evidence. Nevertheless, curiosity grasped him by the throat and he slowly unfolded it.

It was the same spidery writing as on the wall, and written again in Welsh he guessed. He laid it out on the floor and carefully pored over it by the light of the now drastically diminishing candle.

> Paham mae dicter, O Miss Trimble,
> Yn llenwi'th lygaid duon di?
> A'th ruddiau tirion, O Miss Trimble,
> Heb wrido wrth fy ngweled i?
> Pa le mae'r wên oedd ar dy wefus
> Fu'n cynnau 'nghariad ffyddlon ffôl?
> Pa le mae sain dy eiriau melys,
> Fu'n denu'n nghalon ar dy ôl?

Except for the words, 'O Miss Trimble', he couldn't make head nor tail of it. However, those words alone spiked his interest and he was electrified by the thought this might be a clue. Was it a document listing the tortures she'd put him through, whoever he might be? Or a diary of events, a plea for help?

He noticed a lot of question marks in the passage but they told him nothing. The candle was starting to splutter and die, so he hastily pushed the brick back into place and swept the dirt into the corner along with the dead spiders, flies and filth.

After carefully folding everything together, he stood up and turned to leave the closet, just as the candle gave out. As he paused briefly to let his eyes adjust, a sudden gust of cold air hit him from the front and instantly the hairs on the back of his neck stood up in alarm. In front of him, between himself and the believed safety of his bed, stood the large shadowy figure that had plagued him nearly every night. A black shade among shadows, Danny could only just about make him out, but he was there. The air cooled rapidly, and though afraid, Danny was now also curious.

"Put it back," the figure said, speaking English, the anger palpable.

Danny felt like a thief caught in the spotlight when the figure addressed him. "What is it?" he asked after winning the fight to simply throw it back into the closet and dash for the bed.

"Put it back or your mother will get hurt."

"Tell me what it is. Perhaps I can help you," Danny pleaded, taking a step back as the figure flared into flame and shouted at the top of its voice, "No!'"

Regaining his composure, Danny slipped the handkerchief into the breast pocket of his pyjamas, next to the picture of his mother. The thought of her laughing face boosted him, and somehow, regardless of what the demon or ghost had shown him over the last couple of days, he felt stronger, braver -

indestructible somehow.

"Tell me what it is. I want to help. Is it Trimble? Did she do something to you?"

With a shout of anger and a flash of heatless fire, the figure advanced on him. Danny backed into the closet and was already against the wall when it pushed through him as if he wasn't there. An immense pressure waded into him and exited through his back into the wall. A myriad of images danced in his head, of Trimble, Astaroth changing to a goat, the Reverend shouting, a noose, a knife, his mother smiling …

Suddenly the cold was gone and with it the fiery figure. Confused but no longer afraid, had he just won a small victory?

Checking to see if the handkerchief and the picture of his mother were still in his pocket, he walked gingerly to the bed and lay down. The facts now muddled by fatigue and adrenalin, he attempted to sort through the experience. Why did it burst into flames when it felt angry or annoyed? Why was there a noose and the knife in his thoughts when it passed through him?

He concentrated on what felt certain. The ghost wanted the handkerchief back, that much was sure, and also that his mother was safe. She had boosted his resolve and inspired him to ask the questions,. Or had he imagined it? The high of the adrenalin gave way to the dark doubts of his psyche and suddenly he wasn't sure. Had he imagined it? Had the thought of his mother's smile given him hope or was it just curiosity that had moved his tongue?

Perhaps the dark menace was tormenting his mother right now he pondered, just before sleep pulled him into blackness.

The door slammed shut and instantly Danny was awake, instincts screeching at him in alarm.

His breath wafted like steam in the moon's faint watery light and a slight tremor passed through his bladder. Pulling up the bed clothes and covering his mouth, his eyes slowly grew accustomed to the dark corners of the room. IT was back and at that moment he didn't feel as brave as earlier. He'd been ambushed by sleep and now, after being bluntly woken by the slamming door, he felt vulnerable and scared.

It was freezing again and the small voice at the back of his mind needlessly reminded him the window was closed. Not daring to move, and waiting for something to happen, his mind raced in unspoken prayer nothing would.

Slowly the temperature changed and it seemed the cold was retreating towards the closet. He could feel it ebbing away like a tide, almost pulsing as it withdrew. It was leaving, he told himself, willing it to be true.

Unexpectedly a small puff of cold air hit his face and he jerked back as something whispered hatefully into his ear, "Make no mistake, your mother's with me Danny, and she's burning in hell for all the bad stuff she did for you."

Instinct overcame reason and Danny dashed under the covers, knuckling his mouth in silent, absolute terror; wishing for death so this horror could end.

# 19

Sergeant Evans had laughed warmly when Sandra asked to use his bike, but he congenially relented. "I suppose a walk in the fresh air will do me some good, then, but don't overdo it, and try not to change gear going downhill, the chain comes off."

She pushed it up the hill - it was simply too steep to pedal - and then on as the road levelled out. Sandra wasn't sure what she was going to do but she knew something had happened up at the house and she felt a need to see Danny, or at least ask if he had turned up.

Sergeant Evans wouldn't countenance that Danny had nothing to do with Beth's disappearance, and when she'd mentioned it the night before, he'd been positively angry.

"Listen now Sandra, this is the last time we're going to talk about this. Daniel Kelly is a bad egg. Not only has he run away several times, he's threatened the Reverend and poor Miss Trimble, stolen a knife from them and let's not mention the other thing that happened. I have a hunch, and we policemen rely on our hunches a lot. My hunch is this: your friend has run away because he has something to do with Beth Thomas's disappearance. Now I don't want to talk about him anymore, he's a bad 'un, don't waste your breath on him."

So, deciding to withdraw and plan ahead without his help, Sandra determined to go up to the house and see if Danny was to be seen. She'd asked for the bike as a way of shortening the journey. It was all very well to play detective, but she still had homework and chores to do, and a set of wheels would cut the journey time down radically, especially on the way back.

As the church came into view she looked hard to see if Danny was out and about. Her hope was he'd be working in the grounds somewhere. She had no desire to knock and ask to see him, but would do so if necessary. Straining her eyes, she saw a head in a part of the wall that had fallen in, leaving a dip in its length. She was sure it was him and she pedalled faster.

Leaning the cycle against the wall, she approached the dip and looked in. She very nearly squealed in delight to see him and gleefully called his name. Turning to look in her direction, a smile befitting a sun god broke his face as he said her name. "Sandra, what are you doing here?"

"Checking on you," she laughed, then said seriously, "You do know what that awful Trimble woman has been saying about you, don't you?"

"What exactly?" he asked warily.

"Well, all I know is Beth Thomas – the girl who's friends with Huw and the others? – well, she's missing and Mister Evans, I mean Sergeant Evans, is sure you have something to do with it. Trimble told him you run away all the time, that's why he thinks you have something to do with her disappearance."

"But I haven't seen her in ages!" he exclaimed.

Sandra made shushing movements with her hands, "Yes, I know, but you're in his bad books after all that's gone on here …"

She let it hang there and Danny blushed deeply. "Does everyone know what happened? Because it's not true," he asked almost petulantly.

"No, I heard Sergeant Evans telling Mrs Evans but I haven't told a soul."

Danny chewed over his embarrassment. Sandra was the last person in the world he wanted to hear of his illicit entanglements, but it seemed as fate would have it she was to be one of the few who did. Why was life so unfair?

Seeing his awkwardness, Sandra broke the silence. "Well, I don't believe it personally, but Sergeant Evans did, and he's the one we need to get on our side."

Danny's face lit up. "You don't believe it?"

"No, of course not, silly. So how are we going to convince him?"

Danny fished hurriedly in his pocket and brought out the handkerchief with the piece of paper. Taking the paper out, he gave it to Sandra, saying, "I found this in the closet last night. I've no idea what it means but it's got Trimble's name on it." He contemplated briefly telling her about the ghost but decided against it. He didn't want to pollute her trust with stories of the supernatural. Perhaps he'd have a chance to tell her another time.

"What is it?" Sandra asked regardless.

"I've no idea. Have a read of it. It makes no sense to me except the words, 'O Miss Trimble'. Do you know the story about the boy who ran away from the dairy farmer last year?"

Sandra nodded, "Yes, Beth told me."

"Well, I think they have something to do with it. Trimble is … she has a way of …" He didn't know how to put it and Sandra's nonplussed face didn't help, so he dived straight in. "I think he was here and he either killed himself, or they killed him."

Sandra's look of shock almost caused him to back-pedal, until she gasped in amazement, "He was here? How do you know?"

Thankful she hadn't questioned his theory, and his mind in overdrive as to how he could explain himself without any mention of the ghost, he said, "Well, there's all the writing in the closet and the dairy's only down the road. Plus Trimble said to me he had probably just run away as the farmer was always beating the kids that stay with him, but Dafydd told me Jones Milk is a nice man."

Unconvinced but unwilling to give up, Sandra took the piece of paper and nodded slowly. "Right, I'll give this to Sergeant Evans and see what he has to say then."

"Look, I know it doesn't look like much, but there's stuff going on here I can't explain," Danny said, shrugging. "When you give him the note, just ask him what it means. Don't say it was from me or from the runaway. Just keep it simple and wait for him to decide on what to do, okay?"

Nodding, she opened her mouth to say something but a bark from the house shut her up. "You'd better go," Danny said. "Her dog can be unfriendly if he wants to be."

Sandra, eyes wide in alarm, hurriedly said, "Right, I'll go, then. Don't want you being in trouble. I'll come back tomorrow, if you want."

"Yes, of course. Tell me what he said. Now go, quickly!" he said, shooing her away. She straddled the bike – it was a man's cycle and she didn't know how to mount it without looking inelegant – and pushed off. Danny turned to see Astaroth galloping towards them. Unsure of his intent, but fearing the worst, he shouted, "Quick Sandra, pedal. He's coming!" before the dog hurtled past him and over the dip in the wall.

Snarling horribly, it pounded after the girl, who, on looking back and seeing the galloping monster catching her up, put on a burst of speed that took her over the brow of the hill and downwards. Gravity and her pumping thighs carried her away down the road at what looked to Danny like a dangerously fast rate. However, given the option of dicing with the control of the bike or relying on Astaroth's good nature, he knew which choice he'd have made.

Astaroth stopped running when he saw she was now too far away for him to catch and turned to glare maliciously at Danny. Though the dog was far away, its intent seemed vicious and Danny backed up towards the house. Slowly the dog ambled back, his baleful scowl emphasised by the trail of angry drool dripping from his fangs.

Walking backwards, eyes focused on the dog, Danny bumped into the surprisingly sturdy Miss Trimble. "Watch where you're going please, Daniel," she said as he jumped forward again on contact with the housekeeper. Facing her, he dropped his eyes, the guilt of his discussion written all over his face.

She was dressed in her usual uniform of black skirt and stockings, high heels and white blouse, with one hand on her hip, hair down and her glasses in the other hand. It was all Danny could do to smother his ache. Why did he want her so? She had shown only cruelty and malice towards him since his arrival, and yet he only needed to see her strike a certain pose with her hair down, and he wanted her. It was madness.

"Who was the girl?" she asked pleasantly.

"Sandra, from the village. She came with me from Liverpool. She's staying at Sergeant Evans' place."

Trimble smiled wanly. "Oh, how lovely for her. How perfectly divine," she drawled. "Now what was the note you gave her? I saw it all from my room, so there's no use denying it."

His mind racing, Danny blurted out the first thing that came to his mind. "A love letter. I asked her to go with me when we get back to Liverpool."

"You're lying."

"Ask her," he bluffed.

Trimble smiled, running her tongue across her teeth. "I will," she said casually. "And if you're lying to me …"

There was no need for her to finish as Astaroth, who had now reached where they stood, gave his customary low growl from behind.

"What …?" Danny asked tetchily, emboldened by the fact someone outside of this madhouse was in his corner and knew he existed. "Astaroth will kill me? Like he did the boy in the closet?" he probed.

Trimble reacted as if slapped. "What do you know about what happened in the closet?" she nearly screamed, raising more growls from the dog. "Has the Reverend told you anything … stupid?"

Pausing to ponder on what to let on, he decided to go the whole mile and see what she said. "No, a ghost did. The ghost of the boy you killed in the closet with your monster dog there." He pointed at Astaroth who simply growled louder in return. He knew he'd shot his bolt when she visibly relaxed. "You don't know a thing, boy. We haven't killed anyone, so go to your room and stay there until I call you for tea. I think the Reverend may have to have words with the Sergeant after all."

"I'd like to be there as well. I want to talk to the

Sergeant too."

Trimble's jaw dropped in shock at his answer, and before she could retort he turned to walk into the kitchen, closing the door behind him.

# 20

The cloudless heavens let the full gaze of the half-moon pour down through the window to light up his room. Gwynfor Davies lay awake in bed, contemplating his best move. It was obvious now he had no place in the whole scheme of things, and he'd even feared for his life today when his housekeeper had confronted him in the living room with that damned dog.

"What exactly did you tell him about Achlad and the closet?" she fumed, her voice a ragged hiss of impatient anger. Astaroth stood at her side, staring balefully at him, and Gwyn knew it was only a matter of time before he'd start to growl. He'd begun to hate that growl.

"I didn't tell him anything. He told me about it," he said, shocked at her tone. "He'd seen a ghost in there, that's all I know. I didn't say a word," he babbled. "He even mentioned the closet."

Trimble looked thoughtful and idly scratched Astaroth's head. "He's seen a ghost, he reckons.

Perhaps he's going insane. Achlad had completely lost it towards the end." She laughed at the memory. "He was insane with desire. He used to cry, begging me to sleep with him. Laughable, really. All I had to do was rub him up a bit, let Astaroth terrorise him now and then, and he snapped."

"He was insane before he came here," Gwynfor added conversationally, thankful she was no longer angry. "Did you know about him setting fire to the orphanage he was in? He was in an orphanage not far from Ruthin but he was too volatile, so they sent him to one in Liverpool where he went completely berserk and set fire to the place."

"I always felt he was a little disturbed," she nodded, "what with being an orphan and all that. I thought it was because perhaps that dairy farmer was touching him up as well. They're all a bit funny those farmyard types, especially the Welsh ones, or so I am told." She laughed at that memory as well. "You boys are all so easily misled. I didn't know about him lighting fires, though."

"But how did Daniel know about the closet?" Gwyn asked.

"Perhaps we really are haunted," Trimble suggested, putting a finger to her mouth, a gesture Gwynfor had always found mildly erotic. "I wouldn't be surprised. It says in the book the spirits of previous victims come back when we start working up to the ceremony, and it is in two days time."

"It says what?" he asked.

"The book, it says when we finally prepare to do

the ceremony properly, the spirit world will know, and the ghosts of all our earlier victims will come and watch, jealous they died for nothing, I suppose."

She smiled brightly as she said this but a cold fear gripped Gwynfor's guts at the thought. Had that been the feeling he'd experienced yesterday in the orchard? The souls of the men he'd killed over the years coming back to the church? Watching him, following him? Was that why Astaroth had gone around the church ground wall and not through the back gate, because he knew the spirits were there? The thought followed him all day and into the night, and now, in the wan light of the moon, Gwynfor's imagination went into a frenzy of dreadful scenarios.

Every time he closed his eyes visions swirled before him of men laid out in a pentagram, naked but for a cord around their necks, knotted tight to stop the airflow, faces black with hypoxia. It had all been so easy, so rehearsed, a process where the only unpleasantness had been the cleaning up and disposing of the bodies. And even that had been performed by the worshippers. Now his imagination, emotions and visions, convinced him they were back. Sleep still came for him during the wee hours, but the torture to his psyche was unabated. Guilt, the mother of all nightmares, cast her weighty spell and cursed him, unfolding dreams of tramps with black tongues, their clothes sodden in piss and shit, their necks bruised and misshapen, banging at his door, demanding entrance, food, his soul …

The nightmare provoked a strangled cry, waking

him. Sweat-bathed and feverish, the Reverend grabbed the glass of water by his bed and gulped it down in one. Must get away from here; must leave, he was going insane. What had started as a money-spinner with perks was now a full-blown nightmare, and it was high time to slip away with as little fuss as possible.

Mind made up, he lay back and thought the matter through. He'd need money of course - that was the prerequisite of any escape. Trimble had taken control of all the money and had locked it away in her room. What if he reasoned with her, if he told her straight he wanted away, she should give him his half and they'd go their separate ways? There was easily over twenty thousand pounds in the kitty, enough for them both. He could leave the country, go to Canada perhaps - he'd always fancied Canada. Maybe start a church up there as well. It had all been going swimmingly until Trimble had stuck her oar in and turned it serious.

As he talked himself into approaching her with the idea, he gradually appreciated the fact his plan was a pipedream that would never happen. Trimble would no more give him his half than she would give up her plans. The money would have to be written off if he was to leave, so what could he do - turn himself in to the police? Tell Sergeant Evans everything and come clean? Maybe claim insanity and be given a life sentence in some hospital with pretty nurses?

He shook his head sadly. That would never

happen either. He'd be hanged as a mass murderer, regardless of the fact all those poor souls he'd drugged and then peacefully strangled had been granted an escape from their daily misery. Life for some people is torture and for those mental derelicts who had known only the ruthless side of society, he reasoned their deaths had been a mercy. However, in a court of law they would see only a monster, a Satanist who killed the helpless souls who had come to him for help.

There seemed to be no way out. He was doomed to remain at the vicarage until Fiona decided to move on, or command her damned dog maul him to death. If only the Bishop hadn't found out about their ceremonies, or better yet, if only they'd been a little more discreet in the first place. Then a thought hit him. Wouldn't the Bishop welcome a chance to be rid of the black sheep in the diocese? Perhaps he should make an appointment with him and ask to be sent somewhere obscure.

He'd once heard of a vicar renowned for being a sodomite being sent to Rhodesia the day after he was caught with a choir boy doing extra organ lessons. He smirked at the memory of telling Trimble about that and how they'd laughed themselves sick at the double-entendre. He cleared his mind of the memory and decided he'd go to the Bishop the next day. He'd tell him everything and demand he be sent to Rhodesia, or Timbuktu, or wherever - he didn't care - just away from Old Colwyn, from Wales, from bloody Great Britain. Who knows, if he made it sound bad enough perhaps he'd be sent that day.

Gwynfor felt better now he had a plan, regardless of how tenuous it was. The Bishop would keep a confidence, being one of the new breed, the political sort who wanted the world to think all was well on his watch. Fortunately, he was also a bit soft, too well-mannered to start a scandal, so there shouldn't be any problem there.

The room was unusually warm and Gwynfor kicked the sheets off, went to the window and opened it. He gazed up at the crescent of the moon, hope flickering in his heart like a new candle, weak and spluttering. Yes, he'd do that tomorrow, go to the Bishop and plead his case. Of course he'd spare the details about the murders, but would tell him the rest; the ceremonies, the black masses, the sex, everything. Then perhaps, just perhaps, he'd escape this madness.

Something in the orchard caught his eye. In the pallid gaps between the shadows of the trees he thought he saw a dark face looking up towards the window. But he blinked and it was gone. Bending out of the window for a better view, he squinted into the greyness of the night. With a gasp of horror he jerked back when the image reappeared. The face looking up at him was almost black, like the victim of strangulation. An involuntary gasp of shock shook the Reverend, followed by a wave of dizziness and he looked away, grasping the windowsill to steady himself against falling out.

Daring to look again, there were more faces,

multiplying. Filling the orchard was a crowd of shadowy forms staring at him. Men, all men, all in a dishevelled state, their eyes bulging, tongues lolling out, faces blue or black, all silently accusing him with their unflinching glares. Horror, unchecked and ravenous, took over as he backed away from the window, his hands clawing mouth and face, bladder voiding silently down his leg. They were here. They wanted him. They wanted vengeance.

A low growl stopped his retreat and he turned to face Astaroth. The growling ceased but the snout stayed frozen in a silent snarl as a voice in his head spoke to him, its tone ancient, as old as creation, and weighted with unfathomable malice. The words gripped Gwyn's spine, paralysing him, leaving him in no doubt the hound before him held the spirit of a demon.

"Running won't help you. Your crimes are recorded and you are marked preacher, marked for damnation. You can enter his realm as a sinner to the fires or as a king among the devil's own. But running will not help you." The hound eyed him for a second more and then turned to amble out via the door. His head swam and unconsciousness waited at the back of his mind like a leaking damn, threatened to burst through and engulf him.

And then he was awake, lying in his bed. Sunlight shone through the window and a bird sang its morning melody for the entire world to enjoy. Had he dreamt the whole thing? Had it really been a nightmare?

He noticed the window, open to the world, and he knew it hadn't been a dream after all. The cold clamminess of his pissed pyjama trousers confirmed his worst thoughts. The window had been closed when he went to bed; damnation was his reality and yet in the light of day he couldn't find it in himself to believe it.

He'd have to see the Bishop today, he had to get away.

# 21

"Ah, Gwynfor, do come in." It was Vincent Meredith, the Bishop's secretary who answered the door. A fussy looking man of late middle age, he was unmarried, effeminate, and known as a pedant and scandal-monger in the Church institution. Gwynfor always suspected it was him who had architected his dismissal from the church, regardless of how soft he'd landed after the fall.

"Is the Bishop in? I really must speak with him," Gwyn asked nervously.

"Why, whatever's the matter Gwynfor? He isn't in right now but do come in. I'll make us some tea and perhaps I can help you."

He opened the door wide and stepped back for Gwyn to enter.

"When is he due back, do you know? It really is very important."

Meredith put his hand to his chin and affected a look of concern, unable to hide his glee and curiosity at what could possibly have made the man in front of him so edgy. "I'm afraid not for a couple of days. He's in Birmingham right now at a Bishop's seminar. He should be back early next week at the latest."

Gwyn's heart sank. Rushing out of the house this morning with the laughable excuse he'd given Fiona ... surely she suspected something; and it had all been for nothing.

"Gwynfor do come in, you look terribly worried. Perhaps if you told me what this is all about I may be able to help."

Nodding at the invitation he stepped over the threshold and into the Bishop's parlour. Why not? He had nothing to lose and he knew the Bishop's secretary was capable. With all his eggs in one basket, this one attempt at getting away was all he had. If Gwynfor went back now he doubted very much his housekeeper and that demon dog would let him live.

The secretary came into the room bearing a tray with a tea set. After pouring the tea, he sat down and crossed his legs in a decidedly feminine way. "Now then, Gwynfor, what seems to be the problem?"

"Vincent, I don't know where to begin," he started. He'd already decided to leave out the whole murder thing. He knew Meredith would have no problems handing him over to the police and he'd actually enjoy the scandal. No, he'd keep it safe. "Simply put, I have to get away from my housekeeper. How can I put this ...?"

"Miss Trimble? Why ever would you want to sack Miss Trimble? She works for free and has quietly serviced you ... I mean served you and the Church for nigh on twenty years if I'm not mistaken." Meredith smiled at his false faux pas and Gwynfor inwardly rolled his eyes at the childish innuendo. The secretary thought he knew what was going on with Fiona, they'd been the mainstay of his gossip for years, yet in reality he didn't know the half of it.

"No, I need the Church to send me away." A glimmer of an idea hit him and he decided to use the secretary's lust for tittle-tattle to his advantage. "She's sex mad. I simply have to get away from her. Vincent, she wakes me up at all hours for sex. She's insatiable and I can't take it anymore."

Meredith's eyes lit up in glee as Gwynfor expounded on the many and varied perversions his housekeeper demanded of him, and how he, with the interest of the Church in mind, indulged her with the strict instructions nobody should ever know.

"But I can't do it anymore, Vincent. I'm a simple man, a man of God with a country soul who can't condone this anymore. If we throw Miss Trimble out she'll surely cause a scandal, something the Bishop would be very angry about I'm sure," he added to remind Meredith of his place.

"Yes, yes, of course. Wouldn't want that, then, would we? So what are you asking precisely, Gwyn? Spell it out for me, please."

Gwynfor sat forward, his elbows on his knees and his head bowed. "I need the Church to send me away. Anywhere will do, I don't care where it is. But

I need to go now, today. I can't stand another night in that house with her." He contemplated trying to force crocodile tears, Meredith would have loved that he was sure, but decided against it. He shook his head again, as if in remorse for all he'd done, and exhaled loudly. "I can't go back, Vincent. There must be somewhere you can send me. I've only got the clothes on my back, I've no money, no possessions. I'm begging the Church to look after me as I have looked after its flock all these years." He paused for effect, then looked up with the most sincere expression he could muster, expecting to see sympathy - the gloating pity reserved for enemies who have fallen on hard times, but nevertheless sympathy - only to be met with the coldest smile he'd ever seen in his life.

"You pathetic worm, Davies. Who are you kidding?" the Bishop's secretary crowed. "I've known what's been going on up at that church since the first stories reached my ears all those years ago. Who do you think persuaded the Bishop to allow you to stay in the church, eh? Me, it was me who talked him into it!"

Gwynfor couldn't hide his shock or control his artless tongue, "You knew?"

At this the secretary burst out laughing. "Knew? Of course I knew. I know everything that goes on in this diocese. But mostly I knew because Miss Trimble, Fiona, told me."

His mouth like a gasping cod, Gwynfor's shock was complete. "She told you? Why?"

"Because we both serve the Great Beast whose name is Satan, Abaddon, Mammon, Beelzebub, Belial, Mephistopheles, whose armies are legion and whose dawn now breaks the horizon." He picked his teacup up and stirred it absently as he spoke. "I'll be there tomorrow for the ultimate feast. We'll sacrifice the helpless lamb under your roof and our riches in this world will be innumerable, but in the next world eternal! Gwynfor Davies, go back. You'll find no succour here. Your name is known in the realm of Hell and you have nowhere on this earth to run to. Join us or burn for eternity. Now get out."

Listening as if in a daze, Gwynfor stood up and slowly backed away, his fear and bewilderment now controlling his thoughts. "You're in league with her as well?"

Rolling his eyes in exasperation the Bishop's secretary calmly sipped his tea and sat back in his chair. "No, you still don't understand, do you? This goes ahead, you can't stop it, and if you want to save your immortal soul I suggest you get with the plan." He tutted and shook his head. "Go back, Gwynfor. I'll see you tomorrow at the ceremony. Close the front door on the way out, please."

•

Danny decided the coast was clear and filled the bath with warm water to wash his clothes and himself. Trimble was shopping in the village with Astaroth, the Reverend had been gone since this morning, so he felt it was safe.

Reaching for the carbolic soap and scrubbing board, he paused to look out the window. The view was breathtaking and he sighed at its grandeur, sad in the knowledge that to enjoy it he had to endure this madhouse. He turned to the tub, knelt down and started to scrub. Hanging the wet clothes on a wash stand next to the open fire, he hoped the shirt would be dry before Trimble came home. He didn't want to be half-naked when she returned.

His thoughts drifted idly to Sandra and the trust and friendship she had shown him recently. They hardly knew each other but she had proven herself to be a brick when all the world seemed to be against him, and he was grateful. It seemed stupid to consider since she was pretty with a dazzling smile and nice blonde hair, but the main emotion he felt when he thought of her was gratitude. Was he so miserable he couldn't even think about a girl in 'that way' anymore?

In a flash his mind changed gear and his thoughts fell on an image of Trimble, her hair down, blouse open, whispering in his ear. A guilty twinge flitted through his groin and he tried to cast the picture out his head by scrubbing his collar harder against the board.

His clothes now washed, except for the trousers which were simply too heavy to hand wash, he slipped off his pants and sat in the bath. Scrubbed and clean, he hung them on the side of the tub and lay back. He hadn't had the house to himself before, and the peace and lack of worry and stress, allied with the warmth of the bath water, soon had him falling to sleep's calming hold.

The key rattling in the back door woke him and he sat up straight, startled, as Trimble bustled into the kitchen carrying a bag of shopping with Astaroth prowling close behind. She stopped in her tracks when she saw Danny, then smiled cruelly.

"Someone's been waiting for us, Astaroth." She laughed and Danny involuntarily pulled his knees up to his chest. Putting the bag on the counter, she unhurriedly took off her jacket, hung it on the chair, then walked over and squatted down on her haunches to speak to him.

"So, now that you're cleaned and scrubbed, what am I going to do with you?" she asked, stroking a loose hair back from his fringe.

Danny held his tongue. A myriad of incompatible emotions clashed inside of him. He hated and feared Trimble, ashamed she was seeing him nude. And yet, somehow, bewilderingly he desired her, craved her approval, hoped for her assent. The possibility of her catching him in the bath had been at the back of his mind all day.

Half of his psyche prayed it wouldn't happen, the other half that it would. Now she had, his heart embraced guilty delight at the situation.

She let her hair down and flicked it back over her shoulder, took her glasses off and smiled. The effect was startling and Danny crushed an impulse to pull her to him and kiss her. Her perfume once again dimmed clear thought and his need for her to touch the heat between his legs took precedence over everything.

As if reading his mind she put her hand in the water and held him tight. "Oh, you like that, don't you?" she breathed into his ear, massaging him as she spoke.

"Yes," he gasped, his voice husky and thick.

Eyes closed in pleasure, he didn't see or hear Astaroth as the creature approached the pair of them. She let go of Danny and he opened his eyes.

"But I'm afraid Astaroth doesn't like me doing it to you, you wicked boy." She affected a disappointed pout and looked at him with cow eyes. "Sorry, Daniel, but we don't want to make him angry now, do we?"

Alarmed at the turn of events, he pushed himself back as the dog approached, a silent snarl on its lips.

"Now, now, Astaroth, it wasn't his fault. Let's not take our anger out on the young man just because he's more handsome than you."

She laughed as she spoke, provoking a quick snarl that made Danny jump in the water. "Come on, let's go. We'll leave him to clean himself up." The dog gave a last snarl, then turned and padded out after her.

Swallowing hard, Danny put his head back and closed his eyes. He knew what she was trying to do to him and yet he also knew if she beckoned, he'd come running.

The combination of her open sexuality and inaccessibility fired his urge to have her, a feeling he had never known, and it was driving him insane with yearning.

He had to be with her, away from prying eyes and snarling fangs.

# 22

She found the Reverend in the living room, downing whiskey from a large tumbler. Smiling knowingly she sauntered over and knelt before him. "How was your day, Gwynfor? Did the Bishop see you?"

"You knew? How did you know I was going to see him?"

"I figured you'd try and get away before tomorrow. I knew you had no money, I also knew you'd never go to the police, so I phoned up my friend Mister Meredith from the post office in the village and he mentioned you'd had a chat."

"I never knew he was one of yours, I really didn't. I thought the Bishop simply let us stay here to escape the scandal, and all the time he has been protecting us," Gwynfor shook his head.

"He isn't one of mine, he's one of yours Gwynfor. You started this, you made the first sacrifices and now you want out? It's madness, believe me. Tomorrow you'll thank me for holding you here, I promise you." She put a hand on his knee and reassuringly rubbed it up and down his thigh. "Tomorrow we'll be able to go back to how things were, Gwyn. Before Astaroth came, before all this, the only difference is we'll be rich beyond our wildest dreams. Then I'll be yours again, as we were." She turned her hand and raked her nails into his flesh, which brought a flicker of a reaction.

"It will never be as it was before, Fiona," he said tiredly.

"No, it'll be better, I promise you. The book has shown me the way. Astaroth is here because of the book. The whole situation here with Daniel, how he came to us, how he made his own prison here, it's all pre-ordained. This was meant to be, Gwyn. It's going to happen whether you want it to or not."

Gwyn nodded resignedly and took another sip of his whiskey. He was stuck there anyway, what was there for him to do? And what if she were right?

What if this was the real thing and Satan actually was going to reward them with untold riches?

"Right, fine, I have nowhere to go anyway, so how are we going to do this? I need you to run through everything so I know what's expected of me."

Eyes alight with approval, Fiona slapped him playfully on the knee and stood up. "Well, it isn't going to be nice, I can tell you that now, and it's going to be dangerous Gwynfor. You're going to have to be strong and we're going to have to follow the rules in the book properly. So brace yourself for a bit of unpleasantness."

Gwyn nodded uneasily but said nothing.

Trimble started to pace around, counting points off on her fingers as she spoke. "Firstly, the guests. I've only invited those who I know are serious about this, so we're only going to be thirteen, fourteen with Astaroth, which is perfect actually."

Gwynfor mentally calculated how much money they would lose in lost tribute from the people not invited, but held his council on the matter.

Trimble continued, "We'll do it at midnight. I know it sounds dramatic but it's in the book. We'll have to turn the cross upside down and we'll bleed him on the altar."

"Are we going to drug him?" Gwynfor asked, his earlier pessimism lost to the planning.

"No, that's the unpleasant part. We'll break his legs with a hammer or something, his arms too if he gets too much. Lay him on the altar and at the right time slice his throat."

Gwynfor blanched at the scene she just described, and Trimble decided to lay the whole thing on him so he would be prepared for what was to come.

"Gwynfor, now listen as this is very important. We break his legs, maybe his arms, and then tie him down. We'll strip him and lay him on the altar. First we nick a vein and fill a cup with his blood. It's very important we don't spill any at this moment. We close the wound, I'm only planning to make a small cut, so a plaster should do, and we present the cup or glass of blood to Astaroth. He will drink it and then give us the okay to make the sacrifice proper. Then we simply slit his throat and throw the blood over the altar, and that's that, riches and a place on a throne in the afterlife."

"Albeit a throne in hell," Gwyn muttered.

"Yes, quite. However, there is one last but very important issue here. Before Astaroth drinks the blood, we're not allowed to let one single drop hit the floor."

"Why?"

Trimble shrugged, "Well, in the book it states if the victim's blood is spilt before one of the devil's princes accepts it, it's no longer a gift or a proper sacrifice, because then any old murderer could make an offering and Satan wouldn't know if it was truly from the heart or not. It has to be confirmed, if you will, that it is an offering before we pour it over the altar."

Nodding thoughtfully, Gwyn asked, "What happens if we do spill it?"

Raising her eyebrows in a sort of facial shrug, Trimble's voice was ominous, "The spirits of all those people we killed in Satan's name, the ones roaming the plane between here and the afterlife, will come, claim the blood, and then claim the person they blame for their death."

"But that was me!" he cried.

Trimble nodded, "Yes, it was. They'll take the one who they think brought about their demise, and send him to hell as a sinner, to burn forever. So we'll have to be very careful if we don't want this to go horribly wrong."

An uncomfortable silence hung between them. Gwynfor was deeply aggrieved he would be held to blame, and also slightly irritated at the way she had so casually slipped in his eternal damnation if they made a mistake. Trimble was visibly displeased by his lack of enthusiasm.

Finally Gwynfor swallowed hard, asking, "Do we have to make a sacrifice? What's so special about tomorrow anyway?"

Trimble stopped pacing and let her hands drop. "Yes, we do have to make a sacrifice. We've been doing it now for how long and suddenly you want to stop? No, we're doing this and we're going to do this properly, once and for all."

"And why tomorrow?"

Trimble nodded, confident he had accepted the situation. "Okay, tomorrow is August the first, the feast of Lammas. Lammas was originally a Celtic celebration but the Christians took it over, as they did with nearly everything. It means 'Loaf Mass' and it celebrates the first bread made with the newly harvested grain. Understand me so far, Gwyn?"

"Yes, I see. Do go on," he said, shocked he'd never heard of it.

"The Celts also used to sacrifice animals and people. We'll be celebrating our own mass with the idea of it being a play on the Christian breaking of the bread and the body of Christ."

"We're going to sacrifice the lad because the

Christians break bread and call it the body of Christ?" Gwyn asked, perplexed.

"Basically, yes. That's all you need to know, to be honest. There's a lot more in the book but basically, slit the boy's throat and all our earthly and unearthly wishes will be granted."

Shaking his head in dismay, Gwyn stood up and went to walk out of the room.

"Where are you going, Gwynfor?" she asked sternly.

"To get rotten drunk. I need it," he said without looking back.

# 23

Sandra fingered the piece of paper gently, running her eyes over the words as if somehow she could derive a meaning from them. It was hopeless and she knew it. Welsh was so alien, so different to the English language, the only words she could make out were, 'Miss Trimble', which helped nobody, especially not Danny.

A picture of Danny grinning happily sprang to mind when she said she hadn't believed what she'd heard. She didn't really believe it either, though she was sure something had happened with Trimble, just not what everyone was saying.

The kitchen door opened and Sergeant Evans walked in the house. She'd already decided not to tell him the note was from Danny, because technically it wasn't; he'd found it and given it to her to pass on.

"Sandra!" he said when he saw her, a smile fixing itself on his face. "Do me a favour, put the kettle on would you please?"

She nodded, smiled back, and obediently filled

the kettle to put it on the stove. He sat down and started unlacing his boots while Sandra prepared the teapot. As she poured the water onto the leaves, she said, "Mister Evans, would you look at something for me, please? A friend found it and I don't know what it means. It's in Welsh."

Sitting back up, he exhaled heavily and nodded. "Of course. What is it?"

Wordlessly she handed over the piece of paper and the Sergeant studied it. She looked for a reaction on his face, a hint it was something against Danny's captors, as they'd become in her mind.

He raised his eyebrows briefly and put it down. "Who wrote that?"

"I don't know, it was found," she said, not really willing to go further into any more detail.

"Well, whoever wrote it seems to have a crush on Miss Trimble, the housekeeper up at the old vicarage," Evans said, smiling bemusedly. Then a dark cloud passed over his expression. "Who gave you this? Have you been up to the vicarage? Is that where you went to on my bike?" Cornered, Sandra tried desperately to think up an excuse but the Sergeant answered for her. "It was that Kelly lad, wasn't it? Is he back now? I've got some questions for him."

Head down, shoulders slumped, Sandra nodded. "Yes it was him, but he had nothing to do with Beth, Mister Evans."

"Told you that, did he?" he said sternly. "And you being so nice, you go and believe him!"

"I do, Mister Evans. He isn't like you think he is."

The Sergeant sighed and said in a softer voice, "I know you're soft on him, love, but I'm telling you he's a bad one."

Sandra noticed the kinder tone of voice. He never seemed to be able to be angry with her for long, so she looked asked, "So what does it say, Mister Evans?"

Picking the note up once more, he scanned the page briefly before answering. "Well, if I'm not mistaken, it's the lyrics for a Welsh love song called 'Myfanwy'. But he's changed the name Myfanwy to Miss Trimble. It fits in nicely as well." Off the cuff, he gave a low key rendition of the song, much to Sandra's amusement and observed, "I didn't know your friend spoke Welsh."

"He doesn't. He asked me to ask one of the boys at school to translate it. He says he found it."

"He found it? In the vicarage or on one of his ramblings? Never mind, I'll ask him myself tomorrow, that's if he hasn't run away," he huffed.

"He doesn't run away, though. They never let him go to school. He just works around the church grounds all the time, with the Reverend and Miss Trimble and that dog watching him."

Evans raised his eyes in mock surprise and smiled, "Scare you does he? Astar?"

"He attacked me today. Well, he ran at me and chased me down the road. If I hadn't had your bike he would have caught me as well. He's horrible. I hate him."

The simulated amazement fell off his face, "He attacked you? Astor, the Reverend's dog? That can't be. He's daft as a brush, that one."

Sandra nodded, "He did."

"Well, I've never heard of Astar doing that before. Are you sure he wasn't playing?"

"He ran at me while I was talking to Danny. I just got away in time."

Rubbing his eyes tiredly, the policeman picked up his brew and blew on it before sipping. Nodding at Sandra, he said, "You better not go up there anymore. They're funny things, dogs. They'll take to a person straight away, or they don't. And when they don't it can get scary, dangerous even. I'll go up tomorrow and have a word with your friend. I might just ask him where he found this as well." He tapped the note on the table with a massive sausage-like finger.

Danny pushed the window open and looked into the night, down at the multitude of faces peering up at him. To a man, their features were tortured, eyes bulbous and bloodshot, faces darkened by oxygen starvation, while bloated tongues drooled freely onto their clothes.

It was as ghastly a sight he'd ever seen in his life and yet he felt no fear or ill-will from those below him. He knew they were victims – though nobody told him, nobody whispered those words into his ear, he just knew.

It was summer, but the trees in the orchard seemed to be devoid of all greenery and the pale moon cast spidery shadows among the throng.

"Who are you?" he asked.

"We are the victims of folly, of vanity, of greed," a voice echoed through his head, its tone angry and bitter, yet Danny felt no malice towards him. "They'll kill you too. Get away while you can."

"I can't, the police will hunt me; they want me for murder." And though he felt that was true, somehow he wasn't sure. "Murder?" he tested the word out, mouthing it over and over. Was he really a murderer?

"No," the voice said, "you haven't murdered anyone. There is only one killer, one murderer, one thief who took our souls in the pursuit of wealth and power. You must get away!" The last was shouted and Danny blinked hard …

… and found himself standing in front of the closed window. It took a second or two but then he realised he'd been sleep walking. It was still dark in the room and he peered down into the garden to see if anyone was still there.

The trees held all their foliage and the garden was sombre under the weak light of the moon's thin crescent. There was no one in the garden but he was puzzled, wondering about the dream. Normally they disappeared into nothing five seconds after waking but this one stayed clear in his head. Had Trimble or Astaroth killed all those men? Was he next? Was the ghost in the closet just one of many?

Goosebumps prickled his arms and the back of his neck at the thought of him being held captive by a mass murderer. He needed to get away now more than ever, and he cursed his stupidity for being caught with the knife.

The thing was, he felt so alone. Dafydd hadn't come back with any news about the passage he'd scribbled down and Sandra had only just been given the second passage. He thought about Sandra again and a warm glow filled his insides. At least she was on his side; he felt good about that.

Again the temperature dropped behind him and he turned to stare straight into the face of the ghost in the closet, the figure's left side in shadow, his long fringe falling loosely over his right eye so Danny could only make out his cheekbone and the long curve of his malevolent smile.

Danny backed up and bumped his back against the window.

"What do you want?" he asked, his breath a blast of steam, his voice trembling.

"I don't want anything but for you to leave this house," it answered, the grin curling up higher. "But they," he said, indicating beyond the orchard, "They want you to stay. They want your soul to stay with them forever because they're jealous."

"Jealous? Of me?" he exclaimed. "You must be joking!"

The slant of the smile turned downwards, "No, Danny boy, I'm deadly fucking serious. They're the souls of the tramps and drop outs killed in botched ceremonies. They live in the place between heaven and hell, their souls neither sinful nor cleansed of sin."

Danny's mind spun in horror as the ghost explained further.

"They thought they were being clever, thought they could trick the naive with sex and excitement, but nobody tricks the devil. They couldn't trick me!" The last he shouted into Danny's face, causing him to collapse to the floor, hiding his face as the spectre carried on his monologue. "So get used to the idea Danny boy, get used to the fact your soul is to be cast to hell as a gift to Satan, who'll give you to his minions to do with as they please."

Danny could hear the spirit bending down towards him until finally it was speaking into his ear.

"And your bitch of a mother can sit by as we flay you alive with hot knives and force you to eat your own bowels, you miserable…fucking…worm …"

At the mention of his mother a spark of anger flickered into life. A small voice spoke for the first time in the back of Danny's mind. Who was this ghost? What did he want? Was he the devil?

Danny didn't think so and yet the figure spoke as if he were. Peering up when the ghost stopped talking it was frightening to see it looking down at him, a self-satisfied expression on its face that shocked Danny's anger into life.

He stood up, his back to the wall, eyes on the

figure in front of him. The ghost remained, gloating and at rest. Danny searched for the right words of defiance but nothing came.

The ghost spoke again, his voice deeper than usual, louder, his resentment clear as day. "Why are you still here? Don't you understand they want to kill you? Miss Trimble wants to kill you! Get out now, while you can!"

Two words in the onslaught wedged themselves into Danny's head – 'Miss Trimble'. The writing on the note he'd found, the only words he'd understood, were 'Miss Trimble'. Had the ghost written the words?

The idea broke out before he could stop it. "Did you write the note behind the brick?" he nearly shouted. As if guillotined, the monologue stopped. Danny couldn't make its face out but he knew it wasn't smiling anymore, nor was it raging. He asked again, slowly, calmly, "Did you write the note behind the brick?"

The door to the closet crashed open and suddenly the back wall started to fall away. Heat like a blast furnace roared out and Danny turned to protect himself from it. He glanced back where the closet wall had been and saw thousands of bodies, fighting and screaming in a forge. The noise of the fire was drowned out only by the shrieking of the tormented as their hair burned away, flesh melted off bones, and eyeballs popped in the fierce heat.

"Your mother's in there Danny boy, and that's where you're going if you don't leave here tonight!

Do you hear me? Tonight!"

Grasping at anything to keep himself sane, Danny screamed the question over and over again at the ghost. "Did you write the note behind the brick? Did you? The note, did you write it? Tell me!"

"Get out of here. You don't belong here. This is my house. She is mine!"

Understanding finally clicked in Danny's head. The spectre didn't want him or his mother, he wanted Trimble! He wants me to leave because he wants Trimble.

"I can't leave here, I'm a prisoner!" he shouted back, his voice lost to the noise of the flames and the suffering. "Can you hear me? They won't let me leave!" The figure before him stared back and said nothing, so he shouted louder, "Trimble and the Reverend won't let me …"

Suddenly the closet door closed, leaving the room silent. The ghost had disappeared, everything was as it had been. He glanced again at the closet and whispered, "I can't leave, I'm a prisoner."

"I am too," a tragic voice answered in his head.

# 24

The Reverend was reading the newspaper, so Danny knocked on the living room door to gain his attention. The older man dropped the newspaper to his lap and Danny was momentarily stunned by the haunted expression on his face.

"What do you want, Daniel?" he asked, his voice hoarse with a fatigue that ringed his eyes and plagued his left hand with a tremble.

"I need to ask you a question about the ghost in my closet, if that's alright," Danny probed.

"No, it's not alright. Leave me alone with your stupidity and go and do your chores," Gwynfor blustered, putting the newspaper back up in front of his face.

Danny stayed where he was, the reaction another silent confirmation of his suspicions. He decided on another tack. "Are you a prisoner here as well, Reverend?" he asked.

The newspaper once more fell to his lap, but this time its descent was slower, more controlled. As if accused of some heinous crime Gwynfor stared at Danny in wide-eyed surprise. He swallowed hard and blinked rapidly. "What do you mean?"

Danny looked over his shoulder before saying, "I mean, are you a prisoner here as well? Do Trimble and Astaroth have control over you? Perhaps we could work together to get away."

Gwyn's head swam in amazement; how did the lad know? Had he had contact with the ghost? Was it Achlad or was it one of the ghosts from the garden? He'd been up all night thinking about them, wondering if they had some sort of vengeance in mind.

He coughed before asking, "Explain to me exactly what you mean, Daniel. Who's been putting ideas into your head now?"

Unsure as to whether it had been a good idea to talk to the Reverend about this, Danny decided to let it drop. "Oh, never mind, I had a bad dream and ..."

"And what ...?" the Reverend pressed. "You thought to ask if I was a prisoner here because of a dream? Have you been talking to your ghost again?" he asked, injecting a note of disdain in his voice and yet fearing the answer.

Danny shrugged; the man thought he was an idiot anyway so why not tell him the truth? "Something like that, though it wasn't a dream. I spoke to him normally. He only appears when I'm awake. The men in the garden were in my dream."

As if electrified the Reverend shot up from his chair. "What ... what men in the garden? What did they say to you? Tell me lad!"

Surprised by the reaction, Danny took a step back. "The ghosts, the ghosts of the men Miss Trimble and Astaroth have killed. They're there, in the orchard, angry at what she did."

The Reverend advanced on him and grabbed his arms in a surprisingly strong grip. "That's what they told you? They're after Fiona ... I mean Miss Trimble?" he asked anxiously, sweat now breaking out on his forehead.

Danny wrenched his arms free and pushed him back. "Don't touch me. Don't threaten me. I'm not scared of you."

Coming to his senses, Gwynfor turned around and walked back to his chair. "Yes, I'm sorry. All this talk about ghosts in an old house like this ..." The words trailed off, leaving Danny more puzzled than before. As if coming to some sort of inner agreement with himself, Gwyn nodded at Danny and said, "I'm sorry, Daniel. I have a lot on my mind and I haven't been sleeping very well. Whatever you imagined or dreamt didn't happen, it can't possibly happen because ghosts do not exist."

"They do, Reverend, and you know it too," Danny replied, staring resolutely at him. "The ghost in the closet is jealous. He wants me to leave because he wants Miss Trimble."

"You're delusional, lad!" Gwynfor exploded.

"I'm not, Reverend, and you know it."

"You're not what, exactly, Daniel?" Trimble's voice sounded from the kitchen and Danny wondered if she'd been listening in the whole time.

Astaroth glided past, growling softly as he went by, and the dynamic of the scene suddenly shifted.

"Well, lad, explain yourself. I'd like to know as well," Trimble said, walking towards him from the kitchen.

Danny mentally braced himself and plunged in. "Last night I had a dream."

"A dream? Oh, how quaint," Trimble laughed, but Danny pushed on regardless.

"I dreamt I was looking out of the window and onto the orchard, and it was filled with dead men, ghosts, all with bulging eyes and black tongues and faces, like they'd been hanged, and they said you killed them in botched rituals. Then I woke up ..."

"Enough!" Trimble broke in. "I will not hear such nonsense in my house!"

"It's not your house, it belongs to the church and the Reverend, and you're just the housekeeper here," Danny snapped back, angry at her disdain. Trimble looked set to explode and Astaroth gave a warning growl from his place next to Gwynfor.

"Are you going to let this lad talk to me like this?" she nigh on shrieked, and Danny turned back to see the Reverend advancing towards them, his hands held out in a placating gesture.

"Now, now, settle down here. We don't need to shout at each other," he said, approaching them. "Daniel, now listen to me. This ghost, who does he say he is? Has he mentioned a name to you?"

Danny, outflanked by the mollifying tone the

Reverend was using, stuttered his answer, "No, no, he hasn't. Who is he? Is he the lad who ran from the dairy farmer?"

"That boy was very disturbed, Daniel. The Reverend will tell you," Trimble said, prodding Gwynfor into action.

"Yes, Miss Trimble's right. He came here to Old Colwyn, a troubled young man with a history of violence and arson. He set the fire that made him into an orphan. He also set an orphanage ablaze that took him in. He was never happy at the dairy farm and kept on coming here, which we didn't encourage but we also didn't chase him away." Gwynfor looked to his housekeeper, who nodded for him to continue. "Anyway, one day he suddenly stopped turning up at the door. He came every day and then nothing. We asked around and Sergeant Evans set up a search team to look for him but nothing was found. All very odd. Now how did you come to decide it was him in your closet, when we still don't know if he's even alive? As far as I know, he still hasn't turned up yet. Have you just heard his name somewhere and dreamt the rest up?"

Affronted, Danny shook his head vehemently, "I haven't made anything up, honestly!" He was about to let on the spirit had said he was a prisoner but decided not to. Though he knew they would never let him out of their sight, he didn't want to bring the issue up in case it forced them into something drastic. Despite the drama of the situation, an uncomfortable silence settled among the three of them. Trimble looked to Gwyn, who felt he needed to say something positive about the lad they'd been discussing, as up to now he and Trimble had only spoken about him in negative terms.

The Reverend smiled, as if recalling an incident he was fond of, and said, "I remember one day he arrived here with a song he'd found. He just turned up and started singing it at the door. Terrible timing and completely off key, of course, but it was the thought that counted."

Confused by the sudden change in direction, Danny asked, "A song? He sang you a song? I don't understand."

"Well, apparently he loved the melody so much he went to the local library and asked the librarian about it. He actually hummed the melody for her. The librarian, Mrs Rodgers, a lovely lady from Rhyl, recognised the tune straight away and found him the lyrics, which he copied and came here to sing for us. It was a lovely gesture, a sort of thanks for all we'd done for him. He was especially fond of Miss Trimble."

Alarm bells rang at the back of Danny's mind. "Miss Trimble?" he asked, innocently.

"Yes, we had a special connection, you could say Daniel," she answered, smiling one of her shark smiles that deadened her eyes and bared her teeth. "Right, Daniel, now if you don't mind, I'd like you to start your chores. There's such a lot to do today as we have guests coming later on, and I'd like the Reverend's house spick and span before they come."

Pre-occupied by what he had just learnt and what the spirit had said to him about Astaroth and Trimble wanting to kill him, Danny nodded obediently and started for the kitchen, missing the knowing looks passed between Trimble and Gwynfor.

Gwynfor sighed inwardly. The lad was too trusting. It was almost painful to see him cleaning the kitchen in preparation for the people who wanted to kill him later on tonight. He didn't know if he marvelled at his housekeeper's calm exterior or whether he was disgusted by it. She was planning a brutal murder, one that involved inflicting the maximum pain on a human being, and yet she played the obedient housekeeper part as if born to it.

Astaroth sauntered out of the living room. Gwyn had forgotten he was there he'd been so quiet. For a dog the size of a small cow, he had an uncanny knack of disappearing into the woodwork when he wanted to.

Gwyn thought back to Danny's initial question on whether he was trapped or not. He was, there was no getting away from it, and as unbelievable as it sounded, he would have to take part in the ceremony tonight to save his mortal soul. Something he never really believed in until the last couple of days, and was the reality of his situation right now.

Trimble nudged him, and standing at his shoulder whispered, "Look at him, he doesn't suspect a thing. He's cleaning the house out so it'll be nice for when the people arrive who want to break his bones and gut him." Gwynfor winced at the remark but Trimble patted his behind and said, "Don't go soft on me, Gwynfor. You did that one time too many and that's why we no longer share a room."

Bristling at the jibe, he hissed back, "No man could get it up with that damned dog in the bedroom, watching all the time."

"He can," she nodded at Danny and laughed. "It's just I won't let him do anything with it."

"And Astaroth, can he …?" he asked, his anger riled and looking for a way to wound her.

She turned her head towards him and stared steadily into his eyes, saying, "Yes, he can. And he does."

Gwynfor gawked in astonishment as she walked away from him and up the stairs. A clatter from the kitchen, a curse and a loud feline hiss turned his attention.

"Get out, you dirty little …!" Danny shouted.

"What's wrong now?" Gwynfor asked, walking to the kitchen.

"Reverend," Danny huffed, standing in a pile of pans. "That cat has got to be kept outside. It's always doing its business in the house and it's disgusting. And I always have to clean it up! And now I've just slipped in its shit again and dropped all the pans I just washed."

"Okay, let me help you here," the Reverend said, scooping up some of the pans. "You're right. I don't like the cat being in the house either but cats do what they want, you can't control them," he laughed.

Danny was still a bit perturbed by this new side to the Reverend. The melancholy moribund figure didn't quite tally with the boisterous over-bearing vicar who had picked the evacuees up from the station and taken them to the church all those weeks ago. He wondered what had happened. He also wondered what the song was the lad who had run away from the dairy farm had sung, as it might help in discovering if it was the spirit in the closet. If he had a name, perhaps he could use it when it visited next to scare the bejeezus out of him.

"Reverend, you said earlier the lad who ran away from the dairy farm, the one who liked Miss Trimble, you said he sang you a song. What was it?"

"You wouldn't know it, Daniel. It's a Welsh song, a love song. Why?"

"Oh, just wondering," he shrugged.

"Well, if you must know, it's called Myfanwy."

The name didn't ring any bells and Danny felt a bitter disappointment at not knowing it. Another possible clue lost to his ignorance.

"Yes," the Reverend continued. "He sang it beautifully. He was a fine soprano despite his elder years. Disturbed and violent, but they say music has charms to soothe the savage breast and it certainly had a soothing influence on Achlad."

A name, and a name Danny was sure he'd seen or heard before; but where? As he cleaned, he searched his memory but nothing came to him.

However, he did now know Trimble's name was

Fiona, so the F.T. on the handkerchief was definitely her initials, and that was almost an indictment to Danny's grasping mind.

# 25

She was scared but simply had to see him again to make sure he was alright. Sandra deliberated on how she'd break the news to him about the passage he'd given her only being a silly love song with the name changed, but she decided to cross that bridge when he asked her about it. Until he did, she wouldn't mention it. Sergeant Evans mentioned he'd go up in the afternoon to speak to Danny about Beth's disappearance, so she'd decided to skip school and walk up on her own.

It would mean trouble if they asked at home about her, but she knew she could play on her reputation at school and the fact nobody would ever have thought she would dare stay away from school without Sergeant Evans' permission.

Before long the wall of the church grounds came into view and she paused briefly to see if he was in the garden, and to make sure the dog wasn't there. His head bobbed past and she smiled and made her way towards him.

Danny was sure he was being watched. He couldn't see anything but he wasn't alone in the orchard and it was tangible. Like a blind man in a crowd he could feel their presence but couldn't see them. He thought back to what he'd dreamt the night before and shivered. They meant him no harm the voice said, but they were waiting for his death which made no sense to him at all.

A whistle brought him back to the present. Looking up he saw Sandra waving, so he walked over to her, grinning at her cheery wave.

"Hiya, no school today?" he asked.

"Of course there is. I just decided not to go," she explained, a cheeky smile dancing on her lips. He laughed and leaned against the wall, relaxed and enjoying her good mood.

"So what are you doing?" she asked.

"You'd never believe it, cleaning up the dog dirt from the grass. I have to mow the lawn and it's easier to get rid of it now than clean it off the blades later." He pulled a face and Sandra laughed.

"Sounds awful. Do you do all the work here?"

Danny's laugh died in his throat. "You're right, I do! I've never thought about it, I haven't seen either of them do a spot of work since I've been here. Miss Trimble makes the meals but I do the cleaning up after. In fact I do all the cleaning." He laughed at the absurdity of the situation. Never once had he thought to question her, what exactly did she do with her time besides cook and go shopping now and then? "Ah well, what else would I do with my time if I wasn't allowed to clean up the dog dirt from the garden?" She smiled back at him sadly, and then his face turned serious. "Did you find out about the passage with Miss Trimble's name on it?"

Her shoulders slumped and she dropped her gaze to the ground. "Yes, it's just a Welsh love song someone changed the lyrics to. It doesn't mean anything. I'm sorry, I wish I had more for you, I really do."

Danny nodded, "No problem, I have the other passages here if you don't mind taking them. Did they laugh at you when they translated it?"

"Who?"

"Huw, Bryn the others?" he said.

"They didn't do it, Sergeant Evans read it. If you give me the paper with the other writing on, I'll ask them to have a look, then I won't have to bother Mister Evans unless it really is important," she suggested as Danny dug them out of his pocket and handed them over.

He contemplated telling her about the ghost, whom he was now certain was the one who had changed the song name. On a whim he asked, "Has anyone mentioned the name Achlad to you, or have you seen it anywhere?"

Sandra pondered the question before answering. "No, it doesn't ring a bell. Why?"

"It's the name of the boy who disappeared last year. I was just wondering if it was on the other note I gave you …" His words trailed off as he realised how lame it sounded.

"I don't know. I'll have a look when I'm home. It might be on there."

Danny nodded as another question popped up. "Did he say what the song was called, the original version that is? The one I gave you with Trimble's name on it?"

Sandra nodded, "Yes, but I can't remember it, it was Welsh, a girl's name, I think."

"Myfanwy?" he suggested.

"I don't know, it might have been, he only said it once or twice." She didn't want to tell him he'd actually sung the song for her and she still couldn't remember the name of it, so she left it alone. "Why?"

He shrugged, "It doesn't matter." He then turned around hastily as Trimble called his name from the kitchen door.

"I have to go. Thanks for coming up to visit. It made my day," he said, smiling his wide open grin Sandra found so attractive.

"No, it's okay. I have to go now as well. Sergeant Evans is coming up later to ask about Beth," she said, a little worried he might be scared that he wasn't so innocent after all.

"Good," Danny said and nodded vehemently, to her delight. "I'm looking forward to talking to him with Trimble and the Reverend present. I want to put my case across and I'm starting to get a grip on what those two in there are about, so I won't be so naive. I just hope your Sergeant doesn't go all doe-eyed when he talks to Trimble."

"What do you mean?"

"Well, oh never mind, it doesn't matter."

Sandra was mildly shocked at the accusation but decided to ignore it. She was just happy he had no qualms about speaking to Sergeant Evans. If he had been scared she reckoned her whole world would have fallen to pieces.

"Right, I really have to go now. Thanks for coming around to check on me picking up dog dirt," he laughed.

"It's okay," she answered, then tiptoed and kissed him on the cheek. "For luck," she whispered and turned to walk away.

He raised a hand to his burning cheek and his grin nearly split his head in two. "Thanks. Bye. Don't forget the note," he called after her.

"I won't. Go inside or you'll be in trouble," Sandra laughed and picked up her step down the road. She was right, but he didn't care, and he watched her as she fell out of view as the road turned downhill.

Sandra's good mood subsided at what she saw huffing up the hill on his pushbike. Sergeant Evans hadn't seen her as yet, but as there was nowhere for her to hide it was only a matter of time. She could hear him breathing heavily under the strain of pedalling from her position a hundred yards away, and she wondered why he simply didn't get off and push.

He still hadn't noticed her when he was twenty yards away so, unable to stand the suspense of waiting for him to recognise her, she called out. "Hello, Mister Evans, why don't you just push?"

He looked up, surprised at hearing her voice, but his shock soon turned to a scowl when he registered she was there. "Never mind push it, Miss Smith, why aren't you in school?"

She decided on the spur of the moment to tell the truth and to use his rank, as that had always disarmed him up to now. "I had to come and see if he was alright, Sergeant Evans. I couldn't concentrate otherwise."

There was a brief lull in their conversation until he reached her. "Right, I don't want to hear any excuses. We can talk about this later. Now off to school with you, and if the headmaster wants to give you detention for not being there, I'm all for it, tell him.'"

The words sounded angry but Sandra, with a feminine intuition men will never grasp, knew he wasn't. Putting on a contrite expression, she nodded and said, "Yes, Sergeant," and walked down the hill.

"And tell him to give you it tomorrow. Mrs Evans is making toad-in-the-hole today and that never tastes nice reheated," he called after her. He knew all about reheated food. Police business demanded he know all about warmed-up leftovers. After watching her walk a while, he smiled to himself and shook his head. "Kids!" he laughed, and stepped onto the pedal to carry on with his ride.

He'd thought long and hard about what exactly he was going to ask the young man but had ultimately decided simply to react to his answers.

In his experience, if lads were guilty they normally let their conscience speak for them. So he'd ask what he knew about Beth and her disappearance, and take it from there. He reached the wrought iron gate of the church grounds and stepped off the bike. Sweating in his thick uniform he stood the bike against the wall and unbuttoned his tunic to let some air in to cool himself down.

Removing his helmet, he combed his wet hair over and let his thoughts drift over to Miss Trimble and her intoxicating offer. The fact was, he'd thought of nothing else since the night before when, after hours of contemplating how he should approach the issue, he'd clumsily broached the subject of intimacy with Mrs Evans.

With the lights out and the pair of them in bed, he'd snuggled up to her back and pressed himself against her. Reaching his arm around her, he'd cupped her left breast and tried to kiss her ear.

"John, it's late, I'm tired and we're far too old to be doing that. Now go to sleep like a good boy, you've got a long day tomorrow," she said, rather unkindly he thought, before removing his hand.

And that was that.

After years of dutifully bringing the bread home, of working all hours the Force sent, of playing by the unwritten rules his wife had set down through their long years together, he now realised where he stood with her, and it hurt. He was a man, over his prime but a man nevertheless, and he had needs, needs he'd ignored over the years as Mrs Evans had made it plain sex no longer played a role in her life, and he could like it or lump it.

Buttoning up his tunic, he put his helmet back on and turned to enter the church grounds. He saw Danny in the orchard and walked over to him. He watched him a while as he searched the ground, stopping now and then to pick up whatever he was looking for with old newspaper. Evans realised it was dog dirt and pulled a face of disgust at the thought of handling something like that.

He coughed and Danny looked up. "Good morning, Sergeant," he said easily. "Sandra said you'd be coming around today."

"Oh, she did now, did she?" he said, feeling mildly betrayed at the revelation, though he really should have known she'd say something.

"Yes, I think it'd be better if we went inside and talked to the Reverend and Miss Trimble together. You'll probably want to talk to them as well."

Evans nodded. "Come on, then, let's go inside," he said, feeling vaguely disappointed he wouldn't be interviewing Miss Trimble alone.


Trimble and Gwynfor were both in the living room when Danny walked in with the policeman in tow. "Sergeant Evans is here. He wants to talk about Beth Thomas," he announced.

Gwynfor, the high back of his chair to the door, flinched visibly before calming himself.

Trimble, with the grace of a cat, coolly stood up and offered the Sergeant her chair. "Do sit down, Sergeant. I'll go and make us all some tea," she smiled, then turning to Danny she said brusquely, "Come with me and help with the tray."

In the kitchen Danny filled the large kettle while Trimble watched him. "I don't know what you're thinking right now, Daniel," she said, breaking the silence, "but if you're intent on trying to make trouble with Sergeant Evans, you'll be sorely disappointed. He's on our side and anything you say he'll simply not believe, do you understand me?"

Placing the kettle on the stove, he turned to face her. "What do you mean, Miss Trimble? Why would I say anything to Sergeant Evans about Beth? Or have you been telling lies about me behind my back?"

"You think you're so clever, don't you?" she sneered. "You think just because there's a policeman in the house you're safe. If I picked up this knife," she said, pulling a carving knife out of its holder, "and I stabbed you with it, who'd not believe me if I said you attacked me, and after weeks of sexual abuse I finally defended myself? You're known as a sexual pervert Daniel Kelly, so don't get any ideas above your station."

Danny mulled over her words. She was right: nobody would believe him if he, as he had planned, accused Trimble and Astaroth of killing Beth, a fact of which he was one hundred per cent sure, regardless of the fact he had no proof.

He stared at her and dropped his head in defeat. She had him where she wanted him, and once again it seemed everything was in her favour.

She moved towards him and whispered in his ear, "Now this is what you're going to do. You're going to go outside and sit in the old church until I tell you to come back. Do this and you'll be fine, Daniel. I'll come to you tonight while Astaroth is asleep, and I'll make good on the promises I've made to you, do you understand?"

Confused, he looked back up at her. Trimble's perfume played its heady magic with his loins and the promise of carnal pleasure struck like a hammer against his will.

"Yes, that's right, Daniel, I'll let you fuck me. From behind, on top, any way you want, you can do it to me," she breathed, and once again his power of clear thought fell victim to the drive that curses and defines all men. "However, if you stay here and try to cause trouble for the Reverend and myself ..."

A low growl, the same noise that had turned this house into a place of fear sounded from behind her, and Astaroth stepped into view.

Danny knew he had no choice but to comply. Wordlessly, with the promise of what he'd yearned for since that first day in the tub dancing at the back of his psyche, he left the kitchen and walked to the ruined church next door.

Trimble breezed into the living room, carrying the tray, and immediately picked up on the tense atmosphere in the room.

Evans looked up when she entered but there was no smile on his face, and he spoke gravely, "The Reverend has just told me Elizabeth was here after the day she visited with Sandra. You told me you hadn't seen her since."

"I didn't see her," she blurted. "You must be mistaken, Reverend. Perhaps you saw her here, but I certainly didn't."

Evans looked to Gwynfor, who tried to stay calm but was squirming visibly and wore the shell-shocked face of a caught liar.

"Yes, hum…perhaps you're right Miss Trimble," he agreed unconvincingly.

Evans sighed. "Look, did you or did you not see her?"

"I think so. I'm not sure now, to be honest Sergeant. Sorry, and I know it sounds silly, but I really didn't attach much importance on seeing her. These kids come here all the time to steal from the orchard and the likes. I don't mind it and that's why I don't take much notice."

He shrugged when he'd finished and Evans, irritated by the flippant answer, frowned angrily.

"I don't think you're taking this as seriously as you should be, Reverend," he said testily. "Just to clarify things here, a young girl has gone missing, I'm trying to ascertain who saw her last and you can't remember. With all respect to your station, Reverend, that's just not good enough."

"Yes, yes, I know. Okay, now I've thought about it, I think the last time I saw her was when she came with Sandra. Yes, that's it, that was the last time I saw Elizabeth," he stuttered, blinking nervously.

"Reverend," Evans exhaled, "Miss Trimble told me you were away on the day Sandra and Elizabeth visited, at the Bishop's place if I remember correctly. So, unless you've made a mistake about that day as well, you couldn't have seen her then either."

"No, Sergeant, I think I may have made the mistake," Trimble smoothly glided into the exchange. "I'm sorry, the Reverend did meet with the Bishop but I think I mixed the dates up."

"There you have it, Sergeant," Gwynfor exclaimed, elated at his housekeeper's interjection. "Miss Trimble got the dates wrong. I did see the girls when they came here and that was the last time I saw Elizabeth." A picture flashed in his mind of earth falling on her ripped body, on her face, covering her open eyes and falling into her mouth, and it was everything he could do not to physically shudder at the recollection.

Sergeant Evans looked at the pair of them and couldn't believe the hunch that was building momentum at the back of his mind. No, not these two, they couldn't have, surely? "Okay then, so we have that settled. Where's Daniel Kelly? I need to speak to him as well."

Gwynfor nearly collapsed in relief but gripped himself and looked to Trimble. "Is he still in the kitchen Miss Trimble?" he asked sombrely.

Trimble put on a confused expression. "No, he

went outside, said he was going for a walk." She looked pointedly at the policeman. "He said you two were finished, that you'd interviewed him already on the matter."

"He said what?" Jumping up from the chair, Evans ran out through the kitchen and into the back of the house. "Well, I'll be damned," he muttered, scratching his head as he scanned the orchard.

"Pardon me, Sergeant?" Gwynfor asked. "I didn't quite catch that."

"He does know something about poor Elizabeth, I'll lay my month's wages on it. Why would he skip off like that?"

Trimble dug Gwynfor in the ribs and smiled slyly at him when he looked back at her, indicating with her head he should leave them.

"I think you're right Sergeant," she said, taking a step forward to stand next to him as the Reverend retreated inside. "Why would he run away like that if he didn't know something. The boy isn't just stupid, he's evil."

Still scanning the grounds of the church, Evans nodded and looked down in astonishment as he felt her hand intertwine with his. He looked back to check if the Reverend was there, and when he saw he wasn't he squeezed lightly on her slim hand with his massive paw. "I thought about what you said, Fiona," he said matter-of-factly.

"And?" she asked in a low tone, trying desperately not to grin, the delight at how easily she had ensnared him bubbling in her chest. Men were so weak.

He swallowed hard. He was crossing a line that had at one time in his life been unthinkable, and yet he felt it was right. "I'll gladly meet with you one day, but we'd have to be discreet," he whispered.

"Oh, John," she gushed, the hilarity of the situation forcing her to put a hand to her mouth in mock delight. "When, when can we meet? At yours or here?"

The thought of betraying his wife in their own bed seemed abominable to him and he blurted, "Here. The village is too crowded. When are you alone?"

"Tomorrow. Come tomorrow afternoon. He won't be here then and we can …" He nodded his understanding and turned to go back inside. "You won't be sorry, John, I promise you," she intimated in a husky voice.

Looking ahead, he nodded, businesslike and serious. "I know, Fiona, I know. But we must be discreet. I don't want anyone being hurt, as I'm sure you don't either." He turned his face to look at her and gently stroked her cheek. "Where were you before I met my wife, Fiona?"

"I was here, I've always been here. Here for you. But now we can make up for it and you won't be sorry, John"" She gagged inwardly at the laughably kitsch dialogue and the ham acting; it was all too rich.

He stroked her cheek a last time and nodded, as if terminating the conversation.

She watched him walk back inside and Astaroth came to stand next to her, growling quietly as if passing comment on what he'd just witnessed. "He won't be sorry," she muttered to him.

"He'll be dead," Astaroth finished for her, a dark voice in her head.

Sandra went straight to the headmaster's office and apologised for not being there that morning.

"Well, where were you?" he asked, an irritated frown marring his forehead and spoiling her hopes he'd take her absence lightly. She was one of his best students after all.

"I wasn't feeling too well this morning, but now I feel a lot better, and so I thought I'd come back to school." She'd decided a white lie was for the best at that moment. If Sergeant Evans decided to check, well she'd cross that bridge when she came to it.

The look of irritated doubt dropped into a smile and he ushered her good-naturedly out of his office and into the corridor.

"Mister Gerrard, does the name Achlad mean anything to you?"

Rubbing his chin, the headmaster looked thoughtful before answering. "Achlad, wasn't he the first bat for the Colwyn Bay Cricket Club a few years ago?"

She shook her head, "No, wasn't he the boy who disappeared last year?"

"Oh, yes, very tragic. Why do you ask?"

"Well, I was just wondering about him and what happened." Then to explain the question, "I heard his name being talked about and it set me thinking about him. Did he die?"

Mr Gerrard's hand moved to his mouth as he contemplated how much he should tell her. "Well to be honest Sandra, I don't really know. He was a bit of a funny lad who was always absconding from the dairy farm where he was put up, or so I'm told. Then one day he simply vanished. There was a manhunt for him of course, but nothing came of it. He had a lovely voice, though. He sang 'Myfanwy' once at the Thanksgiving Festival in the new church. It was quite beautiful. I'd never heard the song sung by a soprano before and yet there it was, glass clear, simply beautiful." He looked back down at her and smiled. "But I have to admit, he was a strange lad. Now off you go and don't think any more about him," he said, gently guiding her out and into the corridor.

It was dinner break so she looked for Huw and his gang. They were kicking an empty can around, and they ignored her and carried on playing when she found them. She stood and watched for a while, considering the best way to approach this.

They were nice boys, and she knew Huw was soft on her, but like all boys they were quick to pour scorn on anything a girl had to say, especially Geraint with his dirty comments and wandering eyes.

Dafydd noticed her first. He stopped playing and walked over to her. "Have you heard anything about Beth? Is she at home ill or has she run away?" The other lads stopped playing and joined him.

"I haven't heard a thing. She went up to the old house, the vicarage, and that's the last anyone saw of her as far as I know." Her lip trembled at the thought of Beth and where she might be right now.

"What are the police doing? I bet that old vicar's got her," Bryn said vehemently.

"Sergeant Evans went up there but he said she isn't there." She decided to omit the part about him implying Danny had something to do with it as she felt the policeman had simply been misled.

"Right!" Huw said decisively. "I say we go up to the old poofter's house tonight and see what's what. We'll have a sneak around. Perhaps we'll find something."

Sandra was thrilled and fearful in one go. She was delighted they wanted to help find Beth but scared in case Astar found them first. The more she thought about him running after her, the more she realised how much danger she'd been in. "What about the dog, Astar? He attacked me the other day, well, chased me."

As one the four boys smirked in unconcealed amusement. Of course it was Geraint who scoffed out loud, "Scared in case he tried to shag you, was it?"

"No, really, he was barking and he ran after me

to bite me!" Her protestations only made the boys laugh harder as Geraint started to hump Bryn's leg and howl loudly. Embarrassed by their scorn, Sandra blushed in anger.

Huw, seeing Sandra's hurt, said above the laughing boys, "Don't worry, Astar's harmless. We all know him. We'll go up tonight and have a look. I'll tell you what happens tomorrow."

"But I'm coming with you!" she exclaimed.

"No way!" Geraint and Huw said together.

Huw carried on, "We'll go up tonight, and we don't need any girls hindering us."

"And being scared of humping dogs," Geraint laughed cruelly.

"I'll tell you what happened tomorrow, okay?" Huw finished.

Sandra knew there'd be no arguing so she nodded curtly, turned and walked away.

# 26

He was just dozing off when the door opened and Trimble slipped into his room. He'd gone to bed early, as he always did since his arrival.

The early mornings and long days took their toll on his young frame and by seven every evening he was ready for the realm of Somnus, even though it was still light.

"Astaroth is sleeping Daniel, so I thought I'd come to see you," she said standing before him, the light of the window creating an aura around her, shining through the sheer nightdress and concealing nothing.

She slowly undid the top buttons. Danny, eyes wide in nervousness, mind swimming both with desire and self-loathing, watched silently as she dropped the garment and stood before him, nude.

Long dark hair fell over slim shoulders, and as she coyly looked down and to her side, he let his gaze move further down. He stared in fascination at the small but still pert breasts that sat above her barely visible ribs, her dark nipples stiff, excited. Down past a taut flat stomach that sat between the twin sentinels of her protruding hip bones, to the dark triangle between her legs.

With the natural grace bestowed on every slender woman, she glided forward and pulled the sheets back. "You're still dressed, Daniel," she purred, looking at his pyjamas trousers and the swelling under the material.

He whipped off his top and lay back as she wordlessly tugged at the bottoms. Now naked, he lay still as she gazed at his body.

"I know you won't believe me," she breathed, her voice soft, yet loud in the silence, "but I couldn't come to you earlier. Astaroth is so jealous, so possessive ..."

She let the sentence go and lay next him.

"Daniel, I know I've been bad to you but I know you still want me, to be with me, but you don't want to make that move, you don't want to show you forgive me," she murmured sensitively, stroking his face lightly and letting her hand dance slowly down his chest and stomach. "So I'll do everything. You don't have to forgive me, just as long as you say you believe me. I want you to tell me you believe me. That you believe me when I say I want you, and it was Astaroth who kept me away from you."

As she grasped him between his legs, he did believe her. He hated himself for it. He knew she was playing with him but he didn't care. He wanted her, needed her, and at that moment all that counted was burying himself in her soft velvet folds and shallow lies.

"Yes, yes, I believe you," he gasped, and she immediately covered his mouth with hers, her tongue darting into his mouth as she efficiently straddled him. She was wet and ready, and his engorged shaft slid effortlessly into her, eliciting a gasp from both of them.

There was no slow build-up, no tender start. He reacted to her furious kissing and thrust his hips as fast as he could. She pulled his head to her breasts and he slurped noisily on a nipple.

Trimble sighed, squeaked and moaned in reckless abandon, and a small voice at the back of Danny's mind wondered about waking the Reverend, or Astaroth.

He pushed back from her to breathe and, horrified, saw his breath like a plume of steam shoot out of his mouth. He nearly choked with shock as he realised the temperature had sunk, which could only mean one thing. Trimble, her eyes closed in concentration, mouth half-open in a silent moan of ecstasy, was oblivious to the drop in temperature. He leaned right back and looked to the closet. For an insane split second he thought he saw the silhouette of a man in the window, but he blinked and the figure was gone.

Trimble looked down and stopped grinding onto him when she noticed his expression. "What's wrong?" she asked, "Why is it cold in here?"

Danny thought to tell her, tell her everything

about the ghost and all he'd seen, but despite the cosiness of their intimacy the steady hand of caution held his tongue.

"Daniel?" she asked, puzzled by his inactivity, but he stopped her questions with an urgent teeth-banging kiss, then buried his face into her breasts again, blocking out all thought of jealous lurking spirits.

Though still inside her, he could feel himself softening with the distraction so he cleared his mind and pictured Trimble's body, her breasts, the turn of her hips, her tight flat stomach, the warm clammy welcome between her legs.

Pulling her to him, his hands grasped her slim waist and he pushed her down onto him while visions of her naked figure passed through his mind. He clenched the muscles in his groin as he reached climax and shot into her with a gasp of release.

Trimble soon followed, quivering and gasping in her own fulfilled ecstasy.

After what seemed like an immensely long time to Danny, she collapsed over him, breathing hard and sweating. Eyes closed in the warmth of post-coital bliss, he caught his breath and tried desperately to think of something to say, which seemed to be the least he could do. However, he found there was nothing to say. He felt this had been promised to him from that first evening as he stood naked before her in the bath tub.

Wordlessly she sat up and looked around. "It's so cold in here, is it always like this?"

Her earlier warmth all but forgotten, the arrogant housekeeper edged back into her voice. Before he could answer she dismounted him and wordlessly gathered her things to leave. Confused, and not a little rejected, Danny watched her as she pulled the night gown over her head and punched her arms through the sleeves.

Businesslike and cold, she ordered, "Up early tomorrow Daniel, so go to sleep, please. I don't want to have to come and wake you." Then, as quickly as she entered, she left, leaving Danny to contemplate what had happened, and why, as he gushed into Trimble at the apex of their act, a picture of Sandra's innocent smile appeared unbidden in his head.

With Trimble gone and the house quiet, sleep crept up on him like a silent assassin. Though it was only just past eight, he couldn't keep his eyes open anymore and so gave in and drifted off.

He dreamt of the closet, his mother and Achlad, the victim of a demon's tricks and a housekeeper's malice. It was dark when he woke with a start. Something or someone had touched his cheek and the vague impression he'd felt was one of kindness.

"Mam, are you here?" he asked the darkness, but nothing answered.

He struck a match and lit his candle. Wide awake now, he knew it would take a couple of hours to go back to sleep, so he decided to check out the closet again.

Swinging his legs out of bed, he froze when the voice began. Not audible, it was in his mind, and he knew automatically who it was.

"You have no idea who you are messing with," it said.

"Achlad? Is that you? Is that your name?"

"You know it is," the voice hissed as the form slowly materialised in front of him. "I told you to leave, to get away from her, but you wouldn't and now ..."

"Now what?" Danny asked heatedly. "Who are you, why are you here? What do you know of anything?"

"What do I know?" Achlad laughed maliciously. "Let me show you."

Danny was instantly hit by a mental picture of a lad about his age but of larger build, a lad completely besotted by Trimble, standing at the doorway asking to do small jobs for her.

Then Trimble showing him his room. "You can stay here, Achlad. Perhaps if you're a good hard-working boy, I can come visit you at night."

Danny's heart cracked at the sight of complete gratitude Achlad gave her, a puppy to her whims. Next they were in the orchard, together and alone. He was singing, his high soprano voice at odds with his large frame.

Trimble looked on, smiling encouragingly, but as soon as he shut his eyes to concentrate on the song she sniggered cruelly at him.

Danny recognised the music. It was the one he'd

heard in his first few days there, the melody slow, haunting, a love song or a hymn of mourning.

In the next scene the lad was in the bath tub, standing naked before her, hand between his legs, pumping furiously as she watched. A blush of shame rose to Danny's face at the memory of what he had gone through, what had happened in front of her all those weeks before. He noticed Astaroth watching from the kitchen door, behind the boy, its snout in a silent snarl, and yet Danny was struck by how it seemed as if Astaroth was grinning.

The next scene was in the living room. Achlad was on his knees, begging Trimble for something while the Reverend looked on. His tear-wracked pleas were broken by sobs and whimpering as she arrogantly looked down at him.

"Please, please, I beg of you!"

"No you dolt, it wasn't about love. I'm not going to fuck you. I was playing with you."

"You mean last night, you and me, you touching me there, it was nothing?" he asked, shocked.

"Yes, nothing, I do it all the time with men. You're all the same, putty in my hands. Did you really think I was going to do it with you? I wasn't going to fuck you, you imbecile. Now get up, you're embarrassing me and the Reverend."

The Reverend however, looking anything but embarrassed, was clearly having a hard time controlling his amusement.

Achlad looked to the ground and backed up again, determined to see this through. "Miss

Trimble, I love you and I want to marry you."

"Marry you? You disgust me, you sicken me, you worm," she said and laughed dismissively.

"But I love you. Please, marry me. I love you."

"Not if you were the last man on earth," she sneered, laughing as she walked away.

Danny caught Trimble winking at the Reverend, her smile a mask of hideous gloating, and to his surprise he winked back.

The next scene played out in front of him. Achlad watched from the shadows in the corridor as Trimble sent the Reverend away.

"Gwynfor, don't be tiresome. I haven't slept with the boy, and when I do it'll only be to compound his misery. There'll be nothing in it, now go."

"But, Fiona, I thought –" he stammered, but she cut him off.

"No, leave or I'll be forced to ask Astaroth to make you leave. Go now!" The last was shouted, accompanied by the now familiar low growl.

Dejected, the Reverend walked away.

The boy waited and inched towards the open bedroom door. There was movement, the sound of someone changing their clothes, taking something off. Danny felt a quiver of anticipation at the idea Trimble was getting undressed, but it wasn't his own yearnings, he knew it was Achlad's.

Achlad stopped, his back to the wall as another sound gradually grew in volume. It was the soft rhythmic creaking of the bed, slow at first but gradually intensifying in pace.

Sweating in expectation and yet ignorant of what was happening, Achlad clutched his chest to build up the courage to look around the corner.

Danny, knowing something bad was going to happen, willed him with his whole heart not to do so. He moaned in pity as he read the other boy's thoughts while he speculated on what Trimble was doing. Danny winced physically when Achlad came to the conclusion she was doing the same as he did every night after prayers, and the thought of catching her at it thrilled and terrified him in equal measure.

The rocking noise grew louder and faster, and Achlad giggled silently when he caught the sound of grunting, almost snarling.

Horrified, Danny sensed the boy wondering what she would say when he walked in. Would she invite him to join her? Would she just let him watch and beg his silence over the matter?

Achlad thought briefly about what she had said to the Reverend and reckoned she was just saying it to pacify the fool.

Looking on, an impotent spectator to a tragedy he knew was about to happen, Danny hid his face as Achlad swallowed his grin and stood taller to enter the room. He watched as he pushed away from the wall and walked into the light of the open door.

Danny's heart thudded to see Achlad's face drop at the scene before him. Danny moved past him to look in and inhaled in shock himself.

There was Trimble on her elbows and knees, naked, her face in a pillow, with Astaroth, his huge paws either side of her shoulders, thrusting behind her. His vision tunnelled on her face as she turned in their direction, screwed up in pain, lust, exhilaration, while the huge wolfhound, his tail a waving flagpole, looked to be almost draped over her back. Astaroth drooled freely onto Trimble, her head and neck wet with his slaver as he snarled and grunted in his exertion.

Bending over, Achlad retched loudly at the sight and Danny instinctively stood back in case he vomited. He looked up, and to his horror Trimble had opened her eyes and was watching Achlad. Astaroth ignored him, maintaining his punishing tempo against Trimble.

"Seen enough to know where you stand in life, Achlad?" she coolly called over to him, her voice jerking with Astaroth's thrusting.

The boy finally gave in and spilled his stomach onto the floor, and Danny shook his head in stunned disbelief.

The next scene was in the kitchen. Achlad was sitting in the bath tub, weeping uncontrollably, holding a huge knife over his wrists. "No, don't do it!" Danny shouted, forgetting he was witnessing scenes that had already passed.

Achlad sawed once, twice, three times, and a jet of blood fountained out, spraying the tub and floor in bright oxygenated red.

Whether it was the sight of his own blood from traumatic shock, Danny didn't know, but Achlad lost consciousness almost straight away. The Reverend ran into the kitchen, shouting wildly in panic. "Fiona! Fiona, come quickly!"

She ran down the stairs, pulling on a dressing gown over her naked body. Danny expected Astaroth to turn up but he was nowhere to be seen.

"Oh," Trimble said and rolled her eyes. "Stupid boy."

"Bandages, get the fucking bandages out, woman!" Gwynfor shouted, and Trimble who had now affected an air of bored indifference, sighed and walked to the medicine cabinet.

"Here," she said, throwing a roll over to him, and he bound the boy's wrists tight, stopping the blood.

"Thank God he cut across the wrist. It's deep but it should heal. Will you look after him while I go call an ambulance?"

Trimble sighed, "He doesn't need an ambulance. There's hardly any blood there. Give him some sweet tea and we'll put him in bed. He'll be fine by tomorrow."

The Reverend looked up.

"He tried to kill himself, Fiona. He won't be okay. We went too far. You went too far with your acting," he said patiently.

"Too far, Gwynfor? What are you on about? We're going to sacrifice him in two days time. We need him to be depressed, miserable. It's the only way the Great Beast will see his soul as a gift. We haven't even started properly yet!"

Gwynfor stood up. "What more do you want to

do to him? He's completely broken. He wasn't the brightest of buttons in the first place but now he's lost it completely."

Trimble leaned back against the kitchen table, her hips forward and one slender leg poking out of the bath robe. Despite the scene, Danny found his eyes wandering up the exposed limb, conscious she was naked under the thin material.

"Gwynfor, this is how it's set out in the book. We capture the victim with sex to the point he's obsessed with me, or whoever plays the role. We humiliate him, beat him if necessary, but always keep him on his toes with the promise of love. Up to now things have gone well. The night he's to die he's given what he's craved, to lure him into a false sense of safety all will be well. Then on the same night, we take him to the place he's to be sacrificed and give his soul to Satan. He'll need to be pacified but the main thing is he's not just terrified when we slit his throat, he has to be in pain, confused and hurting. We need as much negative power as we can draw out of him to claim our reward."

Danny, like the Reverend, stood bewildered at the revelation.

"You cannot be serious," Gwynfor said.

"I'm deadly serious, Gwynfor. The others know what needs to be done. In two days time we'll take him out and slaughter him like the pig he is, and then we'll be rewarded by riches and power beyond our wildest dreams."

"But that's inhuman!"

"No more inhuman than strangling drugged-up tramps for money and sex, Gwynfor. But this time we're going to do it right, this time Satan will look on us as prospective royalty in his realm, not as sinners to be cast to the fires."

Unsure, Gwynfor shrugged. "It's the idea of pain I don't like. I have killed people, yes, but they were drugged or dead drunk, and they didn't feel a thing. This is different, Fiona, it's evil."

Trimble snorted a laugh of complete contempt. "You mean to say the murders of countless young men in the name of the devil for money and sex wasn't? We're doing this my way, Gwynfor, and if we do it right, we'll only have to do it the once. Now wake him up and get him upstairs." She threw him the smelling salts. "Use these. This charade has gone on far too long."

Danny looked to the prone form of Achlad, still in the bath tub, his wrist bandaged and slowly moaning in his stupor, and an infinite sadness hit him. He closed his eyes briefly and opened them to find himself in his room. Achlad was in the closet, naked, and was standing on a chair muttering to himself. Danny knew something bad was about to happen. Achlad had bound a tie to the bar that ran across the top four coat hangers and was testing his weight against it. He worked carefully, mumbling incomprehensibly, yet intent on the job in hand. With no fuss or ceremony, he slipped his head through a loop in the tie and kicked the chair away. Danny cried out when he saw him jerk against the knot, yet the material held.

Powerless to do anything about it, Danny watched as the dejected boy kicked and struggled, mind wishing death, body instinctively fighting for life. His face turned dark red and his eyes now looked fit to burst out of his head. Gagging like a cat spitting hairballs, Achlad slowly started to lose the fight to stay alive. The struggling faded as his face grew darker. Then he stopped. Silence.

Stunned by the violence just witnessed, Danny turned away and closed his eyes, only to wake up and find himself in his own bed.

The ghost of Achlad was gone but the meaning of what he had been shown struck him like a thunderbolt. The plan with Achlad had been for sex on the last day, luring him into thinking he was loved, welcome and safe, and then murdering him in some sick ritual. Trimble's earlier visit tonight was merely to put that same plan in motion with Danny. Tonight was, if the ghost wasn't lying, the night they'd come to kill him.

He jumped out of bed to get dressed and escape. There couldn't be more than a couple of hours left before they came, and regardless of what Sergeant Evans said about him going to jail, he must leave before it was too late.

The suitcase was under the bed but he decided against taking it. The weather was mild so all he'd really need was a jacket to keep warm at night.

He pulled on his long trousers, second best, and a shirt and pullover. It would be too hot in the day for those but he had no idea exactly where he was going to go, and who knew how cold the nights would be if the weather turned?

Pulling out the picture of his mother, he looked at it for a moment and spoke to her in his mind. "I hope you can see I'm not as bad as they all think I am, Mam. Look after me." He kissed it and popped it into the breast pocket of his jacket.

A plan came to him when he was ready to go. He'd leave here, head east towards Liverpool and join the army. Quite possibly he could get in without any papers. There was a war on, so it had to be possible, right? From there he didn't know what he was going to do. It depended on if he survived the war he supposed.

Picking up his boots and carrying them for stealth, he slowly opened the bedroom door. In the gloom was Astaroth lying on the floor in his own room, apparently asleep. Danny made to tiptoe past him. The dog rattled off a warning growl but Danny ignored it.

Astaroth growled all the time when he slept, and he was probably dreaming. As if in answer to his disregard of the warning, the huge dog sprang up to face him.

"Easy there, boy," Danny said. "I'm just going downstairs for some water."

He felt stupid explaining himself to a dog, until a voice, rumbling and pitiless, spoke in his head, "You're not going anywhere. Get back in your room."

Danny froze. Had he just imagined that? He knew there were strange powers at play here, far out of the ordinary, and yet still, after all he'd seen and experienced, he still couldn't grasp the dog could talk to him.

Astaroth spoke again in his mind. "Get back in there now or you will die in this corridor, now rather than later."

Danny deliberated on whether he should just run, until he heard, "I will catch you and I will eat you alive. Don't try to run, boy. Others have plans for you. I just want to rip your guts out and devour them while you die slowly and painfully."

The dog moved forward and out of the shadow to peer at Danny. Astoroth glared his malice and Danny knew there would be no escape.

Hungry drool dripped from the silent quivering snout and it seemed Danny could actually feel those cruel fangs piercing skin, tearing, disembowelling him before his own horrified gaze. Wordlessly he shuffled back towards his room under the angry watchful eye of the demon wolfhound.

He shut the door with a bang and turned towards the window, knowing it was too small but it was his only hope. Opening it, he looked out and reckoned perhaps he could get through it if he tried hard enough. The fall on the other side wasn't that far. He could easily jump down; just getting through posed the problem.

Hoisting himself up onto the windowsill, he considered how to accomplish the task without falling headfirst.

But the voice spoke again, "My eyes are everywhere, boy. I'll know if you try to get away, and I'll catch you, drag you down and devour you from the inside out."

This time it laughed, a cruel malicious sound that cut to his quick.

Looking back down, there were the eyes the dog had spoken of. The souls of the people in the garden were standing their silent watch, their stares unwavering, locked on him as if waiting for something. He fell back and away from the window. There was no getting away. He was trapped, until Trimble, at her leisure, came for him.

# 27

She sat on her bed with all the pieces of paper laid out around her. The first were the prayers; the second, the piece with the smaller passages; and the last, the song with the lyrics changed. It seemed hopeless, especially in light of the conversation she'd had with Sergeant Evans that day.

"Sit down Sandra, there's a good girl," he'd said, smiling reassuringly and yet obviously angry with her. She'd sat opposite him at the kitchen table and waited for his anger to surface. It didn't.

Instead, with the air of a man fed up with not understanding what was going on, he said, "Okay, tell me, tell me everything. I have no idea what's going on with you and that boy, but I need to know because he's a bad penny, and though I'm not your father I am responsible for you."

"You won't be angry?" she'd asked, hoping for a smile that didn't materialise.

"I already am, but it's always better to know what I'm angry about."

Sandra nodded and started in, "While I was up there today, Daniel gave me some more passages he'd copied down from the walls."

At that, his hand went up. "Stop right there. I don't want to know any more about pieces of paper. They mean nothing. I want to know why you keep going up to see that boy. I don't understand it Sandra, I honestly don't. A young girl is missing and he absconds. You don't have to be Sherlock Holmes to realise this is very suspicious behaviour. Beth was your friend and he might know something about her disappearance, so why would you want to be friends with him in the first place?"

His voice had steadily risen in pitch during the tirade and Sandra, who had decided the only way forwards was to remain calm, let him talk.

"Now if I were you young lady, I'd be asking myself why young Mister Kelly has done a disappearing act. Why is he never in when I come around? I'll be writing a report today and it'll go to Bangor constabulary. In it I'll be naming your friend as the chief suspect in what might turn out to be a murder case. So, I don't want you going up to the vicarage anymore, as the last thing on this earth I want is to lose you to a madman who's preying on young girls. Have I made myself clear on this?"

"But there's more to this than meets the eye, Sergeant Evans."

"No, there isn't, Sandra. I know what's going on, and though I can understand it, I don't like it and won't tolerate it. I don't want you hurt by this boy."

The dam of her patience broke and she crossed her arms to speak. "What ... what is going on?"

"Well, alright then, young lady, if you want me to be plain, you're sweet on the lad, maybe you like his bad image or it's just you both come from the same place, I don't know. But you're sweet on him and you refuse to believe the evidence before your own eyes."

Sandra's fuse blew. "That's not true!" she said, jumping up from the table.

Evans, realising the whole conversation had run exactly the way he didn't want it to, also stood up and put out two pacifying hands. "Now, Sandra, calm down. I didn't mean it in a nasty way. That's just how it seems."

But it was too late. Staring at him in anger, she fought with herself not to make the same accusation against him in regards to Trimble. "I'm going to my room, Mister Evans. I have homework to do," she said, and walked out, a model of controlled rage.

And that had been the end of it. He'd never believe her and even though she'd told him Beth had gone up to the house, she knew the Sergeant had already decided on who the villain was.

Picking up the passages she looked at them blankly, seeing only two words she understood - the 'Miss Trimble' in the song lyrics. It was hopeless, especially as Sergeant Evans wasn't going to read the new ones Danny had given her.

A tap at the window broke her concentration. Another and then another, until she opened the window to see who it was.

She looked down to see Huw, Bryn, Geraint and Dafydd, and hurriedly opened the window to them.

"What's happened? Did you find something?" she asked anxiously.

"Not yet," Huw answered for everyone. "We took a vote and decided you can come with us, if you want."

"Really?" she squealed. "I'll be right down."

She turned and walked to the bedroom door.

There was no way Sergeant Evans would let her out this late. It was nearly ten at night and she had school the next day. So, clutching her heart, she tiptoed out onto the landing and down the stairs.

The Sergeant was in the living room, waiting with Mrs Evans for the 'Ten O'clock News'. After slowing taking her jacket off the hook, she crept past the door and into the kitchen and outside. In the back yard she could hear something zip past and hit the street sign, and guessed correctly it was Dafydd in a tree with his catapult.

She shook her head. Boys of his age were always either climbing trees or throwing stones, or both, what was wrong with them?

"Dafydd, come down. Mister Evans will hear you and come out," she hissed loudly. About to argue until Huw shot him a warning glance, he wordlessly climbed down.

Huw said, "Right, we'll go up to the church first and see if we can see anything. We might find something there, then we'll have a look in the orchard, and maybe we can see something through the windows."

Bryn nodded. Geraint and Dafydd said, "Right," in unison and Sandra shrugged.

"Okay, but before we go, can you take a look at these please?" She held out the three pieces of paper for Huw to read.

He scanned the sheet with the song text first and pulled a face. "What is it? What's it meant to be?"

Sandra told them about the writing Danny had found and how he couldn't read it.

Dafydd looked a little sheepish when Sandra mentioned he'd thrown the second sheet, the one with the Lord's Prayer in Welsh, away - but moved swiftly on to the last one. "This is the last page he gave me. He doesn't understand it. Neither do I, obviously. Can you read it?"

Huw turned to the last piece and read through the passage, his face turning to shock as he did so.

"Is this real? Did he copy this off a wall in the house?" Sandra nodded. "The first, *Pam eu bod nhw'n gwneud hyn i mi, mae hi'n gwybod fy mod i'n ei charu hi, pam, pam?* means, 'Why are they doing this to me? She knows I love her. Why, why? The second says, *Pam eu bod nhw mor greulon efo fi?* and that means, 'Why are they so cruel to me?' The third one, *Dwi'n ei charu hi ac yn fodlon marw er ei mwyn hi felly mae hi'n ymwybodol o'r cariad sydd gennyf* means, 'I love her and will die for her so she knows my love'. Sandra, what is going on up there?"

Sandra, too shocked at what she'd just heard,

had nothing to say. "I don't know, but poor Danny's up there with them."

Huw looked up from the sheet and said, "The last one is a bit longer and it's really weird, *Ni fyddaf byth yn ei gadael hi. Fi sydd biau hi, Duw am gwaredo, neu'r diafol satan, rho'r ddynes yma i mi a mi roddaf innau fy enaid it*, and that means, 'I'll never leave her. She is mine, as God is my witness, or the devil. Satan, give me this woman. I will give you my soul'." He lowered the paper and looked at Sandra gravely. "I don't like it. That scares me, that really scares me."

Sandra nodded.

"Let's go and show it to Sergeant Evans. He can come with us then, as well," Dafydd broke the silence.

"But he thinks it was Danny who took Beth, even though it wasn't," Sandra said glumly.

"Not if we show him this. He has to see there's something wrong up there when he reads this," Huw said, holding the sheet of paper up for all to see.

"I don't know. If he sees me outside I'll get in trouble."

"Let's do it," Geraint declared. "You might get in trouble but Danny might be dead if we wait here too long."

It was a dramatic statement. Sandra knew instinctively he'd said it to annoy her, but it set the boys in motion and she had no other option than to go with them.

Huw knocked on the door and Sandra pushed

past him and opened it. "You'd better all come in. Shoes off, please," she said, dreading the next meeting with her host.

"Well, it won't be long now and they'll be in Paris if this keeps on," Sergeant Evans was pointing out to his wife when Sandra walked in the room. She coughed to gain their attention and said, "Mister Evans, would you come to the kitchen please? We need to talk."

He'd thought they were going to have another discussion about the boy, so he nodded at Sandra and winked at his wife before standing.

He walked into the kitchen and was shocked to see five children waiting for him, but he quickly regained his composure. "Right then, boys, what can I do for you all?"

Huw had decided to lay everything out in a certain order, and so he spoke, holding the three sheets of paper to his chest. He laid the first on the table. "Sergeant Evans, have you seen this piece of paper before?" he asked gravely.

Evans looked down, recognised the altered song lyrics and rolled his eyes. "What in heaven's name is wrong with you all? This means nothing. It's a song some love torn lad wrote, probably your Mister Kelly in my opinion," he stated pointedly at Sandra.

"Yes, but Sergeant, Danny doesn't even speak Welsh, never mind write it," Geraint broke in, causing the policeman to frown at the tone of his voice.

"Now listen, you lot. He probably copied the

words down from some book or other. The same goes for the prayer."

"But he couldn't have copied these down from anywhere," Huw said, handing him the last note of four passages.

Evans scanned through them. "Is this a joke? If it is, I can tell you all there are heavy penalties for wasting police time," he lectured, though somewhat half-heartedly.

Sandra had the impression the Sergeant simply didn't want it to be true. Maybe there really was some truth about his feelings for Trimble.

Huw gave him the last piece of paper and said, "This is the first note he gave Sandra, the Lord's Prayer. At that time he didn't know who Achlad was."

Evans took the page and read the first few lines before stopping. "So?" he said. "He's in a church. The place is built on old bibles."

Sandra wondered where Huw was going with this but kept her peace when she saw the look of triumph on Huw's face.

"Sergeant, what was Achlad's second name? Does anyone here know?"

Bryn and Geraint shook their heads, but Dafydd piped up, "I know, it was …"

Huw cut him off with a hand to his mouth.

"Rhys, no Rhysolt, no wait, oh I can't remember," the policeman said.

"Right, none of us can remember his second name because we all just knew him as Achlad, so how could Daniel know it if he copied these words from a bible and not from the wall, like he said he did?"

Evans looked puzzled and Huw's beam grew even broader as he triumphantly pointed at the sheet and said, "Look at the bottom of the prayer, Sergeant. It's written there."

Evans looked back to the page and gasped. There, at the bottom of the passage was the name Achlad Rhydderch. He looked back at the five and nodded. "Alright, I'll go up there tomorrow and ask about it."

"No, we have to go up there now. Tomorrow could be too late. It was for Beth and this Achlad. They could be killing Danny right now!" Sandra blurted, eliciting a sceptical frown from the Sergeant.

"It's too late now young lady, and it's too late for you to be running around with boys. Now get to your room. I'll take these pages up to the old vicarage tomorrow and that's the end of the matter!" the police Sergeant exploded, leaving a shocked silence in the wake of his flare-up.

Huw smiled encouragingly at Sandra and winked before saying, "It's okay Sandra, you go to bed. We're going up to the church to have a look around, maybe throw some stones and make a lot of noise."

Sandra's eyes opened in shock and she smiled warmly when she realised what he meant.

"You'll do no such thing, young man!" Evans

turned on him. "You'll all go home this minute, and that's an order. If I find you've been up there tonight I'll charge you with causing an affray."

"You'll have to catch us first, Sarge," Geraint laughed, clicking on to what Huw wanted to do.

"So if you want us, you know where to find us," Huw finished for him.

Evans looked down at the pages again, mentally turning over what he held in his hand. "So you really think he didn't have anything to do with young Beth's disappearance and it was the Reverend who had something to do with poor Achlad as well?"

"Him, Trimble, or both," Huw answered for everyone.

"I'm not convinced, I don't know the time frame of when these notes were written, and I don't know what Achlad has to do with Beth at all! In fact, you've come to me with nothing concrete whatsoever. How do you know Kelly didn't know Achlad in Liverpool? They both come from there."

Huw sighed, "Sarge, we're going up there to have a look around. You can come and arrest us if you want to but we're not leaving until you do."

"Don't be clever, lad," Evans reproached him, and then as if coming to a decision within himself, "Right, the only reason I'm going up there now is because I don't want you lot causing trouble." A collective sigh of relief met his words, until he added, "But I'm going up there alone. You lot all go home now."

"Sergeant, it's after ten at night and they have a

big dog there. We're coming with you, either with your blessing or simply following a hundred yards behind."

Rolling his eyes in pained acceptance, the Sergeant conceded, "Alright, but you do as I tell you, no arguing, I'll go put my uniform on."

# 28

Fiona Trimble lay on her bed in only her underwear and sighed in satisfaction at how things turned out. If she could have purred she would have. It was going to be a long night, but if all went to plan, and she saw no reason why it shouldn't, by dawn she would hold all the power a Prince of Hell could offer.

She thought back to that fateful day when she found poor David Price hanging in the garden. Such a fine specimen of a man he was. She'd swallowed her initial revulsion of him when she discovered his easy ways and infectious good humour. He'd been doled out a lot of bad luck along the way and yet he still held tight to his integrity.

True attraction finally arrived when she saw him stripped to the waist, chopping wood in the garden. From afar she watched his tireless shoulders, arms, back and chest as he split through one bough after another. His rhythm was almost sexual and she knew she had to have him, but just the once and very discreetly. The tattoo on his chest fascinated her and she decided to ask about it as a way of gauging if he had any feelings for her. Gwynfor would have gone mad if he knew her intent.

"Oh, that," the woodsplitter said, smiling a broad toothy grin that disarmed her, melting her heart immediately. "I had that done just after the war, a whole lifetime away. I'm done with that now, though. It didn't bring what I thought it would."

"What do you mean?"

"Devil worship. It was a scam, a fake. I'm embarrassed by it now if the truth be known." He shrugged and grinned apologetically, hefting the axe and burying the blade in the chopping block before picking up his glass of water.

"What exactly did you hope it'd bring you?" she asked, eyeing his chest muscles while pretending to look at the picture.

"Answers mostly. I needed to know if God and the Devil really were what I thought they were. After Belgium, my wife leaving me with the kids, then the Spanish flu, I just didn't know anymore. I still don't but I'm finding my way slowly, I think you and the Reverend have shown me the way forward. I'll never forget the kindness you both have shown me."

Trimble could recollect her feelings of embarrassment at those words and his gratitude.

She'd felt such a fraud, almost dirty with betrayal, knowing even as they talked Gwynfor was contemplating planting evidence of theft on him and reporting it to the police.

"Charity's all very well, Miss Trimble, but I'm

fed up of him eating us out of house and home," Gwynfor proclaimed to her after one whiskey too many. "We'll wait until he's finished all the jobs that need doing and then he's out before winter. Can't be having tramps in the house at Christmas, it's un-Christian!"

But life took a different turn and suddenly Trimble found herself in possession of a book that changed her whole outlook on life. *The Devyl and his Hellifh familiars* had been the key to opening up her direction in life. Until then she had been happy to drift along as aimlessly as a butterfly through a storm. As she digested the instructions, the order of ceremonies and the promises made therein, she realised what she most desired in life was within reach. She wanted power, something that had never been granted to her outside of the bedroom.

Oh she could control men up to a point, as could all women who knew how to use their sex, but she wanted real influence and the real authority only money and standing could provide. This book assured the reader, if performed correctly, a sacrifice to Satan would bring wealth and influence. That became her focus, her purpose, and although they'd not yet done it completely right, finally tonight, with this one named Danny, she would deliver on what she set out to do all those years ago.

Breathing deeply she could feel herself being energised, an almost sexual lift, aroused by the pending culmination of all her desires. One evening of unpleasantness and it would be over. She'd get rid of Gwynfor and move out of the vicarage to a house with electricity and a gas fire.

A mild stirring in her loins and a moist warmth made her smile to herself. She slipped a finger into her panties, and closing her eyes in pleasure let the tip move up and down her warm cleft. Astaroth entered the room excitedly wagging his tail, but a noise from outside made then both stop.

"It's the guests. Let's get ready," she said to the dog, who whined briefly, then turned to pad out of the room.


Danny also heard the guests arrive. He went to see from the bedroom window, but they were coming from the other side of the house so he couldn't see anything. Back to the bedroom door he peered out. Astaroth was gone.

Opening the door a bit more he pushed his head through and looked both ways. No one was in sight. It was now or never, so he went back to grab his jacket and quickly pull on his boots.

The sound of the front door opening made him freeze and the voices moving into the living room chilled his spine. He could hear the Reverend speaking, addressing them in a muffled voice. For an idiotic second he stopped walking to listen to what was being said, but he shook himself and picked up his things to go. The floor creaked horribly on the landing, causing him to pause in his stride, however the Reverend droned on and Danny decided to go for it. At the top of the stairs he took a breath and began the count. He knew they'd see him, as the door to the living room looked directly on to the foot of the stairs (one), but there was no choice but to make a dash for it (two). He envisioned his route and hoped Astaroth, by some impossible chance, wouldn't be awake to stop him.

"Three!" and he was off. Taking the stairs two at a time the descent sounded like thunder, but he was out of the front door before any of the mob could make a move. Glancing over his shoulder he saw their impotent gaze from the open doorway and felt like yelling in triumph as he sprinted between the gravestones and the orchard.

Pushing toward the wrought iron gates which were now a symbol for his freedom, disaster struck on four paws. Over the roar of his beating heart and bellowing lungs came the growl of pursuit and the lightning fast drum of pads on stone.

Chancing a look back, he yelled in dismay as Astaroth leapt onto him. The dog tumbled into his legs and bit deeply at the back of his thigh. With a scream Danny went down, turning to face the dog. His fist connected with the side of its head but the hound shrugged it off and continued to tear at the bite. Through his pain and dismay, in the distance he saw the crowd running towards him.

An distant part of his brain wondered why the running people were dressed as monks. Astaroth's tooth grated on his leg bone and in a paralysing blaze of pain, merciful oblivion took him.

He came to under a sky of hoods. Hands held him down as his legs and arms were bound. The wound in his thigh pulsed and his trousers felt wet. "It must be blood," he said aloud, but nobody answered him.

"Pull him around. I think it'll be better to do it side-on,"" a voice he vaguely recognised as Trimble said, and he was roughly thrown onto his side.

When he was bound tight, the sea of hoods backed away and he was left on the ground where Astaroth caught up with him. Eyes searching upward he counted thirteen people, all hooded and robed, the only indication of identity was the size of their hands. A slow chant started up and one of the gathering, a woman by the size of her hands, gave a hammer to the biggest among them.

"Immobilise him so he enters His realm in the same agony he'll experience for eternity," she said. It was Trimble's voice and he shook his head when the understanding of the words sunk in.

"No, don't do it, don't do it," he cried out frantically, struggling against the bonds that held him. Kicking out with his legs he rolled over and over, until the crowd was commanded to hold him fast on his side.

The man with the hammer stood over him and Danny caught a glint of white as he smiled. Raising the weapon above his head, he paused to make sure he couldn't hit anyone else.

"Do it!" Trimble ordered from the side, and the

weighted head came down with a sickening crunch against the side of Danny's thigh.

The pain rendered him unconscious before he could even cry out, and his last sensation was of splintered bone ripping up through his skin. Out cold, he was rolled over onto his other side, and just as he surfaced again into awareness the head smashed down on his other leg.

This time he let rip and howled his pain at the top of his voice. Astaroth who sat patiently watching the proceedings, lifted his head and howled with him, causing the crowd to laugh. A wave of nausea swam in his head and he vomited on the shoes of the man who swung the hammer.

"Filthy swine!" the man said, kicking Danny in the face.

"Put a gag in his mouth and let's take him to the church. Bind that wound tight. It's not allowed to drip blood anywhere, it's important," Trimble ordered.

The crowd moved in again to hoist him up onto their shoulders. A woman stuffed a wad of cloth in his mouth and he nearly choked on it as she rammed it down with a small stick. Roughly they grabbed and hoisted him.

Danny screamed as the broken bones in his thighs grated against each other, but this time cruel oblivion would not spare him his agonies.

The procession marched towards the church, thirteen robed believers and their trussed and suffering sacrifice, his tormented screams of anger, fear and pain strangled by a rag. Finally a dog, large, shaggy and ponderous, followed them, his head down as if exhausted, the blood of his victim around his snout.

Abruptly he picked his head up as if recognising a new scent on the wind. With one look at the procession he dashed off towards the house.

# 29

"What was that?" Sandra asked as they trudged up the steep hill towards Peulwys. They all listened as it happened again.

"Sounds like a dog howling," Geraint said.

"A bloody big dog," Sergeant Evans muttered to himself. "Astar, howling? Now that is a first," he said to the rest.

He was still angry the kids had forced his hand, but on an instinctive level he knew something wasn't right up at the old church, so it wouldn't hurt to have a look and keep the peace. Mrs Evans always said he was too soft when it came to kids, and now he believed her.

They crested the top of the hill and the church walls came into sight. "Thank God we're over that hill," Evans said, stopping for a breather.

He looked back and out across the bay. Admiring the crescent of lights that pinned out the line of the bay, he ruminated on how evil or insane someone would have to be to commit a violent crime with this view at their back door.

"You ready, Sarge?" Huw asked, breaking his reverie.

Shrugging, the Sergeant turned and walked on towards the old church. On reaching the gates he turned to give his orders. "Now listen, I'm going up to the house. I want you to stay here. I'll ask them about Achlad, and if I have the impression there's something not right going on, I'll arrest them. But you stay here!"

They nodded solemnly, so he turned and plodded towards the front door. He wouldn't be arresting anyone today but he knew that would keep them at bay. He'd thought a bit more about whether Kelly knew Achlad before, but he doubted it, and even if he had why would he write his name under the prayer? Why not use it in a more direct way? That fact, taken together with the four shorter passages that didn't have his name on, was very strange indeed.

He'd soon be at the bottom of it, he reckoned, as he knocked loudly on the front door. Nobody answered, so after trying again he decided to see if there was a light on inside.

It always struck him as strange they didn't have electricity here. The whole of Colwyn Bay had had it since the beginning of the thirties, and yet here the church decided not to invest in it. "Most strange ..." he thought as he nearly ran into Astaroth.

"Hello, old boy," he said, smiling and reaching out to pat his head. He jerked it back when the dog snarled angrily at him. "What's wrong, old boy? It's me. Don't you recognise me?"

A sound from the old church attracted his attention and he looked up to see a flickering light through one of the broken windows. Straining his ears, he thought he could hear some sort of religious incantation.

A growl brought him back to the present.

"You stay here, boy. I'm going to have a look in there," he said, moving around the large dog, but Astaroth blocked his way.

"What's wrong, Astar? Don't tell me you've gone mad as well," he sighed, not alarmed as such, just curious as to what had happened to the hound's usual good nature.

He looked up to the church again but decided to make his peace with the dog before going in there.

Astaroth growled once more, so he bent down and put his hand out for him to sniff it. The dog stopped growling and moved his nose up to the proffered hand.

"There's a good lad," he said and curled his forefinger into a hook to scratch his ear.

With a quick snarl and a lightning bite, Astaroth nipped his hand. Evans jerked it back and looked at it again when it started to sting terribly. His head swam as his eyes focused on a bloody stump where his forefinger had once been.

"You bit me?" he said, more puzzled than shocked by what happened. He looked back down at the dog who was now growling in a very menacing way. "You bit me!" he said again, this time in anger, and aimed a kick at the dog's head.

Astaroth ducked under the leg and shot in to bite him in the groin. Evans let out a high-pitched scream and fell as the weight of the dog pushed him over. He batted ineffectually against its head, feeling the teeth crunch again and again as the hound bit through the thick material of his uniform trousers. The wicked fangs ripped through flesh and cloth like soggy paper, spattering blood, and finally puncturing the femoral artery in a large fountain.

The numbness of shock and blood loss set in and Evans soon felt no pain, just a dreadful weariness and a willingness to get it over with. The ground around him was slick with his blood and yet, when he looked down his body to see the huge head eating him alive, he knew he didn't want to die and found within himself the will to fight.

He remembered his truncheon and reached into his pocket to pull it out. Astaroth saw the hand movement and went for his arm. Pulling the weapon free he hit out, narrowly missing the dog's snout. It was a miss that enraged the beast and Astaroth pounced again, landing on top of him as he bit his face.

The dog's lower fangs caught the flesh under his jaw as Astaroth ripped his head up. Just before the policeman passed out from the shock and pain, he felt the skin of his face being torn from his skull.

Astaroth guzzled the limp segment of fat and skin that was once a face in a single bite. Then, bloody and frenzied, he stood to meet the new threat that had fallen at the corner of the house, not twenty feet away, and was now scrabbling to be off.

"Come on, let's go to the church. He won't do anything today," Huw said.

"No, wait, he's come this far. Surely we should do as he says," Sandra countered, but she knew their minds were already made up.

"Come on," Geraint sneered. "You stay here Miss Goody-Two-Shoes. We'll go check out the church."

Huw, Bryn and Geraint moved off together, leaving Sandra at the church gates.

"I'll stay with you Sandra, just so you won't be alone." It was Dafydd, and at that moment she could have kissed him.

"Thank you, Dafydd. At least someone's on my side here."

"We all are, Sandra. It's just that they want to check out the church –"

A high pitched scream cut him off.

"What was that?" she whispered.

"Don't know," Dafydd whispered back. "I think it's the Sergeant. It came from the house."

"Oh no," Sandra moaned and instinctively ran towards the house.

"Sandra, come back!" Dafydd shouted, running after her.

The screaming suddenly stopped, and in the

close dark of the night she could hear the snarls and slap of a large animal eating. As she stood at the front door the sound came from around the corner, and Sandra knew she had to look to make sure Sergeant Evans was alright.

Peering slowly around the corner she saw Astaroth standing astride the prone form of the police Sergeant, blood pooled around them, and the dog was busy pulling at something on the man's head. With a jolt of disbelieving horror she realised it was his face, and gasped as it threw its head back to swallow the skin and flesh whole.

Gagging silently in fear, she turned to get away before he noticed her. Dafydd clattered into her back and they both fell to the floor in clear view of the feeding hound. Scrabbling to stand and get away, she looked up and saw Astaroth in the light of the moon, blood-smeared and snarling, a beast from her worst nightmares turning towards them.

"Quick, round the corner and up the big tree!" Dafydd squeaked, and they both sprinted around the corner to the large tree that overhung the vicarage, scrambling up and into its boughs.

Astaroth stood below them, staring sullenly.

Dafydd looked at Sandra as they both gulped for air. "That was close." Suddenly Dafydd jerked and nearly fell as an angry hiss from the branch next to him startled the pair. Trimble's cat, belligerent and feral, stalked towards them, caterwauling its hatred as it approached.

"Go away!" Sandra shrieked as its angry

remonstrations grew louder, making it sound baby-like and eerily human.

Astaroth barked from below and the cat stopped to hiss its ire at him. Dafydd ripped a branch from the bough and deftly prodded the cat off-balance while it spat at the dog. Falling gracefully and landing on all fours, the cat had just enough time to direct its rage at the children before the murderous Astaroth snapped it in its jaws and crunched into its spine. Tossing it into the air, the dog then caught its head in its massive jaws and bit through the neck to drop the head on the floor at its feet.

Sandra wailed in dread as the lifeless body kicked its final spasms and pumped the last of its blood out the stump of its neck.

Baying for their blood Astaroth stood on two legs, his front paws on the tree, and Dafydd was sure he'd soon try and climb after them.

The barking stopped and the huge hound cocked his weighty head, as if hearing something very faint. Without a sound he fell back down and dapped off.

"He's gone," Dafydd said, still breathless.

"Oh God, how awful! That poor cat," Sandra whined, burying her face in her hands to weep in horror at what she had just seen.

Dafydd put a comforting hand on her arm. "Sandra, look, there's Daniel," he whispered.

From their position in the tree they could see through the empty arches of a big window, its glass long-since knocked out by storms and stone-throwing children. They could see right down and into the church.

Danny was laid out naked on the altar, surrounded by robed people all joining hands and murmuring.

Sandra, shocked at the sight of Danny naked, asked the first thing that came to her head. "What are they doing?"

"I don't know. He's nude and tied up. You can see everything!" Dafydd said, disgusted. "Stop looking, Sandra, it's rude."

Despite herself Sandra had to laugh at his reaction. "I know, I'm sorry. I won't look again," she said, half-smiling despite the situation they were in.

"Look, Astar is heading towards the others!" Dafydd exclaimed, pointing in the direction of the other three boys by the church.

Huw saw the huge hound galloping towards them and screamed at the top of his voice, "Run!"

He was perched on Bryn's massive shoulders when he noticed the dog, and after taking one last peek into the church he jumped down and ran. Sprinting through the graveyard, they were up and over the wall before Astaroth had a chance to catch them.

Dafydd watched with a sinking heart as they ran down the hill towards the village. Astaroth looked back at the pair still in the tree, then dismissed them as he entered the church.

"What do we do now?" Sandra asked.

"Let's get down and get the police from the village."

"No way. I'm not leaving this tree. That dog will come for us," Sandra said, crossing her arms, her voice as shaky as her knees.

"Well, someone has to go and get them. We can't do anything from up here," Dafydd pleaded.

"No, I can't," Sandra admitted.

"I'll go, then."

"No please, don't leave me. Please," she begged.

Dafydd knew he couldn't leave her, and besides, he didn't really want to leave the safety of the tree with that dog patrolling the area. He decided to wait a little and ask her again before the people in the church came out and pulled them down from the tree.

"Okay, we'll wait, but we'll have to leave before they come out."

Sandra nodded and looked away, ashamed of her fear.

# 30

Trimble was thankful the cowl hid her angry expression. She didn't want Gwynfor to see it and spoil the ceremony with his pouting.

He'd refused point blank to break the boy's legs and it was just lucky that Michael Jones, the butcher from Abergele, was glad to oblige. He was renowned for his sadistic streak.

The rumour in town was he'd been caught torturing animals at the big abattoir in Mochdre, the other side of Colwyn Bay. There was a major scandal and after losing his job there, he opened up a butcher's in the village.

Jones volunteered once to strangle an earlier victim with his bare hands, something Gwynfor had been far too squeamish to allow, so Trimble believed the story about him losing his job. Fiona had often wondered what it would be like to strangle a naked man, helpless before her, his life in her hands, begging for mercy while she throttled him slowly, enjoying his death.

She shook her head and thought back to the hammer blows on the boy's legs. Unflinching from the task at hand, the huge butcher had swung down and she had nearly laughed at the face Gwynfor pulled at the sound of the break. She saw Mike in a new light now. Perhaps he'd be a better partner than that weak fool Davies.

The boy had screamed like a girl as they carried him into the church, begging for them to leave him, not to move him. The little worm; in her opinion, just for that pitiful behaviour he deserved to die.

Since Daniel passed out and they took the bindings off him, and stripped him. He wouldn't move now. The breaks in his legs were far too painful. He'd be paralysed by the pain.

Astaroth entered the church and everyone stopped. His eyes glowed and his body shuddered slightly, the fur seeming to move as if being pushed outward. Trimble stepped towards the huge wolfhound, and bowing her head said reverently, "All is prepared, Master."

Looking back up when she sensed a change in his stance, she gasped as he rose up to stand on two legs, his body morphing before her eyes.

She glanced behind her to see if the others were watching but they stood dutifully where she had directed them in a half circle around the altar. Shaking her head in excited disbelief, Trimble smiled broadly as she watched the wolfhound change into something between a man and wolf.

Danny came to. He'd blacked out again when they carried him inside, the pain from the broken bones forcing his mind to shut down.

His mouth was sour from vomit and a raging thirst glued his tongue to his palate. The excruciating beat pulsed from his legs, making him dry-heave. And as he tried to sit up, the recollection of what happened hit. The movement prompted screams of pain and the robed acolytes to rush forward; strong hands pushing him back down.

In the background he could hear a murmuring incantation, and lying with his back on the altar his head hung off the side and upside down. The bindings were gone but his damaged legs destroyed any hope of fighting or running away. The delirium of pain made the embarrassment of nakedness the furthest thing from his mind.

Looking around, he tried to make sense of what was happening.

It was dark, but in the circle the candles put out some light and he could see the ring of hooded figures surrounding him. With faces hidden and hands clasped in front of them, he had the impression they were waiting for something, or someone, to appear.

One of them stood separate from the others, looking away, toward the entrance to the church. Though he could only see the back of the robes, he knew it was Trimble. She was talking to someone, beckoning them to come inside.

Another wave of dizziness and nausea broke over him but he dared not move because of the drilling throb of his broken legs.

The chanting gained in volume and the person outside the circle slowly turned and faced the altar. It was Trimble, and as she raised her arms to say something candlelight glinted off the wicked-looking blade exposed in her waistband.

He knew what was going to happen but he couldn't fathom it. They couldn't really want to kill him, surely? Not the Reverend, not Trimble. She had slept with him only hours before.

The figure behind Trimble moved into the circle of light and Danny screamed in fear. It was Astaroth, but on two legs, his body transformed into a half-man half-wolf form only seen in the posters for horror movies. Standing on two powerful dog's legs, the beast was easily seven foot tall. Its thin waist widened out into a massive chest and tree trunk arms hung from powerfully built shoulders. Dreadful talons replaced the dog paws on its front legs, and its head now looked streamlined and wolfish.

Instinctively Danny squirmed to get away and screamed out loud at the pain.

Trimble diverted her attention away from the beast and glared in Danny's direction. "Quiet you maggot. How dare you scream in his presence!"

It wasn't just the victim who was scared. As the beast moved into the circle of flickering candles gasps of astonishment, wonder and fear welcomed him, and he paused to pose for their adoration and dread.

Gwynfor pulled his hood up to have a better look. He had never dreamed a demon actually existed; now one stood in front of him.

Astaroth turned his head and stared into Gwyn's eyes. Instantly a vision of himself on a throne surrounded by slaves and treasure of all kinds hit him, and he understood. He now knew Trimble had been right. If they did this precisely as it was written in the book, he would be rewarded. She had been right the whole time and he cursed his stupidity for doubting her.

The demon's eyes moved to the next person and suddenly Gwynfor's mind was his again - scared, doubtful, and wondering what happened when Astaroth held him in his gaze.

Danny whimpered in pain and fear. He knew his life was over and the presence of the demon before him confirmed his destination was hell, just as Trimble said. This was real, the demon was real, and the pain was real. He had nowhere to go and all sense of defiance left him as Fiona Trimble, a woman who had slept with him, enjoyed him, shown him his first physical intimacy only hours before, approached with the knife.

As swiftly as only thought can be, Danny pictured his life before he came to the house in Wales. His mother and their small flat above the pub. School, the boxing club, watching Liverpool with mates through the slats in the fence, seeing Sandra for the first time. Sandra. His mind stayed on the picture of her smile. If he had to die, he'd die with that image in his head.

He felt the cold metal on his neck and opened his eyes. Trimble looked down at him, disgust and loathing on her face. How many times had he seen that expression since he'd been there? He didn't know, but he did know he'd never once seen his mother look at him that way.

He thought back to the picture, how he'd love to look at it just the one last time. After all he'd been through - the fear, the confusion, the pain - he just wanted to see the old photo once more.

His gaze fell on his clothes on the floor next to the altar, thrown down in a pile when they'd stripped him for the ceremony. His jacket lay on top of the small mound, and poking out from the breast pocket was the white corner of the photograph.

Trimble wasn't looking at him. She and her congregation were watching the demon as he gazed intently at each of the robed acolytes in turn.

Danny decided to try for it, and stretching out his fingers brushed the corner of the picture. He pushed down more, ignoring the searing agony from the movement, and tweezered the snap between his middle and forefingers. Bringing it up to his chest, he closed his eyes, and breathing heavily against the pain waited for his death.


Gwynfor could sense the fear in the church. Everyone, except for Trimble, was terrified of what was now in front of them: a beast, a Prince of Hell, called up to accept a sacrifice.

Though the demon's gaze had soothed his dread for a short while, his doubts returned as the beast moved on from him to the next attendant. If there really was a hell, then would that mean there was a heaven? Was it still too late to save his immortal soul? Didn't the Bible say he only need confess his sins and show humility, and all would be forgiven?

One look at the brute before him told him there was nothing he could do, even if he wanted to. Its huge frame dwarfed everyone, radiating power and intimidation. He closed his eyes and hung his head.

He'd been a fool all these years and now he'd pay the price for it. He was going to hell unless he did something. But there was nothing he could do.

Trimble felt the raw energy pulsing out of Astaroth, electrifying the air around him. She knew the time had come to claim her place on a throne in hell, so she approached the victim before her, broken, bound and wallowing in his own misery.

The knife was ready, and with one clean cut she'd collect his blood, offer it to Astaroth, and be welcomed into the underworld as a queen.

All she needed was his word or sign, the blade would make a nick in Danny's throat, and she'd fill the glass with his blood and offer it to Astaroth. Looking back up towards him she saw the huge beast nod his head to her.

"Give me the gift," he said, his voice as low as the pit of hell, and twice as old.

As Astaroth's voice rumbled through the old building Gwynfor saw the look of raw fear that now gripped the congregation.

His focus darted from one person to the next, watching the tremble of panic course through them. They had wanted this, but like himself they hadn't really believed. The only one who seemed to be revelling in the ceremony was Trimble; the others looked ready to bolt.

His thoughts danced on the edge of reasoning about how, if there was a hell, there had to be a heaven, and he couldn't let the notion go. All those years he'd not believed and now, in one swathe of supernatural reality he'd seen it was all true.

He had to give himself wholeheartedly to the ritual. He didn't want to end up in hell a sinner, to be burnt and prodded with pitchforks. He wanted to be a king. He nodded to himself as he made the decision. There was no going back. He was in for everything, his soul counted on it.

Danny held the picture of his mother next to his heart and the vision of Sandra in his mind as the knife jiggled around on his windpipe, the blade quivering in Trimble's excitement.

She held a glass up and bent towards him.

"Don't move, Daniel. I only need a glass of your blood and all will be well," she lied.

Danny, not believing her for a second, and yet hoping with his whole heart she spoke the truth, did as he was bid and held still as the knife nicked a vein in his neck and the blood seeped out into the glass.

After what seemed like an hour but was only a couple of minutes, the glass was full, and while holding a cloth over the cut to stop the bleeding, she proclaimed, "Here is the blood for your Master, Prince of Hell! Take this as a sign of our devotion to him so he may reward his followers as he sees fit!"

The glass of blood, held up and presented to the demon, looked black in the Spartan light of the candles.

Astaroth took a step forward to accept it, then stopped to look up and out of the window to the ancient tree that claimed the side of the church. Suddenly the glass shattered in Trimble's hand and the blood exploded out over her wrist and onto the floor.

Horrified by the spill, Trimble screamed in rage and looked up to see the two children in the boughs of the great oak. The girl Sandra looked down in silent terror, panic etched on her face like a papier-mâché mask. The other was pulling something back with one hand. Then he let go.

Thwack!

A stone sounded against her head and Trimble fell to the floor, out cold. The boy who fired the stone punched the air in triumph and fumbled in his pockets for more ammunition.

Gwynfor looked at Astaroth, who turned towards him and said in a voice that turned his bowels to water, "The blood is lost, the sacrifice improper. Hell awaits you, sinner."

The Reverend looked aghast at the demon, and falling to his knees he pleaded. "No, it wasn't me. I didn't know what I was doing! You have to believe me. I didn't want this. I didn't want any of this!" he begged, his terrified voice ratcheting up in volume and pitch. "It was her, she wanted to do it all, she was the one."

But as the spirit of the demon left this world and Astaroth morphed back to his original form, he found himself talking to a dog, a good natured wolfhound who wagged his tail, panted and blinked in confusion.

The demon's metamorphosis back to a dog acted as a trigger for the other acolytes to leave en masse. They sprinted out of the church, into the night in a flurry of robes and fear as Gwynfor watched them in silence on his knees from his place in front of the altar. Trimble's body stirred but she remained unconscious.

The dog padded over towards Danny and whined, licking his face. "Yes, you're a good dog," he whispered, rubbing his ears and head.

"Danny!" a shrill voice ripped through the church, and Gwyn looked up to see the girl and one of the boys from the village running towards them.

Danny, seeing Sandra, automatically covered

himself with his hands. The boy and the girl ran past the kneeling Reverend, and as she bent over to hug Danny he screamed in pain. "Don't touch me, don't touch me!"

"I'll go and run to the post office, they have a phone. I can telephone the ambulance and the police," Dafydd said in a rush.

"Yes, do that," Sandra nodded. "I'll wait here and cover him up."

Gwynfor stood up, amazed they hadn't spoken to him or even registered his presence, and watched the young lad run off towards the door.

As if hitting a brick wall, he stopped abruptly and began walking back towards the altar. Gwyn peered into the darkness and yelped in fright as a man's head, then the rest of its body moved into the light. The first figure was closely followed by a second, and then a whole row of them advanced forward.

Their necks were uniformly scarred by the strangulation that cost them their lives, and Gwynfor knew it was the horde of victims he'd given up to an imaginary demon in the mock ceremonies. There were so many of them he wondered at how they had got away with so many murders for so long.

The boy now back at the altar, raised his catapult, ready to fire.

The group of spectres stopped fifteen feet away from the Reverend and the first one to enter into the light spoke in a painfully cracked and hoarse voice. "We've come for you so we can be free."

Gwynfor decided to mount a defence and gamely took one step towards them on trembling legs. "I was the one who set you free. You were all, to a man, prisoners to alcohol and your own plagued minds. You owe me. I did you a service. I treated you as equals. I gave you your pride back before I set you free of this world."

His words were greeted by stony silence and Gwynfor, ever the optimist, wondered if his words had hit home.

A crack noiselessly appeared at his feet and ran up through the space in front of him until it reached the line of his victims. Intuitively knowing what it was and yet refusing to believe it, he stared at the break in amazement.

Trimble came to. Holding her head in one hand, she stood and looked at the crack as it began to widen. There was a gust of hot air and the wail of a billion souls caused them both to stand back.

"What happened?" Trimble asked, her voice weak.

"The boy shot the glass out of your hand," Gwyn said, turning to point at Dafydd who was holding his catapult in their direction. "He knocked you out and then Astaroth left."

"But that means they …"

"Are here for my soul, yes," the Reverend said, almost smiling.

The crack opened up like a trapdoor and they both stared aghast into the abyss below. Flames engulfed the souls held captive therein and their shrieks caused Gwynfor's bladder to finally fail.

The horde of vengeful dead mutely filed around the pit, roughly pushing past Trimble, who willingly stood back to watch in fascination until they stood either side of Gwynfor. Grasping hands held his arms tight and yet he put up no protest, resigned to his fate.

The spokesman for the horde passed sentence on him, shouting at him from the other side of the pit over the clamour of the damned below. "For stealing our lives before our time, for casting us into limbo to wait for judgement, for playing with our souls as if they were your personal property, we condemn you to burn in hell for all eternity."

A shove and Gwynfor fell screaming and flailing into the pit. A blast of fire exploded from the hole as if trumpeting his demise, and then all fell silent. Quietly the ghosts of the men began to dissipate into nothingness, and Trimble, Sandra, Dafydd and Danny watched in shocked silence as they disappeared. The gaping hole remained.

Trimble turned towards the three at the altar.

She picked up the knife that had fallen from her grip when she was knocked unconscious and weighed it in her hand. "You little fuckers," she hissed, her crisp English articulation amplifying the menace in her curse. "I had everything under control, everything, and you spoilt it all." She moved around the hole in the floor and approached them slowly. "But you'll fucking pay you little bastards! You'll be sorry you messed with me, because when you're burning in hell I'll be laughing at you, looking at you and laughing when they rip your skin off and make you eat it! When you're impaled on a pole through your arse, I'll be there, watching from my throne and laughing!" she screeched, stopping a metre before them.

A soft draft of cold air surrounded the area around the altar, snaking in between them. Together they somehow tracked its path, despite it being invisible.

Words whispered from the darkness, sibilant and sly in their mocking tone. "Miss Trimble," it hissed.

"Achlad!" Trimble and Danny whispered in unison, one in wonder, the other in fear.

From the back of the church echoed a voice singing in a choirboy pitch.

> Paham mae dicter, O Miss Trimble,
> Yn llenwi'th lygaid duon di?
> A'th ruddiau tirion, O Trimble,
> Heb wrido wrth fy ngweled i?

From the darkness of the shadows, Achlad, the tortured boy who had hanged himself, appeared, the high pitch of his singing voice conflicting with the size of his body.

Trimble saw him and dropped the knife in shock. "No, I didn't kill you, you killed yourself!" she whispered, repeating it to the approaching spirit. "You killed yourself. I had nothing to do with it at all!"

Her protestations were met only with the mournful lyrics of the Welsh love song.

> Pa le mae'r wên oedd ar dy wefus
> Fu'n cynnau 'nghariad ffyddlon ffôl?
> Pa le mae sain dy eiriau melys,
> Fu'n denu'n nghalon ar dy ôl?

The song at an end, Achlad now stood at the opposite end of the pit. "Miss Trimble, you forget the wording of the book."

"What do you mean?" she asked, her voice as feeble and shaky as a new born.

"If the ceremony goes wrong, we take whom we think is responsible for our death. So I'll take you four, as I feel you all have a hand in it."

Trimble turned and pointed at the three at the altar. "This is all your fault. If I had finished the ceremony this would never have happened."

Her words caught in her throat as Achlad abruptly appeared next to her. "Fiona, we could have made such sweet music together and yet you chose to push me into madness. For this, you must now enter Satan's realm and burn for all eternity."

He gave one quick shove and Trimble fell screaming into the pit below, her entrance hailed by a furnace blast from the crack and a swell in the wailing of the damned.

Achlad turned to the three at the altar. "Don't make me come for you," he warned as Dafydd let loose a stone that passed through the spirit to hit the wall behind. "You three I have nothing on, and yet I'm still going to cast you to the fires so I can return to hell as a bringer of souls, a prince among sinners. The gateway is open. I need only push you in and take my place among Satan's elite."

Torn between running away and staying to protect Danny, Sandra shouted, "No, we had nothing to do with you, you said so yourself. Leave us alone."

The ghost walked towards them, the crack opening in his wake. "No, you see, if I bring you with me I'll be rewarded. Normally the only way to hell is through death, but now, with this gateway opened up, I can bring you with me and present you as gifts to the devil himself."

Dafydd let loose another stone that passed through him and stood back, looking ready to run.

"Don't think about it, boy. This church is sealed up tight. The only way out is through this portal."

Achlad reached the altar and grabbed Danny's wrist. He jerked him and Danny screamed at the movement.

"You can't do this, Achlad," Sandra pleaded. "Everyone's told me you weren't a bad boy when you were alive. Why are you doing this now? Why are you in hell?"

He turned to the girl and grinned menacingly, "The children I killed when I set the orphanage alight. Their souls demanded I be sent there. So here I am, feathering my nest as it were. Now come!"

He jerked Danny's wrist again and Danny

wailed in agony as he slid to the floor. The pain blinded Danny. His suffering overshadowed everything until he felt his arm being dropped.

Opening his eyes, he was hit by a bright light that forced him to shield his eyes in its intensity. The light dimmed and there, between himself and the ghost of Achlad, stood his mother.

"Mam?" he whispered through the cloud of his hurt.

"Achlad, you will not take my son," she said. "You have no right."

"I have every right. They dabbled in the occult and they will pay the price. There'll never be a chance like this again, never! The doorway to hell is open, they're in its presence, they will be mine!"

Danny's mother looked back down at her son and smiled bravely. Then turning to the two on the other side of the altar, she smiled and nodded at them. "Take care of my son. Make sure he gets to a hospital," she said to Dafydd. "And you, Sandra, my son will need a friend from now on, one who believes him and will stand by him. Will you do that for me?"

Sandra nodded mutely, but the moment was broken by Achlad's cruel laugh. "What are you talking about? They're coming with me. There'll be no ambulance, nobody to hold his hand. They're going to burn in hell together."

"Achlad, I will come with you. Take me as your prize. A soul from heaven to be used as a gift to Satan, but my son and his friends will go."

"No!" screamed Danny from the floor. "You can't do that. Stay in heaven. I've seen what they'll do to you." He broke down, his inconsolable sobbing drowning coherent speech.

Danny's mother knelt next to him and stroked his face, small shocks of warmth radiating from her fingers as she touched him. "I know what awaits me there, Danny. I'm prepared for that, and come the day of judgement my sacrifice will set me free. It may even happen sooner if God wants it. But know this, know I'll always be with you and we will be together some day. Nothing will ever keep us apart."

She stood and Achlad nodded to her. "Ready?"

With a last look at her son on the floor, she smiled and mouthed the words *I love you*, before silently stepping off and falling into the abyss.

Achlad disappeared and the crack in the floor closed with a snap. The church reverberated with the cries of anguish from the broken boy on the ground.

# EPILOGUE

**Sixty-Two YearsLlater**

He stood watching the mourners from a small rise at the side of the graveyard. There were so many of them he wondered if he was looking at the right burial.

Children and grandchildren stood in respectful silence as the vicar intoned the words and prayers of the ceremony. Sandra wept silently as they lowered the coffin into the ground, and the crowd echoed the last Amen of the service and turned to leave. A few even glanced at the small rise where he stood, yet they saw no one.

Never feeling as good in life as he did now, he chuckled at recalling the line from a film about 'death becoming him.' Yes, death wasn't that bad after all. He'd religiously attended church after that ill-fated night all those many years ago, praying with such fervour for his mother's soul.

And he was certain if it hadn't been for Sandra

and his best friend Dafydd, he would have long been consigned to a lunatic asylum.

"Danny?" a soft voice from behind him called. He swallowed hard, blinked away the tear that had fallen at the sound of her voice, and turned around.

There, resplendent in white, stood his mother. "I told you the big man upstairs wouldn't let me stay there forever," she laughed, and Danny did too, a smiling laugh tinged with tears of joy and fondness. "Come on," she said, "They're all waiting to see you."

Danny took her hand and they wandered together up to the stars.

# The End

## Acknowledgements

Thanks to:
George for bouncing ideas right back at me and correcting my dire English.
Eleri Brady, who works for Macmillan Cancer Support, and Jessica Brady for the Welsh translations.
Dixie and Bob for the immediate feedback.
The Wangers for being Wangers.
To Wild Wolf publishing for being so damnably cool.
To the brave lads and lasses at 1st the Queen's Dragoon Guards.
...And lastly to my good friend Paul Rudd, for sharing a dream and putting action where words once were.

## ABOUT THE AUTHOR

Richard Rhys Jones hails from the sunny shores of Colwyn Bay, in north Wales. The wrong side of 49, he's married with two children and two cats. He writes, occasionally plays the drums for a hardcore band, and is a passionate supporter of Liverpool and Braunschweig.

Printed in Great Britain
by Amazon